D0886703

Flying Pigs

Also by Brian Battison

The Christmas Bow Murder (1994)
Fool's Ransom (1994)
Crisis of Conscience (1995)
The Witch's Familiar (1996)
Truths Not Told (1996)
Poetic Justice (1997)
Jeopardy's Child (1997)

FLYING PIGS

Brian Battison

Constable · London

First published in Great Britain 1998
by Constable & Company Ltd
3 The Lanchesters
162 Fulham Palace Road
London W6 9ER
Copyright © 1998 by Brian Battison
The right of Brian Battison to be
identified as the author of this work
has been asserted by him in accordance
with the Copyright, Designs and Patents Act 1988
ISBN 0 09 478550 3
Set in Palatino 10 pt by
SetSystems Ltd, Saffron Walden, Essex
Printed and bound in Great Britain by
MPG Books Ltd, Bodmin, Cornwall

A CIP catalogue record for this book
is available from the British Library

Prologue

CAMPAIGN LAUNCHED TO QUASH UNSAFE CONVICTION

William Mason, the man convicted of murdering local bestselling author Glen Watkinson, has died in prison following a long-term illness. Mr Mason, 57, had served just six months of a life sentence.

Tony Fricker, left-wing Labour MP for Saltley South and vigorous campaigner for prisoners' rights, has expressed doubts about Mason's original conviction and is now planning to launch an enquiry.

Mr Fricker said, yesterday: 'I've been concerned about the case for some time. Obviously I can't say much at this juncture, but I feel that an enquiry is called for.' Mr Fricker would not be drawn on assumptions that Mason, because of his terminal illness, had confessed to the murder in exchange for a large amount of money, and would only add: 'That is something that needs to be looked into. I hope the police will welcome an enquiry, so that this matter can be cleared up to everyone's satisfaction.'

Handwell Herald and Post, October 1995

1

FINAL DEMAND FOR PAYMENT. Matthew Shelley studied the bold
heading and then put the bill with the others. He had accumu-
lated quite a pile – one threatened to repossess his car, another
promised court action unless he paid the thirty pounds owed to
the book club, a third warned that his telephone would soon be
disconnected . . .

Matthew frowned and ran a hand through his thick brown
curly hair. Final demands had never troubled him unduly;
after all, several months would elapse before their threats were
carried out. But the final, final ones – now they did bother
him.

His frown deepened, making him look far older than his thirty
years, as he picked up the latest communications from MEB and
British Gas. Those two definitely came into the better-get-
worried category. Eighty-five pounds in total, plus the four
hundred he owed his landlady for rent . . . Matthew let out a
long sigh. Why was it that the postman always brought the bills
but never the cheques?

'A cash flow problem,' he muttered. 'That's all it is.'

Yet again Matthew sorted through the pile of junk mail in the
hope of finding an envelope containing payment from a satisfied
client. There was an enthusiastic letter from a home shopping
catalogue stating that his numbers had been selected to go
forward into the grand draw with a prize of one hundred
thousand pounds. A more subdued message from an insurance
company guaranteeing that he would find peace of mind should
he die in a car accident knowing that his life was insured for ten
thousand pounds. But there was no money.

Matthew was half-way through another long sigh when he
heard the determined clatter of high heels on the carpetless
stairs outside his office. Quickly scooping up the bills, he stuffed
them into his desk drawer. Past experience had taught him
that potential clients tended to steer well away from private

investigators who were financially inept. The knock on the door was firm, confident, and just a shade impatient.

'Come in,' Matthew called, getting to his feet.

The woman fitted the knock perfectly. She was in her mid-twenties, raven-haired, and was five foot eight of pure glamour. Her two-piece black outfit was stunning, and it suited her so well she could easily have slipped out of a fashion magazine.

'Mr Shelley?' she asked, in a no-nonsense tone.

Matthew closed his gaping mouth and nodded. 'Yes, that's me. How can I help you?'

'I came here to hire your services, but . . .' She looked him up and down. His long unkempt curls, his faded blue jeans and crumpled sweater seemed to bother her. 'Well, let's just say, you're not quite what I expected.'

He laughed lightly. 'And what *did* you expect? A cross between Sam Spade and James Bond?'

The woman settled into a chair while Matthew waited for an answering laugh that failed to materialise. He noisily cleared his throat.

'No, I mean, nowadays we have to blend in with the crowd. People think my job's all excitement and romance, but you'd never believe – '

'What do you know about the murder of Glen Watkinson?' the woman cut in.

Matthew sat down and stared into the middle distance, his lips pursed. 'Absolutely nothing,' he finally said.

'Famous author?' she prompted. 'Scrap yard? Crushed in one of those machines they use to break up cars?'

'Oh yes, got you,' he said, snapping his fingers, suddenly alert. 'His body was crushed to a pulp, and there was no way the pathologist could say who it was.'

'You're close, but you see the police found two teeth that had survived intact and work done of them was identified by Watkinson's dentist.'

'But how did the teeth escape being crushed?'

'Because they weren't in the car.' She leant forward. 'Listen, three days after the murder a man named Billy Mason confessed to the killing. He claimed he'd met Watkinson in a pub. They'd had a few drinks and then left together. Mason's story was that

Watkinson made sexual advances to him. He lost his temper and punched Watkinson twice. Then when he went to help him up, Mason found he was dead.'

'And all this took place in a scrap yard?'

'No, outside it. Mason panicked, dragged the body into the yard, shoved it in a car and then went home. For the next few days nothing happened, and then the press broke the story that Watkinson was missing. Mason cracked and just walked into the nearest police station and confessed. The police had one hell of a job finding what was left of the body, but they did and Mason pleaded guilty at his trial.'

'That's right, I remember now,' Matthew said. 'Mason received a life sentence with a recommendation that he should serve at least twenty-five years.'

The woman sat back in her chair. 'Absolutely correct.'

'So, where's this leading?'

Her tone became conspiratorial. 'Billy Mason died of cancer in the prison hospital three weeks ago. Just six months into his sentence.'

Matthew looked blank.

'Well, don't you see?'

'It's not smacking me in the face, no.'

'Rumour has it, Mr Shelley, that Mason knew he was terminally ill before the murder even took place. Now, suppose someone wanted Watkinson out of the way. It's just possible that this someone killed him and then paid Mason to hold up his hand to the murder.'

Matthew drummed his fingers on the desk. 'But why would he do that? Surely, with a few months left to live, the last place he'd want to spend them would be in prison.'

The woman gave a shrug. 'Maybe he wanted to leave his family well provided for.'

'A bit like dying in a car crash on your way to work,' Matthew muttered.

'Sorry?'

'Nothing.' He studied the woman's attractive face. 'Do you know all this for certain, Miss . . . er . . .?'

'I don't know anything for certain.' She rummaged around in her shoulder bag. 'Look, Mr Shelley, my name's Karen Chandler

– here's my card – and I'm a freelance journalist. I've been hired by *Profile* magazine to do a series of articles about the case.'

'To prove that Mason was innocent?'

'Not necessarily. My brief is just to bring the case to the attention of the reading public.'

'And you want me to help you?'

Matthew's mind was racing. Already he could see final demands with PAID stamped across them in a nice bright red.

'It could take some time,' he mused. 'And I don't come cheap.'

'But the editor said you did.' The words were blurted before she realised, and Karen's face flushed. 'I mean, well, she said you were reasonable, actually.'

'I charge two hundred pounds a day, plus expenses,' Matthew said, hoping for a reaction.

He got one. Karen's jaw sagged and a look of disbelief contorted her pretty features. Had he blown it?'

'But on a case of any length,' he added, hurriedly, 'it's only a hundred pounds a day, plus expenses. And I hardly run up any expenses – honestly – in fact, none at all, sometimes.'

Karen Chandler had to wait to use the payphone, for it seemed that a woman and her two small boys had set up home in the booth. They had been in there for ages, and the woman appeared to be not in the least concerned by Karen's aggressive pacing.

She was waiting to speak to her editor and in between shooting glares at the woman Karen allowed her gaze to fall upon the Victorian building which housed Matthew Shelley's first-floor office – if it could be called an office. And what about the man himself? Surely the magazine had made a mistake.

Karen's patience was evaporating fast and, exhaling loudly, she placed herself in the woman's line of vision. Immediately, the door to the booth was pushed ajar.

'I'll have to go now, Rita,' the woman said, loudly. 'There's some snotty-looking cow outside, and I can't think.'

The receiver was slammed down and, pushing the children ahead of her into the street, she emerged with a mocking sneer. Karen gave a derisory snort and backed into the booth.

'Go and cash your giro,' she muttered, as she dialled the

magazine's number. Soon the clear crisp voice of her editor could be heard.

'Hello, Judith Ward here.'

'Hi, Judith, this is Karen.'

'Karen?'

'Karen Chandler.'

'Oh, Karen, of course,' Judith gushed. 'You'll have to forgive me, I was miles away. How are things going?'

'This Matthew Shelley . . . are you sure he's the best man for the job? To be honest, Judith, he comes across as a first class – '

'Of course he's the best man for the job,' Judith snapped. 'In fact, he was hand-picked. What don't you like about him?'

'Oh, I don't know . . .' She toyed with the telephone flex. 'He reminds me of a sixties pop singer . . . jeans, sweater, an old anorak. I kept expecting him to pick up a guitar and start singing protest songs.'

'Appearances can be deceptive.' A note of dismissal had crept into Judith's voice. 'Anyway, Karen, I'll brief you tonight. 'Bye now.'

The plush surroundings of the *Profile* offices contrasted sharply with the rundown business address of Matthew Shelley. And no one could ever mistake Judith Ward for a sixties pop star.

At forty years of age she was close to the top of her profession; and the salary which came with that position allowed Judith to indulge her passion for the best in clothes, hairstyles and cosmetics. Her make-up was thick but expertly applied, and it smoothed away the lines on her face until her skin had an almost doll-like quality. She patted the telephone on her desk, and smiled.

'Matthew Shelley is a first class idiot – I'm sure that was the term you were searching for, Karen, dear – but he'll serve our purposes admirably.' She let out a hearty chuckle. 'As, indeed, will you.'

2

Next morning Matthew parked his car on a single yellow line, two hundred yards from his office, and made sure that the disabled sticker permanently on loan from a friend was visible to any marauding traffic warden.

He ambled towards his office, scratching his head in such a way as to make passers-by give him a wide berth. His hair was full of grit and salt, an irritating leftover from last night's job. He'd been working on a divorce case – bread and butter money, as he called it – and had been forced to take refuge in a gritting bin at the roadside after the couple in question had taken umbrage at having their carnal gymnastics immortalized on Polaroid prints.

Matthew caught sight of Karen as he crossed the road and, forcing himself to stop scratching, he shot her a pleasant smile. She scowled in reply and watched while he snaked between the moving traffic.

'You're late,' she said, the minute he reached the pavement.

He looked bemused. 'Late for what?'

She ignored the question and glared at him accusingly. 'I've been standing here for ten minutes, Mr Shelley. God knows what I look like. See that Asian man . . .?' Matthew followed the direction of her glance. 'He had the cheek to come up to me and ask how much I charge.'

Matthew suppressed a smile. 'Sorry, but I don't keep office hours. A lot of my work's done at night.'

'Well,' she huffed,'can we please go up to your office and get to work before people start thinking you're picking me up.'

Matthew was ushering Karen towards the building when he stopped in his tracks. He had spied a small dapper man emerging from the doorway leading up to his office, the sort of chap that finance companies use to have friendly chats with their clients before threatening to break limbs.

Matthew made a grab for Karen's elbow. 'Why do we need the

office?' he said, steering her away. 'It's a nice morning, we can talk in my car.'

'Get your hands off me,' she protested.

But he held on. 'Let's just get to my car and leave . . . please.'

'You'd better let go of me, Shelley, or I'll scream. That Asian guy's still watching me. If he sees us going off in your car he's bound to think I'm on the game.'

Matthew promptly let her go. 'All right, all right, but if we don't get to my car right now, Miss Chandler, in a few minutes' time I might not have one.'

'What do you mean?'

'What I say. Now, are you coming or not?'

She gave a grudging nod.

'Good, hurry up, then.' He propelled her along the pavement. 'Now, about the case, I thought we'd start with the police. I've got a contact there . . . a mole . . . I thought we'd arrange a meet.'

Matthew felt more storm clouds gathering as he ordered coffee in a small café opposite the police station. He stirred the mugs with a spoon chained to the counter for far longer than was necessary in order to delay his return to the table, and to the peevish Karen. Fixing a sunny smile to his face, Matthew placed a mug before her. She snarled.

'Are you telling me, Mr Shelley, that this mole, this . . . this . . . contact . . . is the bloody tea lady at the police station?'

'She's given me a lot of useful stuff in the past,' he argued. 'Do you know something, Miss Chandler, you're a snob. Just because somebody works as a tea lady – '

'I'm a what?' Karen spluttered. 'This has got nothing to do with snobbery, Mr Shelley, this is to do with the need to know. What could a tea lady possibly tell us about Mason, apart from how many sugars he took?'

Matthew sipped his coffee and said over the rim, 'Ethel doesn't miss much.'

'Ethel? Oh, God . . .' Karen closed her eyes and groaned. 'I can see this on TV, you know. Matthew and Ethel – Crime Fighters. Who the hell needs Ruth Rendell?'

'You're very cutting, *and*, I might add, very short-tempered.'

His gaze shifted to the door. 'Here's Ethel, now. Don't offend her – okay? That lady's very special.'

Karen turned and looked to where Ethel was inching her way around the tables. She was in her sixties, grey-haired and tiny, but very noticeable nonetheless in a striking multi-coloured pinafore. She favoured Matthew with a beaming smile and pulled out a chair.

'You all right, love?'

'Not so springfield, Ethel,' he said, with a wink. 'What about you?'

'Oh, could be worse.' She sat down and took cigarettes and a lighter from her pinafore pocket while eyeing Karen with suspicion. 'Who's she, then?'

'She,' Karen said, haughtily, 'is a journalist – '

'She's with me, Ethel,' Matthew interjected with a good deal of authority. 'She's my assistant.'

Karen's mouth gaped open.

'That's all right, then.' Ethel lit a cigarette. 'Right, so you want to know about Billy Mason – '

Matthew nodded and scratched his head. 'Everything you've got.'

'Well,' she said, squinting through the smoke. 'I was there in reception with the tea trolley the night Billy walked in and asked to see whoever was in charge of the Glen Watkinson murder case.' She let out a wheezy laugh. 'Caused a bit of a panic, that did, 'cause there weren't no such case, see. Watkinson had been reported missing, that's all.'

'And what was your impression of Mason?' Matthew asked, speedily making notes.

Ethel drew on her cigarette and exhaled lazily. 'Even at that time he looked ill,' she said. 'I remember thinking he weren't long for this world.'

'So even then he looked as though he was dying?' Matthew probed.

Ethel shook her head. 'Not that ill, no. But with my experience, see, I can spot the signs of . . .' She paused and silently mouthed the word, 'cancer'.

Karen pulled a face and sipped her coffee.

'But I'll tell you one thing,' Ethel went on. 'He was a hard man, that Billy Mason. He held his fists half closed, like he was always ready for action. And I could tell he didn't like the police by the way he looked at them. He wouldn't let them touch him, either.'

'Excuse me for butting in,' Karen said, 'but could somebody tell me what this has got to do with anything?'

Ethel fixed her with a watery stare. 'So, knowing we was in for some action, I got back to the canteen and within half an hour the two coppers that was interviewing Mason came in for three teas. Seems that the man had coughed, owned up to the murder, told them where they could find the body. He said he was glad to get it off his conscience so he could sleep at night.'

Matthew leant forward eagerly. 'But you didn't believe him?'

Ethel stubbed out her cigarette and raised a knowing eyebrow. 'No, I didn't. Like I said, Billy was a hard man, and I found out later that he had some really heavy form. I couldn't see him losing a lot of sleep just 'cause he'd topped a bloke.' She snorted. 'Anyway, the big bosses upstairs were chuffed – not only had they solved a murder they didn't know had been committed, they'd got somebody in the cells for it.'

Matthew studied his notes and took up another frenzied scratching of his head.

'You got nits, love?'

'Not quite, Ethel, no.' He frowned and held up his notepad. 'I've an idea you think there's something iffy about all this – am I right?'

'I do, love, and I've got good reason to an all.' She sat forward and lowered her voice. 'Ada, who does the washing up, has got a sister working at the hospital, and she said that around the time of the post-mortem there was this rumour going around, see, that the pathologist couldn't identify the remains as those of that Watkinson bloke. The two teeth suggested they might be, but that's as far as he'd go.'

'So?' Karen cut in, sharply.

'So, if Billy hadn't pleaded guilty, the police wouldn't have had a case. Which is why they don't want the case reopened by all them "Billy Mason was innocent" merchants.' She pocketed her cigarettes. 'Anyway, that's all I can tell you, Matthew, so I'd better be getting back. If anything else turns up, I'll let you know.'

'Thanks a lot, Ethel, you've been a great help.' He dug a hand into his pocket. 'Here, let me make it worth your while.'

She grinned, momentarily dislodging her upper dentures. 'You don't have to pay me, you daft bugger.' And then she was off. A slight, hunched figure marching purposefully towards the door.

'She didn't even say goodbye to me,' Karen complained.

'You'd better lighten up if you want to get anywhere in this job, Miss Chandler. People like Ethel don't like snobs.'

'But I've told you,' she said, heatedly, 'I'm not a snob.'

'Well, that's how you come across. You just have to relax and look as though you're interested. People open up more if you make them think they're important.'

'Anyway, this whole thing was a complete waste of time,' she said, with a smug smile. 'I've got an interview this afternoon with the detectives who worked on the case.'

'Really? That's good . . . yes, that's very good. While you're there I'd like you to try and get a look at the pathologist's report because at the moment I'm getting two and two adding up to five.'

Karen sighed and rolled her eyes towards the ceiling. 'I think you're reading far too much into rumour and hearsay.'

'Is that so? Okay, why does your editor want to run a story on this, anyway? Because it's news, or because it's about to be?'

Karen shrugged. 'I've no idea, but I do know that lots of people will read into it exactly what you and your supergrass have.'

'Right, Miss Chandler, I'm off. I've a little delicate divorce case to work on.'

Matthew got to his feet, his body language hostile. Afraid that she had offended him, Karen jumped in quickly. 'When shall I see you? We could grab a bite to eat tonight.'

He looked doubtful. 'I'll be pretty tied up until late. Tell you what, if you meet me on the corner of Derby Street at ten we could get something and take it back to my place. You could fill me in on what you find out, then.'

16

Karen brightened instantly. 'Okay, that'll be nice.'

As she watched him leave the café Karen failed to notice a man approaching her table. He was around forty, smartly dressed, and he studied her with a strange glint in his eye.

'Is this seat taken?' he asked.

Karen was looking around at the other tables, most of them empty, and was about to make a sarcastic remark when Matthew's words came back to her. He was right, of course, she would have to cultivate a more friendly disposition. And what better time to start than now?

'No, help yourself,' she said, with a pleasant smile.

Karen watched him pull out the chair opposite, his gaze continually fixed on her face.

'You're not from around here?' he said.

'No, I'm from London. I'm just working here.'

'Things a bit difficult in the big city, then?'

'I'll say,' Karen replied, surprised that she could so readily make conversation with a stranger. 'Whatever you've heard about that place, I can tell you first hand, they don't want to pay for a good service.'

She was about to launch into a description of her journalistic talents and the meanness of London publishers when the man leant forward.

'That at least makes it less embarrassing,' he whispered. 'I thought I was right but you can't always tell.'

'I beg your pardon?' she asked, somewhat puzzled.

He gave her a surreptitious wink. 'How much do you charge, then?'

Matthew finally got to Derby Street at 10.25 p.m. and quickly found that Karen's dislike of standing around on street corners in the dark far surpassed her distaste for loitering in daylight. She was not pleased, and as Matthew followed her strutting silhouettte along the darkened street he wondered whether he really wanted to work with this woman – even for money.

'I don't *believe* you,' she said for the umpteenth time. 'You invite me out for a meal . . .'

'You invited me,' he mumbled to himself.

'And you take me to a crummy fish and chip shop where we have to make do with what's left over at closing time.'

'I helped Mario with his divorce, so now he helps me out sometimes.'

'Well, thanks for telling me,' she said, half turning and giving him a frosty glare. 'I could have died when he asked whether I wanted the two fish cakes or the slightly burnt jumbo sausage.'

'I think you were right to choose the sausage.'

Karen came to an abrupt stop. 'This is not funny, Shelley.'

He held up his hands in surrender. 'I'm not laughing – honest. I've got a cash flow problem at the moment, that's all.'

Matthew turned into a dark alley to their right and motioned for Karen to follow.

She frowned. 'Why are you going up there?'

'I use the fire escape to get into my flat,' he called back. 'Come on, keep up.'

'But . . .? Oh, don't ask, Karen, don't ask,' she muttered, setting off in pursuit.

3

'Put your leg up just a little bit higher,' Matthew said.

'I've got it up as high as it'll go,' Karen replied through clenched teeth. She finally cleared the window sill and stumbled into the darkness of Matthew's room.

'Watch the creaking floorboards,' he whispered urgently.

Karen stopped to draw in a heaving breath. 'Look, I know these are silly questions, and I'm such an idiot for asking them, but why do we have to climb up the fire escape and through your window? And why do we somehow have to try to avoid stepping on the floor?'

'I owe some rent,' Matthew said, flicking on the light. 'If I use the front door or if she knows I'm up here, the landlady collars me.'

Treading gingerly, Karen paced the tiny room and cast a

distasteful eye on the furnishings. It had once been the back bedroom of a large Victorian house and what little space there was Matthew had filled with a single bed, a wardrobe, settee and armchair, and a table with two straight-backed wooden chairs. A small alcove at one end of the room was home to a stove and an enamel sink. Everything was pre-1950s, and none of it matched.

'Hmm, very nice . . .' She gave him an encouraging smile.

Matthew was sitting cross-legged on the floor and tearing into the paper parcels from the chip shop.

'There's your jumbo sausage,' he said, passing it across. 'And mine's the cod.'

Karen sat down and was quite determined not to eat the greasy food, but the salt and vinegar smell wafting up from the paper was making her mouth water. She took a tiny bite of the sausage.

'How did you get on with the police?' Matthew asked through a mouthful of fish.

'They were very informative, actually. I can't remember their names offhand – '

'DS Spencer and DC Cooper,' he cut in.

'Oh yes, that's right.' Karen tried to ignore the thin trail of fat running from a corner of Matthew's mouth, and said, 'Anyway, they assured me that Billy Mason was guilty and there was no point – '

'In anybody looking into the case again,' he interjected for a second time.

'It's bad manners to keep interrupting,' she said. 'And wipe your chin, you've got grease all over it.'

'I just want you to see something, so bear with me.' He paused for a moment to empty his mouth. 'Now, this is how I think your interview went, and tell me if I'm wrong. The police said they were happy that the right man was convicted. They wouldn't show you the pathologist's report but were adamant that it identified the remains found in the scrap yard as those of Glen Watkinson. How am I doing so far?'

'You're spot on, actually,' she was loath to admit.

'Doesn't all that strike you as odd?'

'No, why?'

'Well, if the police were certain they'd got the right man, why be so tight-lipped about the information they've got? There's no reason for them to be so guarded – to my knowledge, nobody's ever thrown doubt on Mason's guilt. In fact, nobody's ever shown any interest in the case – apart from the group of campaigners that Ethel mentioned, and the police are hardly likely to take notice of them. And yet a magazine hires you to do a series of articles about it. It's as if they deliberately want to focus public attention on the case. But, why?'

Karen stared into her chip paper. 'Funny you should say that, the same thought had crossed my mind. Of course the magazine could have sided with the campaigners, but I doubt it – I mean, they would have mentioned it, surely. My brief is to present all the facts to the reader, but I can't see the point because all the contacts *Profile* gave me say the facts prove Billy Mason was guilty.'

'I'll tell you what I think,' Matthew said. 'I think that someone somewhere is frightened the case will be looked into, so they're getting in first and trying to put the conclusion beyond any reasonable doubt.'

Karen let out a caustic laugh. 'We could be getting a bit carried away here. What possible motive could anyone have for that?'

'I don't know, yet.' He chewed thoughtfully on a piece of overcooked fish. 'I tell you what though, Karen – can I call you Karen? – I bet if you told your editor you'd uncovered evidence to suggest Mason wasn't the murderer, she'd pull the plug on the whole project.'

'Do you want me to try it?'

Matthew screwed up his chip paper in a very decisive manner. 'No, let's wait till we have got something first.' He frowned. 'There's something else puzzling me, as well. I can guess why they chose me for the job – but why you?'

'I don't follow.'

'Well, I'm reasonably new as a private detective, therefore I haven't got a track record, so they're probably assuming I'm useless.'

Karen grinned. 'They did hint that you weren't much good.'

'Oh, thanks,' he said, pouting.

'Don't take offence,' she said, hurriedly. 'They just told me not to take too much notice of what you said. I was to look on you more as somebody to ferry me about.'

'That's my suspicions confirmed, then.' He looked her in the eye. 'But you're an experienced journalist – '

'I'm not, actually. This is my first job.'

'You've never had anything published before?'

'I have,' she retorted. 'A short story in the local newspaper, *and* a poem.'

'So, that's it. They think they've got a couple of noddies they can do what they like with.'

There was a knock on the door and Matthew froze, his breath held fast.

'Mr Shelley, are you in there?' Another, more urgent knock. 'Mr Shelley, it's Mrs Perkins.'

'Quick,' Matthew hissed. 'Get behind the settee, it's my landlady.' He scuttled out of sight. 'Come on – quickly – she looks through the keyhole.'

With a weary sigh, Karen joined him behind the settee. 'Shelley, I really don't believe any of this.'

'Look, about money . . .' Matthew whispered.

'I can let you have a hundred pounds, that's all I've got. I don't get paid until the articles are written.'

'Mr Shelley?' Another light knock on the door.

'Go away, Mrs Perkins,' he muttered. 'I haven't got any bloody money and at this rate I'm never likely to have any.' He turned to Karen. 'So I don't get paid until the case is finished?'

'That's about it. If you want to back out . . .'

Matthew leant against the settee, his expression one of defeat. 'By that time, I'll have no gas, electricity, telephone . . . no room, no car, no food, tea, coffee – '

'Oh, don't go on,' Karen chided. 'What do you think I'm living on?' She peeped around the settee. 'Anyway, I think your landlady's gone.'

'She'll be back, don't worry.' He pondered for a moment. 'Hey, I've just had a thought. If we do uncover a good story here, something really big, then you could sell it on the open market and name your own price.'

'Huh, flying pigs.' She grinned. 'That's what my mum used to say when I had big dreams.'

'But this one could come true.'

'And what would be in it for you – eh, Shelley? Half of my new-found fortune? Let's try and keep our feet on the ground, shall we? I'm working for *Profile* and you'd better help me do a good job because if I don't get paid, you don't either.'

Suddenly Matthew positioned himself in front of her, his mouth set in a serious line, and Karen was surprised to see a slight blush colouring his cheeks.

'Confession time,' he said. 'I'm not really a private detective. What I mean is, I am, but what I really want to be is a crime novelist.'

'Really? How exciting. Have *you* ever had anything published?'

'Well, no, I've never actually finished a book, to be honest. I used to sign on and they kept sending me on training courses. I did painting and decorating, which I was useless at, and plumbing – that was a disaster – so I thought, why not set myself up as a private eye? That way I'd get some first-hand knowledge of crime, and I'd get paid at the same time.' He pulled a face. 'Now, there's a laugh.'

Karen exhaled sharply. 'They really have got a couple of noddies, haven't they?'

'That remains to be seen.' Matthew stood up cautiously, his eyes on the door. 'Come on, let me show you to the window.'

'You're coming with me, I hope,' Karen said, hitching up her skirt. 'I'm not going down that fire escape on my own.'

'And I wouldn't expect you to. I'll run you home.'

Karen took off her shoes and was half out of the window, her toes feeling around frantically for the metal platform.

'That's another thing,' she said, her breath fogging the night air as she clung like a limpet to Matthew's arm. 'Why did you park the car so far away from your digs?'

'Because it's about to be repossessed, and I don't want to make it easy for them.' He pushed Karen ahead and she gave a little cry of fright. 'Don't make too much noise going down the steps. Mrs Perkins is bound to guess I'm using them, but I'd like it to be later rather than sooner.'

4

Even quiet side streets lined with first-time-buyer terraced houses had failed to escape the march of those dreaded yellow lines, and Matthew was silently bemoaning the fact as he fixed his disabled sign to the windscreen.

It was a pleasant sunny morning, though, and he intended to enjoy the half-mile trek back to his office. He was getting out of his car, inhaling the fresh smog, when a female traffic warden sidled up. With a cheery 'Good morning,' Matthew locked the car door and hobbled away, his limp highly exaggerated.

Two hundred yards later, he glanced back and saw that the warden was closely inspecting the tax disc of a parked Cortina, her pen hovering ominously over her pad of tickets. Matthew relaxed into his normal walk. On the main road he found Karen pacing the pavement and glancing around as if fearful of being approached.

'Hi,' he said. 'What are you doing here? You could have waited outside the office.'

She took in a breath, her nostrils flaring, and gave him a sheepish look. 'I'm having a few difficulties, and I don't really want to go into them. Suffice to say that I feel happier on the move.'

Matthew fell in beside her. 'I didn't really expect to see you here this morning.'

'I did a lot of thinking last night, Shelley, and I've come to the conclusion that Judith Ward, my editor at *Profile*, is hiding something . . .' She fell silent, and bit anxiously on her lower lip.

'Go on,' Matthew coaxed.

'Well, I know we'd decided to wait, but I couldn't. I broached the subject of Billy Mason's innocence and Judith didn't exactly go berserk – she'd have cracked her make-up if she had – but she told me in no uncertain terms not to pursue that theme.' They reached the office building and their footsteps sounded on the wooden stairs. 'But what I can't work out is how somebody as respectable as Judith Ward could be involved in any sort of crime.'

'Maybe she's not,' Matthew said, unlocking the office door and ushering Karen inside. 'Maybe she's had orders from higher up the ladder.' He scooped up his post and kicked the door shut with his heel.

'But what connection would a high-class magazine have with Billy Mason?' Karen asked, as she perched on the edge of his desk.

'That's for us to find out. Listen, there are certain details I didn't fill you in on yesterday,' Matthew said, flicking through the mail. 'Glen Watkinson wasn't that successful as an author. Okay, he was a name everybody knew, but he wasn't mega-bucks, and his publishers were actually losing money from his poor sales. Now, say he wrote novels faster than the publishers could get them out, say he'd got ten unpublished novels lying around – well, think about it, all the publicity about his murder could have those novels in the bestseller lists in no time.'

Karen let out a loud laugh. 'Are you suggesting that his publishers had him killed to increase book sales?'

Matthew settled at his desk and started to open the letters, his expression becoming progressively more dispirited with each one that was tossed aside.

'Well?' Karen said. 'For goodness' sake, you can't really be serious.'

He gave a shrug. 'They might have considered it could be a good career move for him.'

'Shelley, all publishers, by and large, are very respectable people.'

'Money corrupts,' Matthew said, tossing the mail in the waste bin. 'And lack of it sends you climbing the bloody walls. Not one miserable cheque amongst that lot.' He sat back and studied her. 'Believe me, Karen, ten bestsellers would be enough to corrupt any publisher.'

She still looked doubtful. 'None of this makes sense to me – any way I look at it.'

'Of course it doesn't, because we haven't even scratched the surface, yet. We have to start with Billy Mason. Now, he lived in

Saltley, which is a good fifty miles away from here, but every Wednesday he visited Handwell, regular as clockwork.'

'And was it a Wednesday when Watkinson was killed?'

'Yes, it was. Now, as far as I've been told, Mason always spent the evening drinking in the Queen's Arms. On the night in question nobody can remember seeing Watkinson in the pub at any time, although Mason claims that's where they met. I think our best course of action would be to visit Saltley and find out as much about Mason as we can.' He cleared his throat. 'Look, Karen, I'm sorry to have to ask you this, but that hundred pounds you promised me . . .'

'Oh, yes.'

She sorted through her shoulder bag and fished out a cheque. Matthew made an eager grab for it.

'Now at least I can pay the gas and electricity bills,' he said, with a satisfied sigh.

'Is there any chance you could make a payment on the car?' Karen asked, hopefully. 'Only the walks to and from it are beginning to get me down.'

Matthew flashed her a smile. 'Look on it as exercise for your heart, Miss Chandler.'

Saltley was a former market town that had been granted city status in the 1970s. Its urban sprawl gave way to a rather ugly city centre lined with featureless grey stone buildings. Matthew parked in a side street and they got out of the car to sounds and smells of the surrounding market.

'This is a big place,' Karen remarked. 'Have you any idea where Billy Mason lived?'

'No,' he said, tapping the side of his nose, 'but I'm about to find out.'

The market square was cobbled and Karen was wearing a pair of dark blue high-heeled slingbacks – a sure-fire recipe for disaster. They strolled, with Matthew slightly ahead, between rows of stalls selling everything from fruit and vegetables to ladies' underwear. Every so often he had to stop and wait while Karen struggled to extract one heel or the other from the grips of the rutted surface. Very soon her querulous nature was making a swift return, helped along by big butch stall-holders whose whistles of appreciation seemed always to coincide with her ungainly stumbles.

'How much further, Shelley?' she asked, with an exasperated sigh.

''Relax,' he advised.

Her heel caught again, and this time Karen almost lost her footing. 'I can't bloody relax,' she snapped, 'I'm breaking my neck, here.'

It was then that Matthew approached a bric-à-brac stall. The man in charge was small and wiry, his hair incredibly black and parted down the middle.

'Harry, my friend, how you doing?' Matthew said with a grin.

'Well, if it isn't Matthew Shelley,' the man said, gripping his hand warmly. 'I'd heard you'd been appointed as personal bodyguard to the Queen. How you keeping?'

'Not so springfield.' He pointed to Karen. 'Harry, this is my assistant.'

The man gave her a perfunctory nod and returned his attention to Matthew. 'What can I do for you, son?'

'Billy Mason,' Matthew said from the corner of his mouth.

Karen watched the man's ferret-like face turn pale.

'You must be joking,' he said, shaking his head. 'Listen, my features're none too good, but I'm not looking to get them rearranged – know what I mean?'

'Come on, Harry, you know I never disclose my sources.'

'Maybe not . . .' He cast a doubtful look at Karen. 'But what about her?'

'Harry, meet Karen Chandler,' Matthew said, pushing her towards the man. 'Like I said, she's my assistant, you've got nothing to worry about.'

Harry was shooting sideways glances into the crowd. 'So, what do you want to know?'

'First of all, did Billy Mason have a record?'

'Yeah, but that all came out at the trial, no secret about it. He did three years for GBH.' Harry motioned for Matthew to come closer. 'But what they didn't find out was that Billy ran with the

26

gangs down in London in the sixties. When the fuzz broke them up, a lot of them moved out into the sticks.'

'And that's when Mason came to Saltley?'

'That's right, along with some of the big boys who set up stalls around here. Drugs, prostitutes, protection – they ran all them through the seventies and eighties from behind legit business fronts.'

'And what's the word on Billy Mason killing Watkinson?' Matthew asked.

'I can only tell you what I was told – all right? Apparently Billy knew he was dying and somebody offered him enough money to see his missus through after he'd gone if he'd hold his hand up to the murder.'

'Shelley, that was my theory, exactly,' Karen said, excitedly.

'Keep your voice down,' Matthew scolded. 'Is that all, Harry? You're not holding anything back?'

The man looked away, unwilling to meet his eyes. 'You'll get me topped, you will,' he grumbled. 'Okay, there was another rumour flying around, as well. Apparently Billy had attracted the displeasure of his former bosses, and he had to take the rap for the murder, or else.'

'Or else what?' Matthew probed.

Harry rubbed the stubble on his chin while a frown formed on his forehead. 'That's the part of it that don't make sense. Billy had gone down a bit, it's true, but I couldn't see anybody forcing him into doing anything. He was about as hard as they come, was Bill.' The man chuckled. 'It wouldn't surprise me if he's down there now, spitting in the devil's eye and saying: You call this hot? No, son, old Billy Mason wasn't the sort of bloke who'd bow to pressure.'

'So we can discount that, then?' Karen said, putting down the chipped saucer she was inspecting.

'Not altogether, miss, no. Them putting the rumour about were stepped on pretty hard.'

'So there was something in it?' she persisted.

'Look, love,' Harry said, 'the other word going round is there's a journalist and private detective been hired to look into the case . . .'

'Oh, really? That's Matthew and me,' she said, cheerily.

The man gave a sarcastic grunt. 'You don't say.'

'But how the hell could anybody know about us?' Matthew asked.

'Search me, son. All I heard was you'd been told to find that Billy was guilty so there'd be no need for anybody else to look into the case.'

'That's absolutely right,' Karen said. 'And we can't work out why.'

'Think about it,' Harry advised. 'The Mob was hired to kill Watkinson and then get Billy, because of his limited lifespan, to hold up his hand for it. Now, as things stand, it's case closed. But if the likes of you start poking your noses in the wrong places, finding out too much, it could lead to whoever put up the money to have Watkinson's curtain brought down. My advice to you is, leave well alone.'

'Thanks, Harry,' Matthew said, 'but I need just one more favour.'

'And I think I know what it is.' He let out a resigned sigh and reached for a notepad on top of the till. 'But if you grass me up on this . . .'

Harry scribbled on the pad and slipped the sheet of paper across. Matthew gave him the thumbs-up sign and ushered Karen away from the stall.

'Shelley, can we get on to the pavement? I can't walk on these cobbles.'

'Okay, you go and sit down – there's a form over there – and I'll get us a couple of teas.'

Matthew vanished into the crowd while Karen made her cautious way to the wooden bench. She felt very alone, and more than a little out of her depth.

'What am I getting myself into here?' she asked herself. 'Why don't I simply do what I'm told, take the money and then forget all about Billy Mason.'

'I'm having the same thoughts.' She glanced up to find Matthew holding two plastic mugs of tea. 'After all, here I am, up to my neck in debt, and I'm persuading you to throw away your job and my cut of the money.'

'Why are you doing it, then?'

'I don't know.' He sat down and stared at the bustling marketplace. 'Yes, I do. Somebody, somewhere, has looked at me, Karen, and thought, he's just what we need – even if he's sharp enough to work it all out, he'll still do what's he's told in the end. And I don't like that.'

Karen felt a sudden surge of warmth. She had found a soul mate. 'That's exactly how I feel, Shelley. Those same people have looked at me and thought, she's green and she'll follow her brief to the letter, however much the evidence tells her not to.'

Matthew gave an awkward laugh. 'Shouldn't we be saying something noble now like, we'll always fight for justice and for what's right, refuse to be treated like dunkheads?'

Karen gazed into the middle distance, sipping her tea. 'Shelley, could you answer a question that's got nothing to do with the case?'

'If I can.'

'When anybody asks you how you are, why do you say you're not so springfield?'

'Oh, that's just an extension of not so dusty, meaning, not so bad. Not so Dusty Springfield – get it?'

'Oh . . . oh, I see. You're into sixties pop music, then?'

'You bet I am. But I can't play any because Mrs Perkins would know I was in.'

'I should have guessed, really. I mean, when I watched you going to fetch the teas I saw a strong resemblance to a young Bob Dylan.'

Matthew grinned. 'A lot of people have said I look like him.'

'Is that why you wear scruffy clothes and never comb your hair?'

'Of course not,' he said, clearly hurt. 'The first time the similarity was pointed out, I did everything I could to play it down. I'm not that juvenile, Karen, for goodness' sake.'

5

Matthew unfolded the piece of paper Harry had given him and checked the address. Yes, this was it. His gaze settled once more upon the house before him. It was huge and set comfortably within its own grounds.

'Well, this is the Mason residence,' he intoned. 'Who said that crime doesn't pay?'

Karen's eyes swept across the long terrace with its impressive stone pillars and french windows. She gave out a long low whistle. 'There must be at least six bedrooms.'

'And then some, I'll bet. That house was built at the turn of the century. Around the back would be servants' quarters and stables.'

'So, Billy Mason was no small-time villain, then.'

'No, but I didn't realise he was this big.' Matthew drummed his fingers on the steering wheel, his mind working. 'I wonder when Mrs Mason moved into this place.'

'What, you mean it could have been part of the pay-off?'

He nodded.

'Well, Shelley, one thing's for sure, whoever wanted Glen Watkinson dead was obviously willing to part with a heck of a lot of money.'

'Hmmm.' He shot her an enquiring glance. 'Karen, do you think it might just be possible we're wrong in assuming that the motive for the murder was money?'

'I don't know. What else could it be?'

'Search me.' He unbuckled his seat belt. 'Come on, let's go and have a word with Mrs Mason. She must have an opinion of her late husband's involvement in all this.'

They had tried the bell three times and were about to give up when the thick oak door was pulled open. On the threshold stood an attractive middle-aged woman. Her clothes told of much money but little taste, and signs of brown and grey showed at the roots of her blonde hair. Her smile, however, was warm and welcoming.

'Yes?' she said.

'We're sorry to disturb you,' Karen stammered, 'but we're looking for Mrs Mason.'

'Look no further, love. I'm Dot Mason.'

'Oh, good. My name's Karen Chandler.' She unzipped her shoulder bag and searched for a card.

'Ah ... the journalist. I've been expecting you.' Dot Mason turned her radiant smile towards Matthew. 'And you must be the private dick.'

'Yes, yes, you could say that.'

'Come in, both, why don't you?' She stood aside and ushered them into the hall. 'Let's go through into the lounge. It's this way.'

The woman was probably in her mid-fifties, Karen surmised as she followed closely behind; and there was a real hint of toughness behind that ultra-pleasant manner.

The lounge was the size of an average ballroom, and loaded with antiques. Karen's mouth literally watered as she took in the many splendid objects stashed away in burglar-proof glass cases.

'Sit yourselves down, and don't be shy.' Mrs Mason pointed to an exquisite sofa positioned in front of the open fireplace. 'And relax, why don't you? I'm not going to pull a sawn-off shotgun from under the coffee table and blow you away.'

Matthew gave a forced laugh and sat awkwardly on the edge of the sofa. Karen settled beside him, her notepad and pen in hand. Mrs Mason wandered across to the said coffee table and took a cigarette from a silver box.

'I suppose what you want to know,' she said, exhaling smoke with the words, 'is whether my Billy really did kill Glen Watkinson. Well, the short answer to that is, yes.'

Karen was momentarily thrown by the woman's direct approach, but she was loath to let it show. With brow knitted and pen held ready, she attempted the pose of a seasoned journalist.

'Mrs Mason,' she said, briskly, 'this is all very difficult – '

'Then let me make it easier for you, love. The filth don't want the case reopened because, apart from my hubby's confession, they'd got sod all and they knew it. The only person that could confirm the story is Billy, and he died coughing his lungs out.' She took a long drag on the cigarette and exhaled. 'Now a meddling MP with more time on his hands than sense has taken an interest – so what? He won't alter anything – my Billy's dead, nothing's gonna bring him back. He'll just stir everything up again, and for nothing.'

'Mrs Mason,' Matthew said, 'I don't want to cause you any distress – ' He paused to choke as a great cloud of cigarette smoke wafted across. 'But our investigation might just prove that your husband did kill the man.'

A coarse chuckle erupted from Dot Mason's chest. 'You're a real treasure – Mr Shelley, is it? No, love, the only thing an investigation can do is raise doubts in everybody's minds. And all the do-gooders can spend years talking about another miscarriage of justice.' She stubbed out her cigarette and lit another one immediately. 'They'll probably dig up some dissatisfied ex-copper who'll claim he saw them beating a confession out of my poor Billy.' That nicotine laugh came again. 'My God, I'd have liked to have seen them try it.'

'But your husband walked into the police station and confessed of his own volition,' Karen reminded her.

Dot Mason raised a ruthlessly plucked eyebrow. 'You don't see it, do you? The only person who can verify that is Billy, and he's gone. Love, they can twist the story any way they want to. Now, you might think I'm as hard as nails, but I just want things left as they are, I've been through enough already.'

Matthew started to rise. 'We've upset you, Mrs Mason, and we didn't want that. Would you rather we left?'

'No, sit down, treasure.' She smiled. 'You know, my Billy would've loved you. He always admired good manners.' She settled into an armchair, her legs folded beneath her. 'I reckon I can answer most of your questions without you even asking them. Oh, I'm aware of the whispers, all right – my husband knew he was on his way out and was paid to confess to the killing so he could leave me financially secure. And wouldn't I just love to get my hands round the necks of the whisperers.' Her gaze took in the room. 'We've lived in this house for twenty years, and it's on the market now for just short of a million. Believe me, I don't need any more money.'

Karen's eyes widened as she watched the woman demolish her second cigarette and light a third. She blinked rapidly against the smoke.

'I wonder . . .' she said. 'I wonder if I could ask you a couple of very personal questions.'

'Go ahead,' Dot Mason replied, with an expansive wave of her hand. 'My life's common property . . .'

'Right.' Karen glanced at Matthew and cleared her throat. 'Did your husband know he had cancer before – '

'Okay, love, there's no need to draw pictures. Yes, he knew. His mother went the same way so he recognised the signs – the cough, loss of weight, no strength, always tired . . . Oh, he knew all right.'

'And he definitely told you he murdered Glen Watkinson?'

'That's right. He was sitting where you are now.' She leant forward. 'I want you both to understand something – my Billy was a villain, always had been, always would have been. He and the people he ran with didn't recognise society's rules, they had their own set. So you can forget all the guff about the murder playing on his mind because that was pure fiction.' She settled back, the ashtray balanced on her lap. 'He saw the whole thing as funny, if you must know. I mean, forty years the filth had been running round in circles, trying to nail him for one thing or another. And in the end he just walked in and spilled his guts about something they didn't even know about so as they'd arrest him. He saw it as a clear sign of his superior intelligence. People do come to terms with dying, you know.'

'Just one more question,' Karen said. 'Your husband went to Handwell every Wednesday. Have you any idea why?'

Dot Mason turned away and took in a sharp breath. 'You're getting close to the quick now, love. I presume there was another woman. Forsaking all others was another rule Billy didn't recognise.' She shrugged. 'Still, there was nothing I could do, so for all those years I chose to ignore it.'

'Right, then,' Matthew said, getting to his feet. 'I think we've got all we need, Mrs Mason, and I'd like to thank you for being so co-operative.'

'Any time, treasure, any time. Sure you won't stay for a cup of tea?'

'Better not . . . lots to do.' He grabbed Karen's arm and ushered her towards the door. 'We'll let ourselves out, shall we?'

'Please yourself, love. Come again, if you need me.'

Outside, the gravel gave a satisfying crunch as they marched along the drive. Matthew tutted.

'What's the matter with you?'

'I'll have to wash my hair tonight,' he grumbled. 'God, that cigarette smoke.'

'Do you think she was on the level, Shelley?'

'No, I don't. She put in a good performance as the grieving widow, I'll give her that, but she wasn't totally convincing.'

'What makes you say that?'

'Well,' he said, sniffing at his anorak, 'Billy Mason supposedly punches Watkinson and then finds he's dead. So, he hauls the body over the high double gates, drags it some two hundred yards and then throws it into a wrecked car. It hardly fits in with the man's failing strength, now does it?'

'Hmm, I see what you mean.'

They reached the pair of elaborate wrought iron gates that cut into the high walls bordering the property. Matthew struggled to pull them open.

'At the moment, Karen, I feel we're getting the velvet glove, but if we don't back off soon, I fear it's going to turn into the iron fist.' The gates gave a menacing creak as he closed them.

From an upstairs window Dot Mason watched their car pull away, her expression fuelled with alarm. If only Billy had told her what he'd been up to. But he hadn't. She was completely in the dark.

Damn the bastard do-gooders, and damn the press for encouraging them. She'd had no trouble since Billy went inside, and now it could all start up again.

6

Back at the office Matthew was searching through his second post for cheques, and wondering how to dodge Mrs Perkins for a few more weeks. With the last of the letters consigned to the waste bin, he slumped in his chair.

'The trouble is, Karen, she'll work out that I'm using the fire escape and one night she'll be up there waiting for me.' His telephone buzzed and he snatched up the receiver. 'Matthew Shelley, Private Investigator. How can I help you?'

'I need to speak to Karen Chandler. Is she there?'

'Yes, hold on.' He held out the receiver. 'It's for you.'

'Who is it?' she whispered.

'Forgot to ask,' he whispered back.

She took the receiver. 'Hello, Karen Chandler speaking. Who is this?'

'Judith Ward,' was the abrupt reply. 'You really must get a mobile phone, dear, I've been trying to contact you all morning. It really is most annoying. Hasn't Mr Shelley got one, either?'

'Hold on, I'll check.' She clamped her hand over the mouth-piece. 'Shelley, have you got a mobile phone?'

He shook his head. 'I did have one, but – '

'Never mind, don't tell me,' she muttered. 'No, Judith, we don't have a mobile between us. Perhaps if you paid me an advance, I could get one.'

'You have a very sharp manner, dear, I'd do something about it, if I were you. The magazine pays on delivery – you know that – but I've lined up a series of interviews for you, so if you get on with them and produce some copy, then you'll get paid.'

'And who are these interviews with, Judith?'

'The first is with the chief inspector who worked on the Mason case. The second is with Mason's solicitor, and the third is with a man who shared a cell with Mason while he was on remand. They should give you enough for at least two articles, along the lines of your commission.'

'Okay, fine. Oh, Judith, there's something I want to check out with you – now, I know that Glen Watkinson's publisher was Charlton Press, and I just wanted to know whether *Profile* magazine was part of that group.'

There was silence on the line for a very long ten seconds. 'My, my, aren't you an inquisitive girl?' Judith said, at last. 'As a matter of fact *Profile* is part of the Charlton group. Why do you ask?'

'No reason, I just like to be well informed,' Karen said, lightly. 'Right, then, if you'd like to give me the times and places for the interviews, I can get on and we can all make some money.'

Karen was surprised to find that Matthew knew quite a few of the local coppers. As they hurried along the green-walled corridors at the rear of the police station a number of uniformed officers stopped to pass the time of day, and to leer openly at Karen's trim figure.

'How come you know so many people here?' she asked in a hushed tone.

'It's a long story,' Matthew replied, with a non-committal shrug.

'Most of your stories are.' She grabbed his arm and forced him to look at her. 'Give, Shelley, you're holding something back.'

He sighed. 'Okay. Chief Inspector Mackmin – '

'The chap we're going to see,' she cut in, heavily.

'That's right, him. Well, six months ago, about the time I started the agency, his wife thought he was messing around with other women and none of the other private investigators would touch it – '

'Of course they wouldn't – you don't get the wrong side of a chief inspector.' She folded her arms and gave him a sharp look. 'I've a feeling I'm not going to like what's coming, but go on.'

'I didn't know, did I?' he said, his voice full of righteous indignation. 'There I was, broke, and I'd got people coming round at any time to take away my TV and video. I needed the money – '

'But you haven't got a television, or a video.'

'I know, they did repossess them. But, anyway, I took the case and caught Mackmin with another woman, and now his wife's divorcing him.'

'Oh, great ... bloody great,' Karen huffed. She was pacing in small circles, her arms spread in a gesture of despair. 'You do realise that this won't help our investigation one little bit? He's hardly likely to welcome his marriage-wrecker with open arms, is he?'

'I suppose not. In fact, he's already made his feelings towards me pretty plain. He told all his officers to lean on me, wait for me to put a foot out of place. That's how I got to know so many of the lads. They used to harass me a bit – you know, picking me up for having dodgy indicators or dud lights on the car, breathalysing me every time I got behind the wheel, that sort of thing.'

Karen fell back against the wall and let out a deep sigh. 'So, you've managed to alienate the entire police force, and we're here to ask for information they're under absolutely no obligation to give. You definitely make life simple, Shelley, I don't think. Deep down, you must really like starving and having to hide from creditors all the time.'

Matthew acknowledged her cutting sarcasm with a weak smile and dug his hands deep into the pockets of his anorak.

'Anyway,' he said, 'there's no need to worry. I'm sure Mackmin's getting over it, and it's a good thing to have some form in my job.'

'A dodgy indicator? You call that form?'

'Excuse me, is everything all right?'

The voice startled them, and they turned as one to glance along the corridor. Karen's quarrelsome tone had brought a man from his office. He stood on the threshold, his massive bulk almost filling the doorway. And his rugged face creased into a scowl the moment he caught sight of Matthew.

'Is that man bothering you, miss?' He was clearly hoping for an affirmative.

'No, no, he's with me,' Karen said, approaching the man with hesitant steps. 'I'm Karen Chandler, and I'm looking for Chief Inspector Mackmin.'

'You've found him,' Mackmin responded, flatly. 'He's with you, you say?'

37

'Yes, in a way,' she said, discounting Matthew with a casual wave of her hand. 'He does the odd job for me ... nothing much.' She put on a professional smile. 'You are expecting me . . .?'

The grim policeman stood aside. 'You'd better come into my office.'

Matthew flinched under the chief inspector's stern gaze as they pulled up chairs and settled in front of his desk. Mackmin smoothed down imaginary creases in his immaculate dark grey suit and then took his own seat.

'Now, Miss Chandler, I understand you're interested in the Watkinson murder.'

'Yes, that's right.' She crossed her legs and balanced a notepad on her knee. 'I'm trying to shed some new light on it, actually.'

'That's not the way I heard it.' The words were sharply uttered, but then Mackmin's features softened. 'And although I wish you luck,' he continued, with a genial smile, 'as far as we're concerned, it was an open and shut case. I believe my detectives told you that.'

'They did, indeed, chief inspector, but they weren't very helpful with things like the pathologist's report and forensics.'

Mackmin considered her for a moment and then reached for a folder on his desk. 'We don't usually make those documents available to the public, Miss Chandler, but on this occasion I'm willing to make an exception.' He handed the folder across.

Karen flicked swiftly through its contents before passing it on to Matthew. He could feel the policeman's eyes boring into the top of his head while he studied the documents. Soon, Karen's quick-fire questions became a low drone.

Matthew read that the pathologist had concluded there was no way the remains found in the ruins of the car could be positively identified as those of the author, Glen Watkinson. Every bone, every organ, had been crushed to a pulp, eliminating all identifiable evidence such as fingerprints and teeth. Hair present in the remains was of the same dark shade as Watkinson's but hair samples found at his home were insufficient for DNA purposes, so a positive match was never made.

Two upper molars recovered from the scrap yard were identified through dental records as belonging to Watkinson, but as

38

they were only relatively near to the scene of crime the pathologist found it impossible to reach a definite conclusion. Indeed, along one margin he had pencilled in: *If you've got somebody who's confessed to this, just thank God.*

Matthew turned next to the forensic report. The information there was very condensed. No usable footprints or tyre tracks could be identified. But then, as the crime had taken place at the main entrance to the scrap yard, any evidence would have been obliterated long before the police arrived on the scene.

A small model car had been discovered mere feet away from the murder victim, but fingerprints on it matched neither Billy Mason's nor samples of the author's that had been taken from his home, and therefore the toy was regarded as being irrelevant to the case.

Chief Inspector Mackmin was studying Matthew as he closed the file, and his dour snarl became a sullen smile when the private investigator finally looked up.

'I trust everything is in order, Mr Shelley?'

Matthew swallowed hard and met the chief inspector's hostile gaze. 'Yes, fine. It all seems . . . well . . . fine, really.'

'Chief inspector, I hear what you're saying, loud and clear,' Karen said, 'but surely you must agree there's some doubt about this case?'

'No, I don't,' Mackmin growled. 'A murder was committed, a known villain said he did it and pleaded guilty at his trial. The sad fact that he's no longer alive to keep on reiterating that guilt seems to have brought everybody who thinks they can prove black is white crawling out of the woodwork.'

Karen held up a conciliatory hand. 'I can understand you taking this personally, but – '

'Let me tell you something, Miss Chandler . . .' Mackmin leant forward, his beetle-brows raised. 'I'm at a very nasty stage in my divorce. The lawyers have divided up my house and money – *my* house and money, mind – into two very nice little piles, and they are now looking at my pension for which I have so far worked and slaved for twenty-five years. Can you understand, Miss Chandler, how irritating that is?'

'Oh, yes . . . yes, indeed,' Karen said, nodding vigorously as she watched an angry flush travel across his cheeks.

'And do you know who brought about my downfall, Miss Chandler? Do you know who wrecked my quiet, comfortable life? Why, none other than your little helpmate, Mr Shelley.'

'I did explain at the time,' Matthew mumbled in his own defence. 'I just didn't understand the implications in taking the case.'

Mackmin rose slowly to his feet, his massive body casting a huge shadow over the wide-eyed pair. 'You didn't understand the implications, eh? Well, I'm sure you do, now.' He pulled at his shirt collar, struggling to regain his composure, and slumped back into his chair. 'I used to dream about strangling you, Mr Shelley . . .'

'Really?' The word came out as a squeak.

'Oh, yes . . . very, very slowly.' The chief inspector stared into the distance for a moment, his expression wistful. 'But just as I'm getting over that, just as I'm putting it all behind me, what happens? You turn up again, and this time you're throwing doubt on my professional judgement. Not one stain on my record in twenty-five years, but you want to start the fingers pointing, tell everybody I sent the wrong man down because I mishandled the investigation.'

Karen jumped smartly from her seat. 'That's not what we're implying, chief inspector,' she said, snapping shut her notepad. 'I'm sorry you've reacted in this way, but we're simply asking the truth.'

'I'll tell you what the truth is, Miss Chandler. Billy Mason was guilty as hell, and if you've got any sense you'll leave it there.'

'Is that a threat?' Karen asked, her eyes narrowing.

Mackmin seemed to pull back. 'Look, I'm very busy,' he said, grabbing a handful of papers. 'If that's all I can do for you, I'd like you to leave.'

They made for the door, Karen's stride purposeful, Matthew's more like a half-run. In the corridor, she turned to him.

'I don't think he's forgiven or forgotten, Shelley.'

'No, and I don't think he took to you, either.'

Over at the *Profile* offices, Judith Ward was conducting a hissed conversation into the telephone mouthpiece. The corners of her cherry-red lips were turned down and her demeanour spoke loudly of displeasure.

'Yes, but, Giles, darling,' she said, with a hint of exasperation, 'the little bitch has already worked out that *Profile* and Charlton Press are one and the same.'

'And where does that get her?' a cultured voice purred. 'All right, I was Glen's editor – that's no big secret – but it still leaves her a million miles from the truth.'

'I've just got a feeling about the girl,' Judith huffed. 'And as for that private investigator ... I thought you said he was a complete imbecile.'

'He is, Judith, so you're not to worry. And he's up to his neck in financial problems, so if push comes to shove we can pay him off. Trust me, I know how to pick my people.'

Judith took in a deep breath and voiced her main concern. 'I don't suppose Andrew's turned up, yet?'

'Of course he hasn't, I would've told you.' There was a lengthy pause. 'Listen, if you're really worried about the girl, why not get rid of her? Pay her, say, ten per cent of her fee and wave goodbye.'

'It wouldn't work, Giles, she's beginning to sense there's a big story in this.' Judith bit worriedly on her lower lip, leaving a smudge of red on her expensive capped teeth. 'You know, I'm beginning to worry about Andrew. If he's gone missing – '

'He hasn't gone missing, Judith, he's in touch with his office. So, sooner or later we'll track him down and when we do, when we make him see what he's up against, he'll play ball. Now, do you think it might be time to warn off this Chandler woman and her trusty sidekick?'

Judith toyed nervously with a cigarette packet while she considered the question. 'Yes, Giles, I feel it's time we let them know that too much meddling could seriously damage their health.'

7

There was a certain ambience in all solicitors' offices that made Matthew's blood run cold the minute he placed a foot on the inevitable deep pile carpet. Maybe he associated them with the making of a will, and that in turn brought his thoughts around to death. Whatever the reason, he found himself shivering as he settled into an old but extremely comfortable leather chair, and he pulled his anorak tightly around himself.

He was sitting with Karen in the spacious office of one Samuel Allcock, a wizened white-haired old man who was viewing them over the rims of his half-moon spectacles as keenly as an archaeologist would an ancient relic. Karen didn't like him.

'I can tell you very little about the case of the late Mr William Mason,' he said, suddenly. 'He asked us to represent him at his trial . . .' The solicitor coughed diplomatically into his palm. 'Of course, ordinarily I would refuse to discuss such confidential matters with you, but the head of the Charlton Press has asked me to co-operate as fully as I can.'

'Oh, do you represent Charlton Press as well, then?' Matthew asked, in a deliberately casual manner.

'The practice does, yes.' Allcock's rheumy eyes swept over them. 'Now, what exactly do you want to know?'

Karen gave the man a tight smile. 'Just tell us what happened.'

Allcock shrugged. 'There's very little to tell. I received a telephone call from the police station informing me that Mr Mason wished me to act on his behalf – '

'You'd done legal work for him before?' Matthew interjected.

'No, prior to that occasion, I'd never heard of Mr Mason. And when I asked why he'd chosen me, he just laughed.' The solicitor leant forward, elbows on the desk, fingers steepled. 'When I arrived, I was told that he'd simply walked into the police station and confessed. I found the whole thing very odd, to say the least. During that and subsequent visits, I tried to persuade him to withdraw his confession, to say that he'd been suffering from blackouts, but Mr Mason was adamant. He intended to plead guilty, and nothing I could say would move him.'

'Hmm, I see,' Matthew said. 'It certainly does seem odd, I'll grant you that.'

'So, what did you do, Mr Allcock?' Karen asked.

'There was only one course of action left open for me – I went to the prosecution and bargained for a reduced sentence if my client put in a guilty plea.' He chuckled. 'But they were having none of that. It seems the police and the Crown Prosecution Service had been after Mr Mason for some time, and were determined to put him away for the rest of his life, as it were.'

'Which wasn't long, as it turned out,' Karen mused.

'Not long at all, no,' Allcock agreed.

'Did Billy Mason look ill when you first saw him?' Matthew asked.

Allcock considered the question with a lawyer's caution. 'No,' he said eventually. 'No, I wouldn't say so. He had a cough, definitely, but then he was a heavy smoker. He was of average build, although I confess I did learn later that he'd suffered considerable weight loss.'

Matthew frowned. 'And you say he always maintained he'd committed the murder and was going to plead guilty?'

The solicitor gave a definite shake of the head. 'That's not what I said, Mr Shelley. William Mason at no time admitted to me that he'd committed the murder. He only said repeatedly that he intended to plead guilty to the charge.'

'Did you ever ask him outright whether he'd done it?' Karen asked.

'No, I didn't. Mr Mason's guilt or innocence was of no concern to me. My job was to get him the lightest possible sentence. Of course, if he had taken my advice and retracted his confession, then I would have tried for an acquittal. As it was . . .' He took off his spectacles and buffed them up with a white linen handkerchief. 'As it was, there was precious little I could do for the man. I can only advise my clients on the best course of action to take. If they choose to ignore me, well . . .' He spread his hands.

'Would Mason have got off if he'd fought the charge?' Matthew asked.

'Oh, yes, I believe so. If we could have discredited the confession, which wouldn't have been difficult, the prosecution would have had very little. There was no body, as such – no positive identification, at least – no motive, nothing that could have put Mr Mason at the scene of crime, even.'

'Just one more question, Mr Allcock,' Matthew said, sitting forward suddenly. 'This has got nothing to do with the case, really, but say I had a lot of money and I wanted to fake my own death and vanish. How could I be sure I'd have access to my money after I'd disappeared?'

'And that has nothing to do with the case?' Allcock asked, with a knowing grin.

Matthew simply smiled.

'You would salt it away, Mr Shelley, under whichever name you intended to use in your new life.'

'But, say I hadn't earned it yet. What if it wasn't due to come in until a year after I'd disappeared?'

The solicitor chortled softly. He was very much enjoying this game of suppose. 'In that case, you would leave your estate to someone you trusted implicitly ... and pray to God that your judgement was sound.'

The closer the march of time took him towards the repossession of his car, the more Matthew's paranoia flourished. After they had left the solicitor's office Karen was frog-marched past the vehicle several times before Matthew was satisfied that no one was watching. Only then did they make a run for the car and jump in.

'This is getting silly,' she said, still struggling into her seat belt as they hurtled towards the first junction. 'If they find the car, Shelley, they'll simply let themselves in with their own keys. You don't have to be present, you know.'

'Huh, you have no idea how those people think. They like to gloat. They like to see your face drop when your car disappears into the distance.' He took a sharp left at the crossroads. 'Believe me, you need to have a very sadistic nature to do that job well.'

Karen gave him a long sideways glance. 'There's something fundamentally wrong with you, Matthew Shelley. I think you

44

enjoy adding more drama to a situation than is actually there. You're like a little boy, you really are.'

Matthew grinned. 'What did you make of old Allcock?'

'He gave me the creeps,' she said, shuddering dramatically. 'What with his long bony fingers, and those silly glasses.'

'He confirmed what we suspect, though. There really is something iffy about all this. And don't you think it's too much of a coincidence that Billy Mason used the same firm of solicitors as Charlton Press?'

Karen gave a vigorous nod. 'That struck me straight away. It's almost as if he'd been told to ask for them.' She laughed. 'I don't think you fooled the old man one little bit with your questions about vanishing and leaving the money.'

'I hadn't intended to. We're getting the runaround here, Karen. I'll bet our reactions to everything that's being fed to us are being relayed straight back to Charlton Press.'

'So, you're working along the lines that Glen Watkinson wanted to vanish and therefore faked his own murder.'

'Yep, that's still my favourite.' He indicated right and turned into the sprawling car-park of a public house. 'But you don't agree?'

'Flying pigs,' she murmured.

'We'll see if I'm right, then, won't we? Come on, Miss Chandler, let's put this precious vehicle out of sight and go and meet our third witness.' He drove carefully to the rear of the car-park and came to a halt behind a low wall. 'There, well out of sight from the road.'

Karen fished her notepad from her shoulder bag and thumbed through the pages. 'Now, the man's name is Eddie Roe . . .'

The lounge bar was a mass of red velvet upholstery and brass ornaments, and it smelt as pubs always do in the late afternoon: a mild scent of bitter hops mingled with the welcoming aroma of percolated coffee and the slightly stale odours of lunch.

Eddie Roe was not difficult to spot. He was the only customer, and he sat staring morosely into an empty pint glass while a hand-rolled cigarette burned away in the ashtray. He looked up as Karen and Matthew entered, and licked his lips expectantly.

'Looks like this is going to cost us a couple of drinks,' Matthew remarked. 'What would you like?'

'Gin and tonic, please.'

Matthew counted the small change in his pocket then raised apologetic eyes towards Karen with a solemn shake of his head.

She let out an exasperated sigh. 'Half a lager, then.'

The introductions were made while Matthew fetched the drinks: Karen's lager, a pint for Eddie, and a glass of milk for himself.

Eddie knocked the head off his beer in one grateful swallow. 'So,' he said, smacking his lips, 'you want to hear about Billy. You'll know that I shared a cell with him before he was sentenced. Well, he told me he'd definitely done for that geezer, Watkinson.' He sat back, his job done.

Matthew applauded with gusto. 'Good performance,' he said, grinning. 'Word perfect.'

Eddie's jaw dropped. 'What do you mean?'

'You reeled that off as though you'd just learnt it,' Matthew said, waving his hand to disperse the thin trail of cigarette smoke. 'Now tell us what really happened.'

'I've nothing else to say.' Eddie grabbed his glass, as if fearful that it would be taken from him, and gulped down half the pint in one go.

'Until you've seen your brief, you mean?' Matthew moved closer to the man and gave him a friendly dig with his elbow. 'Come on, Eddie, you're not in a police interview room now.'

'Look, I've told you all I know.'

Without warning Matthew brought his palm down hard on the table top, and the flustered man jumped along with the glasses.

'You've told us damn all,' he said, 'and you know it.'

Eddie turned his pleading eyes to Karen. 'But I can't say no more, miss, it's more than my life's worth.'

Matthew decided to stay silent for a moment in order to make the man sweat. He took a tissue from his anorak pocket and mopped up his spilt milk.

'What were you on remand for?' he finally asked.

'Burglary,' Eddie mumbled.

'And how long did you get?'

Eddie looked away, his expression furtive. 'It didn't go to trial. The witnesses refused to give evidence in the end.'

'Oh? Now, that is interesting. Why do you think that happened, Karen?' Matthew asked with a meaningful sneer. 'Could it be that those who paid Eddie to come here and tell us fairy tales put the frighteners on them? Could it be that those same people were scared of what Billy Mason might have told our friend, here?'

'I ain't going to say nothing else,' Eddie babbled. 'They don't mess about. They'd mark me as soon as look at me.'

'Well, you'd better believe that I'm as hard as they are, if not harder. You get the wrong side of me, Eddie, and I'll give you a lot of grief.'

'Oh, yes? And how are you going to do that, then?'

'I'll tell you how.' Matthew gave him a sly wink. 'You know all those witnesses that pulled out, well, the police might just get them to reconsider, because by the time we've burst the Billy Mason case wide open the people who slipped you the money won't care less what happens to you.'

Eddie considered this, his fleshy forehead creased into a frown.

'And I've got a lot of influence with the police,' Matthew added. 'I speak and they jump.'

Karen just about managed to turn away before the laugh that was bubbling in her chest actually erupted. She pretended to have swallowed the wrong way and spluttered into her hands. Luckily, Eddie was too busy thinking up ways to cover his own backside to notice. He turned his fretful gaze to Matthew.

'You're boxing me in here. Whichever way I jump, I'm in trouble.'

'No, you're not, Eddie,' Matthew said, his tone now reassuring. 'Just tell us what Mason really said in that cell, and I promise we'll never quote you. No one will ever know you told us.'

Eddie looked far from convinced. 'That don't add up. Why do you want to know if you're not going to use it in one of your articles?'

'All we want is for you to confirm what we already know, which is that Billy Mason was forced to make that confession. If you do that, then we can go on and find out why.'

Eddie reflected for the best part of a minute, all the time running his finger around the rim of his empty glass. Finally, he nodded.

'All right, I'll tell you, but if anybody ever finds out – '

'You have my word,' Matthew said.

Eddie's fingers were visibly trembling as he took out another hand-rolled cigarette from a tin on the table. It took him a while to light it, but then he sat back, inhaling deeply.

'To be honest, Mr Shelley, I was shit scared when I found out I was going in with Billy Mason – I mean, he was big time. But I needn't have worried because he was a real gent, and having Billy as a cell mate guaranteed that everybody on the wing left me well alone. Billy always had plenty of ciggies and he wasn't tight with them, neither – '

'Eddie,' Karen said, her impatience barely concealed, 'this is fascinating stuff, but does it have anything to do with what Billy Mason told you?'

'Hear me out, will you, miss? I was coming to it.' He drew in another lungful of smoke. 'Billy had connections, see. He could even get whisky into the cell. Anyway, him and me used to have a snifter most nights. He was pretty tight-lipped most of the time, especially about the murder charge, but one night, after we'd had a few, I asked him why he'd done it. Well, he didn't answer directly, he just sat there on his bunk, staring into space. I got worried, then, I can tell you, I thought I'd gone too far. But after a while he looked at me and said, Eddie, they found my weak spot and that's what you've got to guard against. You think you've got all the balls in your court, he said, and then the bastards go and find your weak spot.'

'And you took that to mean he'd been forced into confessing?' Karen probed.

Eddie gave a shrug. 'That's the only thing he could have meant. He sounded really bitter, and the look on his face made the blood freeze in my veins.' He glanced from one to the other, waiting for a reaction. 'That's all he said – honest to God.'

'I believe you, Eddie.' Matthew finished his milk and stared thoughtfully into his empty glass. 'One more question – who paid you to keep your mouth closed?'

'Your guess is as good as mine, Mr Shelley. It was all done in the nick by other prisoners. First, they told me what was likely to happen if I grassed . . .' He shuddered. 'And then they said they could arrange for all the charges against me to be dropped, and they'd pay me five hundred quid to keep me mouth zipped. But I don't know who the paymaster was, honest.'

Matthew dug a hand into his pocket and pulled out what was left of his loose change. 'Okay, Eddie, go and get yourself another pint.' He counted the money, and then counted it again. 'Karen, you haven't got twenty pence, have you?'

8

Fearing another supper of stale chips and burnt sausages, Karen offered to buy a Chinese takeaway to eat at the office. Over roast duck and pineapple, fried rice and pancake rolls, they discussed what to do next.

'I think we should meet Watkinson's publisher,' Matthew ventured between mouthfuls of rice.

'I agree,' Karen said. 'And I'd like to find out more about Glen Watkinson himself, perhaps talk to his secretary.' She bit into her pancake roll. 'On the subject of his secretary, Shelley – do you think that could be a convenient title for homosexual lover?'

'Who knows? But he could well be the sort of trustworthy person Watkinson might have left his estate to. And if they were lovers – '

There was a knock on the door.

'Come in,' Matthew called.

The door was thrown wide open and two men strutted into the office. They were perhaps in their late twenties, one dark, the other blond, and both were smartly dressed in expensive suits, shirts and ties. Matthew jumped to his feet, assuming they were potential clients.

'I'm sorry about this,' he said, indicating the food. 'What can I do for you?'

'Don't worry about it,' the swarthy one said. He walked

49

towards the desk while the blond one closed the door and leant against it. 'We should be apologising for disturbing your dinner.'

Alarm bells were ringing inside Karen's head. The men certainly looked respectable, but there was something sinister about them. Matthew was quick to catch her vibes.

'Oh, it's okay,' he stammered.

'You must be Mr Shelley . . .' He turned to Karen. 'And you're Miss Chandler.'

They nodded.

'My name's James, and my associate's Nick.' He gave them a charming smile. 'We called in at your home address, Mr Shelley, had a long chat with your landlady. It would seem you owed four hundred pounds in rent . . .'

'Owed?' Matthew queried.

'We paid two hundred pounds of it off.'

'And why would you do that?' Karen asked.

'Because we like to be nice, Miss Chandler.' He took a stick of chewing gum from his pocket and dropped its wrapper at his feet. His unwavering gaze was fixed on Matthew's face as he popped the gum into his mouth. 'You're probably wondering why we're here, Mr Shelley. We're representing certain individuals who are worried about what you're doing on the Billy Mason case – '

'Well, I, for one, am just doing my job.' Karen bristled, her nervousness forgotten.

'Of course you are, Miss Chandler.' He turned to face her, his look intimidating. 'And we're just doing ours.'

'Well, go and do it somewhere else.'

'Leave it, Karen,' Matthew cut in, quickly.

'Very sensible, if I may say so,' the man said, grinning. 'Now we want you both to go off and write about something else. Just leave the murder case where it is.'

Karen leapt to her feet and struck an aggressive pose. 'And what if we don't?'

'Karen, keep quiet,' Matthew almost pleaded.

'I'd listen to your friend, Miss Chandler, if I were you. Anyway, I'm sure you're going to think this over and come to the right decision.' He chewed on the gum, his grin fading fast. 'And bear in mind that we don't like anybody interfering with us doing our job – it makes us look bad. Am I making myself clear?'

Matthew's Adam's apple juddered as he tried to swallow. 'Very clear,' he said, nodding briskly. 'There's no doubt in my mind as to what you're getting at.'

'Good, I'm so glad that's all settled. I hate it when things get unpleasant.' He joined his companion at the door. 'Oh, by the way, Mr Shelley, the two weeks' rent was a gesture of goodwill. Don't let us down.'

He closed the door very quietly, and they listened to the ring of expensive leather shoes as the men made their way down the bare wooden stairs.

'Are you a coward?' Karen spat.

'Only physically and morally,' was Matthew's easy reply. 'But look on the bright side, I've just had two weeks of my rent paid off.'

Karen sat down heavily and pushed her unfinished meal to one side. 'Shelley, I wouldn't blame you if you backed out of this deal.'

He gave her an encouraging smile. 'To be honest, I have thought about it but, what the hell, I think I'll go along for the ride. After all, if people are sending their heavies to threaten us, we must be getting close to something. So, I figure if you get a big story, I'll share in some of the glory and that'll do my reputation the world of good.'

Karen's face fell. 'Is that the only reason?'

He nodded and made a renewed attack on the duck. 'Karen, I'm not going to make any big speeches about what's right and being willing to fight for it. If I'm threatened, my first reaction is to run away – I'm not proud of it, that's just the way I'm made – but I have to balance that with the realisation that I'm in a very dirty business . . . as my next case proves.'

What is your next case?'

He extracted a letter from beneath his takeaway container and held it out to her. 'There's a man living in Fairfield Drive who swears his neighbours bring their dog past his gate every night and deliberately get it to foul the footpath. My task is to get the proof on film so he can take it to court.'

'Ooh, sounds exciting. Can I come along?'

Matthew grinned. 'I knew the glamour of it all would attract you.'

Fairfield Drive was a fairly short road, lined with 1950s-style semis, all identical with small front gardens bordered by low wooden fences and gates that opened directly on to the pavement. Matthew parked the car opposite number thirty-three, the home of his client, and reached on to the back seat for his camera.

'Now comes the difficult bit, Karen. There's just enough light from the street lamp outside the house to get the shot. It won't be brilliant, but it'll have to do.'

'Will one photo be enough?'

'No, we'll need at least four, taken on consecutive nights.'

'Oh, have you got one of those posh cameras that records the time and date in a corner of the photo?'

'Not quite, but I have got the next best thing.' He took a newspaper from his anorak pocket and thrust it into her hands. 'When I'm ready to take the picture, I want you to crouch down on the passenger side and hold up the paper so that I can get the title and date in the bottom of the frame. Then, bingo, we're in business.'

'That's brilliant, Shelley, I'd never have thought of that.'

'Trick of the trade,' he said, his camera trained on number thirty-three.

Fifteen minutes went by – fifteen bitterly cold minutes – and Karen's enthusiasm was eroding fast. She was swivelled around in the seat, watching the road behind, and was about to make a muttered complaint when there was action.

'Man with dog at nine o'clock,' she called out dramatically.

'Okay, on the floor, newspaper above your head,' Matthew answered in a terse whisper.

Karen quickly crouched and allowed him to line up the shot with the *Herald* and its date at the bottom of the viewfinder. Matthew waited for the man to come into shot, and he held his breath while the dog stooped down right outside the gate.

'Beautiful, beautiful,' he murmured, his finger resting on the button.

But when he pressed it and the shutter opened, Karen's face loomed large in front of him, completely blocking out the scene across the road.

'Shelley,' she whispered urgently.

'What the hell are you doing? You've ruined it.'

'Never mind the dog.' She pushed the newspaper into his hands. 'Read that, there.'

Matthew followed her pointing finger. The headline read: LITERARY AGENT VANISHES. In the poor light he narrowed his eyes and scanned the story:

Concern is being voiced by clients of well-known local literary agent, Andrew Dickens, who has not been seen for over a week. Mr Dickens acted for the late Glen Watkinson, murdered eighteen months ago. William Mason, who pleaded guilty to the murder and was jailed for life, died recently in prison. Many Members of Parliament and pressure groups have since raised doubts concerning Mr Mason's guilt. A spokesman for the agency said: 'None of our clients need to worry. Mr Dickens is tying up a very important deal, and therefore he may not be available for some time. In his absence the staff will continue to run the agency to the high standards for which it is known.'

'What do you make of that?' Karen asked, excitedly.

'I don't know,' Matthew said, carefully folding the newspaper, 'but my ingrained safety system's telling me to run again.'

9

The footpath-fouling culprit had no doubt enjoyed a nourishing dinner containing all necessary vitamins and minerals and was probably installed in front of a warm fire by the time the shivering pair drove back across town.

'The heater's gone,' Matthew said, sliding the knob for the umpteenth time.

'You keep on saying that,' Karen muttered as she scowled out of the side window.

'I'll be glad when they do repossess this thing. It's falling apart at the seams.'

Suddenly Karen turned to peer out of the back window. 'Shelley, I'm sure that car's following us.'

'You're really getting into this private eye bit, aren't you?' he said, obviously impressed.

The road they were travelling along was poorly lit, and when Matthew glanced into the rear-view mirror all he could see were the twin spots of dipped headlights.

'Lose him,' Karen urged.

Matthew laughed. 'Lose him? Karen, if I push this heap over forty-five miles an hour it really will fall apart.'

'What are we going to do, then?' she demanded to know.

'About what? There's a car on the road behind us, that's all. You're letting your imagination get the better of you.'

'I imagined those goons last night, did I?' she fired back. 'The ones measuring us up for a pair of concrete overcoats . . .'

With reluctance, but in order to pacify, Matthew pushed his foot down hard on the accelerator and glanced at the speedometer.

'There, we're doing forty. All right now, are you?'

'He's staying with us.'

'I dare say he is. We're hardly in a high speed chase.'

'He's indicating to overtake,' Karen shouted over the noise from the engine. 'Now he's drawing level. Shelley, he's staying there.'

'What's he doing now?' he asked, nervously.

'Oh, it's okay, it's only a police car. He's signalling us to pull over.'

Matthew mouthed a number of choice expletives as he applied the brake and stopped at the kerb. A uniformed officer appeared at the driver's window and motioned for it to be opened.

'Good evening, sir. This your vehicle, is it?'

'Oh, come on, Steve, let's skip the bull for once.'

The office chuckled merrily. 'And what have you done this time to incur the wrath of Chief Inspector Mackmin?'

'He's jealous of my looks and wealth,' Matthew said, heavily.

He got out of the car and dutifully blew into the breathalyser that was immediately handed across. By the time Karen had got out and skirted around to them, the officer was assuring Matthew that he was not over the limit.

'What exactly is going on here, constable?' she asked, heatedly.

'Charades,' Matthew told her. 'Leave it to me.'

'Now, I've warned you about your speed and your rear light,' the officer said with a wink. 'So, now I can have a ciggy while things are nice and quiet.'

He leant against the vehicle and offered the packet around. Karen gave a curt shake of the head and was surprised when Matthew accepted.

'I didn't know you smoked,' she said, her tone accusing.

'I can't afford to most of the time.' He bent over the match in the officer's cupped hand. 'Ah, that's good,' he said, exhaling the smoke.

'I don't get any of this,' Karen said. 'We're pulled over, and now you two are standing there like old friends.'

'We are old friends,' was the constable's amiable reply. 'Look, love, your boyfriend gets up the chief inspector's nose, and every so often he puts the word out that Matthew should be pulled over at every possible opportunity.' He took a drag of the cigarette. 'Give it a few days and Mackmin will have forgotten all about it . . . until the next time.'

'But, he can't do this,' she stormed. 'It infringes our civil liberties.'

Matthew grabbed Karen by the wrist and pulled her to one side. 'Listen,' he hissed over her protests. 'I'm trying to do my macho bit, fit in, be one of the lads – and why? Because I want some information.' He waved the cigarette about. 'I don't really smoke, if you must know, and it's making me feel dizzy, so stop giving me a hard time.'

He wandered back to the car while Karen stood sulking. 'Mackmin's a bit fired up,' he told the constable, 'because Karen there is doing some magazine articles about the Glen Watkinson murder and Billy Mason's death.'

The officer shook his head and tutted. 'I'm not surprised you're drawing flak, then. That's a very taboo subject at the nick.'

'Why's that?' Matthew asked, before attempting a pull on the cigarette.

'Let sleeping dogs lie, is the official policy, and has been all along.' The officer moved closer and dropped his tone. 'A lot of the lads weren't very happy with the investigation, such as it was. But like I said, it was made crystal clear that it was keep-your-mouth-shut time.'

'Steve, are you telling me there was a cover-up?'

The officer grinned. 'I wouldn't go that far, even if I thought there was, but some areas of the investigation didn't sit right, if you know what I mean. It just seemed to a lot of us that Mackmin and the others in the know were too eager to get the case stitched up.'

'But with Mason pleading guilty . . .'

'Yeah, yeah, I know, but even so we still have to make sure we've got the right person. Some nutters will confess to anything.'

'But Mason was hardly a nutter . . . was he?'

The officer raised a knowing eyebrow. 'He was when he'd got a sawn-off shotgun or a machete in his hand.' He frowned. 'I can't really explain it, but there was something about the case . . .'

'The murder wasn't Mason's style?' Matthew prompted. 'The whole investigation was like a jigsaw with half a dozen pieces missing? One of those pieces being the fact that no one ever saw Watkinson's body?'

'Yeah, I suppose so.' The officer flicked away his cigarette end and, with a sigh of relief, Matthew followed suit. 'I mean, Watkinson wasn't your cultured author type. Before he'd written a couple of books and got some money together, he'd been a traveller.'

Matthew's eyes widened in surprise. 'When you say he was a traveller, Steve, do you mean one of those New Age travellers?'

'Yeah, and even after he'd made a name for himself he used to have some of his old mates to stay. They used to park their vans in his front garden – a real eyesore it was. But then his neighbours got together and put a stop to it. In fact – and you might find this interesting – on the day they were more or less forced to leave, Watkinson went with them. He was giving the old V sign to his neighbours as the vans went past their houses.'

'Are you sure about this, Steve?'

'Yeah, I was on duty there. We had a right job getting them to leave peacefully, I can tell you.'

'And when was this?'

He thought for a while. 'It must have been a couple of days before the murder.'

'So it's quite possible Watkinson wasn't even in town on the day he was supposedly being killed.'

The officer gave a shrug. 'You guess it any way you want, Matthew, but as far as I know nobody saw him come back. And another thing that's always bothered me is Billy Mason claimed he met Watkinson for the first time on the night of the murder, but that's not true. A lot of the lads had seen them about together over the previous few months. Billy was well known to us, so he didn't go unnoticed.'

'That's something else that was covered up, then.'

'No, that's the point. Billy said in his statement that he met Watkinson in the pub that night. I was on duty in the interview room when he made that statement, and the way it read he didn't actually say he hadn't known Watkinson prior to that, but it was assumed that was the first time he'd clapped eyes on the bloke. If you ask me, a blind eye was turned.'

Matthew considered this. 'Steve, do you think Mackmin could be on the take?'

'Possible, I suppose. He wouldn't be the only high-ranking officer taking bungs.'

Matthew pushed himself away from the car and gave the constable a grateful pat on the shoulder. 'Thanks, Steve, you've been a great help. And I'll tell you something – we'll keep looking into this until we get to the truth.'

'Matthew . . .' He hesitated. 'Well, just watch yourselves on this one, the Mob's involved in it up to their necks. Take that missing literary agent, for a start. Now, the word is they were after him for some reason. Whether they got him, or whether he's just dropped out of sight . . .' He shrugged and wandered back to his patrol car. 'So just be careful whose toes you're treading on – okay?'

They watched the car pull away, its tail lights glowing red in the darkness. Karen shivered.

'I heard all that, Shelley, and I'm beginning to think that maybe we should leave it.'

Matthew made a slight choking sound, and all colour drained from his face as he turned to her.

'Karen, I feel sick. I think it was that cigarette.'

'Matthew Shelley,' she said, cupping his face in her hands. 'You're every woman's dream . . . I don't think.'

10

'Why does she want to see both of us?' Matthew grumbled.

He was trudging along behind Karen who was negotiating the maze of corridors *en route* to the offices of *Profile* magazine. He had spent a restless night, his stomach still felt queasy, so he was in no mood for being given the runaround.

'You keep on asking me that, Shelley, and it's getting on my nerves,' Karen huffed.

She continued to grumble and moan as the lift made its steady ascent to the twelfth floor, and Matthew left her to it. He was far more concerned with the effect the upward movement was having on his delicate stomach. He burped behind his hand as the lift shuddered to a halt.

'Come on,' Karen called, over her shoulder. 'Let's get this over with.'

He followed her along a passage, the walls of which were lined with framed covers of *Profile* magazine. Smiling faces of Hollywood celebrities and minor Royals stared down at them as Matthew's discomfort grew in the claustrophobic heat of the building. It was as though his sixth sense was at work, picking up an almost palpable feeling of menace, and that unease stayed with him as they entered the sumptuous office of Judith Ward.

The woman was exactly as Karen had described – a richly dressed mannequin. Today she wore a simple black skirt and white blouse that fitted her shapely figure perfectly. Her make-up was heavily applied to a face that looked cold and insincere, even when she smiled. And when Matthew was introduced by Karen, he found that her handshake was limp and perfunctory.

'Please sit down, both of you.' She motioned to a couple of chairs in front of her desk. 'There's someone here I want you to meet.'

A man stepped forward while they installed themselves on the comfortable seats.

'This is Giles Abbot,' Judith said. 'He was Glen Watkinson's editor.'

Abbot was a man in his fifties, with silver hair swept straight back from his forehead. His rugged, heavily lined face was at odds with his smart business suit – Giles Abbot was clearly a jeans and chunky sweater man.

'Hi,' he said with a smile. 'I've heard a lot about you two.'

They nodded, and Karen had to push to the back of her mind the attraction she felt for the handsome editor. She gave a shy smile and averted her eyes to study the top of Judith's mahogany desk.

'I've been called here to explain a few things to you,' Abbot continued, perching on the edge of the desk. 'First of all, Karen, I must confess that *Profile* magazine asked you to do the articles about Glen's murder in order to drum up some publicity for his current and forthcoming books.'

'He had a few books in hand then, did he?' Matthew asked. 'Wrote them quicker than the publishers could get them out?'

'That's right, Mr Shelley, Glen was a prolific writer, and we couldn't publish more than one book a year or we'd split sales.'

Matthew shot Karen a told-you-so smirk.

'But we wanted to keep tight control over the content of those articles,' Abbot continued.

'Oh, we shall, Giles,' Judith cut in, curtly. 'Because if it's not what we want, we won't publish.'

'Quite,' Abbot said. 'But maybe we've been approaching Karen and Matthew with the wrong attitude, Judith. Perhaps if they understand what we're actually trying to achieve, they'll see things in a different light.'

Judith leant back in her chair, a look of exasperation on her hard features.

'Publicity is a very exact art,' Abbot went on, 'and we want it fully focused on Glen. So, if your series of articles centred on the fact that Mason committed the murder, Glen's name would be hammered home all the time. But if you shifted the emphasis just slightly and start questioning Mason's guilt, then he would become the star of the series, with Glen no more than a bit part. Does that make any sense?'

'Oh, yes,' Karen murmured as she stared into the man's alluring eyes. 'I think I can see what you're getting at.'

'You couldn't tell us more about Mr Watkinson, could you?' Matthew asked. 'I don't think I've ever seen a photograph of him.'

'Surely.' Abbot reached behind and took a book from the desk. 'This is the current novel, *Shades of Temptation*. Glen was one of the few male authors who could write extremely good romantic fiction.'

Matthew took the book and turned to the author's photograph on the inside of the back cover. Glen Watkinson's image looked back at him. He had been a slim, well-muscled young man with a darkly handsome face and deep, brooding eyes. His long glossy black hair was worn in a style that barely concealed the gold rings that hung from his ears.

'He's nothing like I'd imagined,' Matthew remarked.

'He was of Romany blood, and he looked just right – women loved him.' Abbot relieved Matthew of the book and handed it to Karen. 'Actually, when I said that Glen was one of the few male authors who could write romantic fiction, that wasn't quite true. I'm sure there are many men out there who could do just as well but if, say, a middle-aged, average-looking author had written the stuff Glen produced then it wouldn't have had the same impact. Glen was the complete package.'

'I heard he was . . .' Matthew had to pause while his stomach growled. 'Sorry about that,' he said, burping slightly. 'I was going to say, I heard he was a little uncouth.'

Abbot grinned.'Wild would be the term I would've used. But that facet of his character simply made him all the more attractive to women. The danger factor, I believe they call it.'

'So . . .' Matthew leant forward, his attitude pensive. 'This New Age traveller, who was a bit of a yob, understood everything there was to know about the finer feelings of women in love.'

Abbot stiffened. 'I'd rather not get into a discussion about the art of good writing.'

'Was he homosexual?' Matthew fired the question.

'No, he wasn't,' Abbot responded, angrily.

'But Billy Mason claimed Watkinson made advances to him,' Matthew countered.

'Then he got it wrong. That was one of the things I had to make very clear to the press after the trial.'

'Shall I tell you what I think?' Matthew said. 'I think Mason was forced into making that confession, and saying that Watkinson made advances to him was his way of getting back at you. He didn't keep to the script – in effect, he was putting two fingers up to you.'

'To me?' Abbot said, his eyes widening with incredulity. 'Are you suggesting, Mr Shelley, that I had something to do with arranging a cover-up?'

'Giles, stop this,' Judith scolded, her fist coming down hard on the desk top. 'You've said more than enough already.' She inhaled deeply to calm herself, and then looked directly at Karen. 'My dear, you seem to be far more receptive than Mr Shelley . . . Maybe you'd like to consider severing the arrangement you made with him and continue writing the articles under my guidance.'

At the very moment Karen cast him a sideways glance Matthew's stomach put up another loud protest. A look of despair momentarily flickered across her face, and then she considered the magazine editor with a determined stare.

'Judith, the articles are worth five thousand pounds to me. That sort of money is very tempting, and I can't afford to turn it down – '

Good,' Judith cut in, briskly. 'So, if Mr Shelley would care to leave . . .'

'But, as I was about to say, I think I'll stay with Shelley. We seem to work very well together.'

Judith's face hardened, and her mascara-bound eyes bulged in anger. 'That's a decision you'll both regret, I can assure you.'

'Are you threatening us?' Matthew questioned boldly.

'I've said all I'm going to say.' She waved her hand in a gesture of dismissal. 'And now, I want you both to get out of this office and out of this building.'

'Gladly,' Karen huffed. 'Goodbye, Mr Abbot.'

Outside the office Matthew gave her a grateful smile. 'Thanks for sticking with me.'

'It was against my better judgement,' Karen assured him. 'And what am I going to do about digs? I can't afford to stay where I am now I've lost the job with *Profile*.'

'There's a room off my room,' he said, tentatively. 'Well, it's more of a cupboard, really. I use it to develop film.'

'That's a great build-up, if ever I heard one.' She allowed herself a grin. 'Is it big enough for a single bed?'

'Oh, yes, no problem.' He started back to the lift. 'Listen, Karen, I'm off to get myself a glass of milk. My stomach's really playing me up.'

'I'd never have guessed,' she muttered, following his slouching figure.

'I know what you need,' Karen said, guiding him into an off-licence. 'A good stiff drink, to relax you.'

Matthew watched her stride to the check-out clutching a bottle of cheap scotch and pausing to pick up a bottle of ginger ale on the way. He was now feeling rather self-conscious about the two of them spending a night under the same roof.

As she paid with her credit card, Karen pondered over the startling fact that she found Matthew attractive, in an off-beat sort of way. He stood there simply begging to be mothered and yet, somewhere beneath that marshmallow exterior, Karen could sense a touch of steel. She firmly believed, regardless of what he said, that Matthew was carrying on with the case because he didn't like being pushed around. And the harder he was pushed, the more resolute he became.

The car spluttered into life on the fourth turn of the key, and the drive to Matthew's bedsit was made without interruptions by police patrol cars or any other inconveniences. As always he parked three streets away, and Karen gave out a series of disgruntled sighs throughout the walk back to his place.

'Where are you going, now?' she asked, when he disappeared along the alley.

'Up the fire escape – where else?'

'But, Shelley, you've had two weeks' rent paid.'

'I know, but I owed four so that still leaves two, which is very nearly three, now.' He exhaled sharply. 'You know, Karen, if I don't get some money soon, I've had it. Mrs Perkins has been very patient with me up till now, but I don't know how long that'll last.'

Frightened by the almost total darkness of the alley, Karen stayed close to Matthew's side as they made the short walk to the rear of the house. The gate leading to the courtyard garden creaked loudly in the quiet night air, and a number of cats howled protests in a territorial dispute while the pair silently made their way to the base of the fire escape. They had just about reached it when a tall thin figure emerged from the shadows. Karen's hand flew to her mouth in order to stifle an involuntary scream.

'Good evening, Mr Shelley, I've been waiting for you.' It was his landlady. 'There's a little matter we need to discuss.'

'Well, hello, Mrs Perkins,' Matthew said, the heartiness of his greeting a little overdone. 'I was just showing my colleague your lovely garden.'

'Oh no, you weren't,' she said, stepping into a pool of light from her kitchen window. 'You were going up the fire escape to dodge me.' She folded her arms. 'Come Friday, Mr Shelley, you'll owe me three weeks' rent.'

'Ah, well, you see, Mrs Perkins, I'm ... er ... I'm just waiting for a new cheque book to arrive. And as soon as it does, I'll slip the payment under your front door.'

'Huh, I've heard that one before.' She remained before him, totally unmoved. 'I'm sorry, Mr Shelley, but I've got to give you a final warning. If you get more than a month behind, you'll be finding your belongings out in the street. I've got people waiting for rooms – '

'But, you can't just turn him out,' Karen exclaimed. 'There's a law against things like that.'

Mrs Perkins pulled tight her old plum-coloured cardigan and threw a defiant glance at Karen. 'And who might you be?'

'She's a work colleague,' Matthew cut in, quickly.

'Well, I hope she's not staying here.'

'Oh, no, no, Mrs Perkins, absolutely not.'

She sniffed. 'I'm glad to hear it. I'm sure I wouldn't want my house to get a reputation like those massage parlours have. I keep letting men into your room, and now you come back with this young woman . . .'

Matthew's stomach gave a sickening lurch as he stared up the metal steps. 'Is there someone in there now, Mrs Perkins?'

'Yes, there is – a gentleman – and I'm beginning to wonder what's going on.' Mrs Perkins stared pointedly at Karen and at the whisky bottle in her hand, then pushed past and hurried off towards the house. At the kitchen door, she turned back. 'Don't forget, Mr Shelley, a month's rent by the end of next week or you'll be looking for somewhere else to live.'

Karen groaned. 'Why does everybody keep thinking I'm on the game.'

'Shush,' Matthew whispered. 'What should we do? There's a man up there, waiting for us.'

'Good, I'm just about ready to tackle anybody.' Gripping the bottle tightly she raced up the fire escape, her shoes sounding on the metal rungs.

'Karen, for God's sake, be careful.' Matthew started after her. She was already through the window by the time he reached it.

'And who the hell are you?' he heard her demand.

'Well, well, that was quite an entrance,' a deep smooth voice replied.

Matthew's insides did another cartwheel as he clambered into the room to find Karen standing with hands on hips in front of a man reclining on the settee. His hair was thick and snowy white, and the lines around his twinkling blue eyes betrayed his sixty years. But his lithe body, elegantly clothed in smart suit and black overcoat, was that of a man years younger.

'Ah, you must be Mr Shelley,' he said.

'Yes, I am. Who are you?'

He gave Karen a kindly smile and rose to his feet. 'Forgive me, my dear, I should have stood up when you entered but I was rather taken by surprise when you came hurtling through the window. Now, I know that you are Miss Chandler, so allow me to introduce myself. I am Jocelyn Charlton, owner of Charlton Press.'

Karen exchanged a wary glance with Matthew. 'And you're here to persuade us not to look into the Watkinson case, I suppose.'

'On the contrary, I'm here to ask you to dig deeper. Please may we sit down?'

Karen sank into the armchair while Matthew positioned himself on the arm. She noticed the hungry way in which the man was eyeing the scotch bottle.

'Can I offer you a drink?' she asked.

Charlton heaved a resigned sigh. 'Thank you, but, no, my liver won't take it any more, I'm afraid. They say the alternative to getting old is to die young and sometimes, my dear, I wonder if that might not be a more attractive proposition.' He installed himself on the settee. 'When you can no longer smoke because of your tired lungs, when you can no longer enjoy rich food because of your ulcers . . . But, still, I digress.'

He fixed them both with a penetrating stare. 'I can see you're waiting for me to explain myself, so I'll come straight to the point. Over the last few years – since I retired, in fact – I've harboured a growing concern for what some people term my publishing empire. You see, I'm far from happy with various members of the staff – Judith Ward and Giles Abbot, to name but two – and when your plight came to my attention I decided it was time to act. I had to ask myself several questions: What are these individuals trying to cover up? Who is pulling their strings, and why? And, lastly, is what they're doing in the best interests of investigative journalism?' He slowly shook his head. 'I think not.'

'What do you want us to do?' Matthew asked.

'Exactly what you are doing now – searching for the truth. The only difference is, I'll be paying you to do so.'

Karen's curiosity was fired. She leant forward eagerly. 'Go on, Mr Charlton, you're beginning to interest me – what do you think Judith and Giles Abbot are up to?'

Charlton thoughtfully stroked his chin, his manicured finger-nails grating across light stubble. 'That's a good question, my dear, and one I'm looking for you to answer. One possibility is that they are in the pay of the so-called Mob.'

'That's definitely possible,' Matthew said. 'We've already had a visit from two heavies.'

Charlton let out a wretched sigh. 'But it doesn't make any sense. Why would they be paying people in my company?' His tone became urgent. 'Mr Shelley, should you and Miss Chandler agree to my proposition, I must insist that you report to me alone.'

They swiftly nodded their agreement.

'Very good.' He delved into his inside pocket and withdrew an envelope. 'I'll pay you one thousand pounds immediately, and we can negotiate a fee for the articles when you have gathered the necessary material.' Karen almost snatched the envelope from his hand, and Charlton smiled. 'My private telephone number is in there, too. Now, remember, you must report only to me. I have a healthy distrust of those in my employ.'

Matthew was staring longingly at the envelope. With some difficulty he pulled his gaze towards Charlton.

'One thought that springs to mind, Mr Charlton, is that if we give you a scoop, it'd do wonders for the circulation of *Profile* magazine.'

'Mr Shelley, you are a very astute young man,' Charlton said with a chuckle. 'And I admit there is something in what you say. Since my retirement I have been less than happy with the way the whole enterprise has been run, and falling circulation figures have proved me right.' Suddenly a harsh glint came to his blue eyes. 'Tell me, where do you plan to start?'

'I've got this theory,' Matthew said, glancing at Karen for signs of derision. 'I think that Glen Watkinson might have wanted to vanish, for whatever reason, and decided to fake his own death. Who was actually crushed in that car, God only knows, but I think Watkinson may have gone off with his traveller friends and is now holed up with them.'

'Flying pigs,' he heard Karen mutter.

'So, the first thing we want to do is interview Watkinson's

private secretary, because if the man has done a runner he might have been a party to it.'

'Good thinking.' Charlton got to his feet. 'Already I can see that my money will not be wasted.' He paused. 'You are aware that you're being watched the whole time?'

'Of course,' Matthew lied. 'I am a private detective, after all.' He paced nervously towards the window. 'You don't happen to know who's doing the watching, I suppose?'

'It could be the police,' Charlton replied, quite matter-of-fact. 'It would seem they too have an interest in concealing the true facts of this case.' He shrugged. 'Maybe money has reared its ugly head for them, as well. Who knows?'

'You think that somebody high up in the police force is being paid off by the Mob?' Matthew asked, an image of Chief Inspector Mackmin forming in his mind.

'In life, Mr Shelley, there is a saying – anyone can be bought, it is just a case of the price being right.' He took a step towards the door, and then hesitated. 'Maybe I should leave by the fire escape.'

'There's no need,' Matthew said.

'Look out of your front window, Mr Shelley. The car that follows you around is parked across the street, I shouldn't wonder. Anyway, keep in touch.'

Without stopping to reply, Matthew threw open the door and peered out of the landing window. Sure enough, there was a large blue Nissan parked directly opposite the house. He could clearly see the outline of a burly man in the driver's seat.

'Is it there?' Karen whispered.

'Yes, it's there, but with a bit of luck, if we leave by the fire escape in the morning, we might be able to lose him.'

When they got back to the room Charlton had gone, and all that was left to tell of his visit was the envelope and the curtains billowing at the window.

11

'I reckon we should split the thousand pounds straight down the middle,' Karen said.

'Okay.' Matthew took a sip of his scotch and gave her a lopsided grin. 'I can pay off three weeks' rent and still have some left for my other bills.'

The whisky bottle had taken a hammering, and Matthew was sprawled in the armchair while Karen reclined rather drunkenly on the settee.

'You couldn't pay some off the car . . .?' she asked, hopefully.

'No need. I've an idea we'll be out of town for some time, so they won't be able to repossess it because they won't know where it is.' He let out a foolish giggle.

'Good thinking. In any case it's about knackered, so they're welcome to it.' She pointed a swaying finger and tried to focus on his face. 'You know, Shelley, something tells me you're not what you seem. You're not the bumbling fool you pretend to be.'

He gave her a wry smile. 'That's the nicest thing anyone's ever said to me, Miss Chandler. You've really got a way with words.'

'Seriously, Shelley, tell me about yourself.'

'Nothing to tell, really. I was born in this glamorous town . . .' He waved his arm expansively and spilled some of his drink. 'I'm illegitimate, you know. I never knew my parents, I was fostered out.'

'Oh, Shelley, I'm sorry,' Karen interjected swiftly. 'I should mind my own business.'

'No need to be sorry. It's something you get used to. What you've never had, you don't miss.'

'That's one of my mum's sayings.' As soon as the words were out, Karen could have kicked herself. Fancy talking about her own mother when Shelley had just told her he didn't have one. She really must brush up on her diplomacy skills. 'Anyway,' she quickly added, 'parents can be a pain at times. Mine definitely were. When I was about sixteen they sent me to a psychiatrist – I'm not joking, they thought I was mental.'

'Yes,' Matthew said, after much contemplation. 'Yes, I think I can believe that.'

Karen gave him a good-natured grin. 'My problem has always been that I can't take orders from anyone, I can't be told, I have to do things my own way.' She lay back on the settee. 'I've always found it difficult to keep a job. I'd start to think the others were getting at me, and then I'd just explode.'

'And your parents thought you were mental?' He shook his head and tutted.

'Shut up,' she laughed, aiming a playful slap in his direction. 'Anyway, I finally came to the conclusion that my best option would be self-employment, so here I am.'

'Working with me.' Matthew smiled and drained his glass. 'I think we'd better get some sleep, don't you? Busy day, tomorrow. You take the bed and I'll kip in the spare room.'

Karen pretended to sip her drink. Now that the time had come she felt embarrassed about undressing. She had hoped that the scotch would take away her inhibitions, but it hadn't.

'I'm the one who's imposing, Shelley, so I'll take the spare room.' She might feel better locked away in there.

'But I haven't had time to put the bed up. I'll sleep in it, I'll be all right.'

They were both determined to use that room and were making ungainly strides towards its door when they stumbled against each other. As their limbs became entangled, Matthew immediately pulled back.

'I'm sorry,' Karen stammered. 'Oh God, this is ridiculous . . .'

Matthew stared at the floor. 'No, I'm sorry, Karen. I just feel a bit awkward, that's all, I can't help it. Christ, at my age, as well. You must think I'm a right toss-pot.'

'I feel awkward, too,' Karen said, softly. 'And I don't think you're a toss-pot, at all.'

They held each other's gaze as Matthew backed away. 'I'd better get to bed,' he mumbled.

'Okay,' She lifted a hand and gave a tiny wave. 'Goodnight, Shelley.'

'Goodnight, Karen.'

Matthew kept edging backwards until he connected with the door. He reached behind and turned the knob, but the moment it swung open a couple of mops and a brush tumbled on to him and then clattered to the floor. While he stood there, rubbing his head, Karen dissolved into a fit of laughter.

'Can I reverse that decision about you not being a toss-pot?'

The sun had hardly risen above the eastern horizon before Karen was out of bed, fresh and alert. She made a furtive trip to the bathroom, ever watchful for the formidable Mrs Perkins. And soon she had showered, dried her hair, and was back in Matthew's room, making much-needed coffee.

While she poured boiling-water on to the rich dark granules Karen listened to the regular pattern of his snores coming from the so-called spare room. Smiling fondly, she knocked on his door. The snores came to an abrupt end, and Matthew could be heard making a spluttered return to the conscious world.

'Who is it?' he called.

'I'm here to cut off your gas,' she cackled, in her best witch's voice. 'A little matter of an unpaid bill.'

'Ha, bloody, ha.'

There followed a lot of banging and crashing, then the door swung open and Matthew emerged, wearing white boxer shorts dotted with tiny red hearts.

'My God, Shelley,' Karen said, peering beyond the door. 'That's only the broom cupboard.'

He glanced back. 'It's smaller than I thought,' he had to admit. 'But I do develop my films in there.'

'I believe you, thousands wouldn't,' she said, with a sceptical look. 'There's coffee on the table, and our friend's still parked outside. I couldn't quite see his face but it looks as if he's asleep, so if we hurry we might get away before he wakes up.'

Matthew gulped down the coffee. 'Right, give me time to shower, then on the way out I'll put a cheque for three hundred pounds under Mrs Perkins' door. That should keep her off my back for a bit. We can bank Charlton's cheque on our way to the office, and then we'll arrange a visit to Glen Watkinson's secretary.'

12

Manfield House was an impressive sight. It was a sprawling fifteen-room residence with greystone walls and huge stone mullioned windows, which dated back to the year 1799. It stood at the heart of a vast meadow, in the shelter of colossal oak trees, their gnarled and twisted trunks denoting great age.

'Wow,' Matthew exclaimed, as he peered through the high security gates.

'Wow, indeed,' Karen murmured, equally impressed. 'I'd give up the agency, if I were you, Shelley, and concentrate on becoming a writer.'

'I'm afraid I don't have Watkinson's charisma. I'd probably end up worse off than I am now . . . if that's possible.'

Karen glanced across the road to where the car was parked. 'Do we drive up to the house, or leave the car there?'

Matthew snorted. 'We'd better leave it where it is. It might be dustbin day, and I wouldn't want to lose it that way.'

Laughing lightly, Karen helped him to push open the gates. They ambled along the sweeping drive, still admiring the scene before them, unaware that a large Nissan car had pulled up outside, its driver watching their progress.

Reaching the large stone porch, Matthew rang the bell which sounded some way off inside the house. After a while the heavy door was pulled ajar and they were surveyed by a dignified silver-haired man.

'Yes?' he said.

'Mr Parr? Mr Roland Parr?' Matthew asked.

The man gave them a dubious look. 'Might I have your names first?'

'Oh, sorry. I'm Matthew Shelley and this is Karen Chandler. I rang earlier to request an interview.'

'Oh, yes, you'd better come in. I'm Roland Parr, and I can spare you half an hour, but no more. I really am tired of the endless questions.'

They were ushered into the study. Decorated in rich burgundy, it was the perfect den for a man with literary leanings. The atmosphere was one of absolute peace, ceiling-to-floor bookcases were packed with immaculate first editions; and before the bay window, overlooking a stunning view of the grounds, stood a wonderful antique desk with an old and much-used leather swivel chair.

'Please, do sit down . . .' Parr waved vaguely towards a couple of chairs with carved backs and hard leather seats. 'Now, tell me what I can do for you.'

They perched on the chairs and Karen got ready to take notes.

'We'd like you to tell us all you know about Mr Watkinson,' she said.

'Glen Watkinson was a very gifted writer . . . a writer who is far from dead.' A wistful light came to his eyes while Matthew and Karen exchanged a glance.

'Excuse me?' Matthew said. 'He's not dead?'

Parr settled into the swivel chair and gave them the full benefit of his piercing glance. 'Great writers live on through their work, and therefore they are immortal – '

'Maybe, but his crushed remains were found in a scrap yard,' Karen cut in, rather bluntly. 'So, although his work may go on and prove to be a nice little earner for others, he's going to have a bit of a job getting about.'

Parr gave a slight, humourless smile, displaying teeth that owed much to dental wizardry. 'You're very forthright, Miss Chandler.'

'I apologise, but I'm having a bad day,' she said. 'How long did you work for Glen Watkinson, Mr Parr?'

'About six years. I joined him prior to the publication of his first book.'

'There's something I'm finding difficult to follow, here,' Matthew said, shifting his weight in the chair. 'We've been told that Mr Watkinson – although a household name – didn't really make a fortune from his books while he was alive, and yet this house must have cost a bomb.'

Parr gave a slight nod. 'I can see the reason for your confusion.

But there are two things you're failing to take into account, Mr Shelley. Firstly when Glen negotiated the purchase of Manfield House, the housing market was in the grip of the biggest slump it has ever known. A massive fifty per cent was wiped off the value of this property, almost overnight.'

'Even so, they still didn't give it away,' Karen ventured.

'Quite, but allow me to continue, Miss Chandler . . .'

He crossed his legs and paused to brush the knee of his trousers. Matthew briefly wondered whether this was done to gain enough time to formulate an answer.

Finally, Parr said, 'Whoever told you that Glen didn't find financial success while he was alive, undoubtedly worked in the publishing business. Am I right?'

Matthew nodded.

'You see, Mr Shelley, publishers are willing to lose money for a time, if they believe a writer is going to make it big with steadily increasing sales. So, if a publisher is making little or nothing from an author on his list, it doesn't always follow that the author was paid a poor advance.'

'Are you saying that Glen Watkinson was paid a small fortune, then?' Karen asked.

'I don't think that is what I said,' Parr replied swiftly. 'I know nothing of the actual payments made. I only know that Glen had the money to buy this house.'

'Not bad for a New Age traveller,' Matthew mused. 'Or should I say, a true Romany?'

Parr let out a throaty laugh, and Matthew found himself gazing into the man's open mouth.

'Mr Shelley, I think the Romany thing owes a lot to poetic licence. It was merely a little publicity ploy dreamed up by Glen's editor and agent.'

'And his agent was Andrew Dickens?' Karen enquired. 'The man the papers say is missing?'

Parr glanced around nervously. 'Yes, that's right.'

'Allow me to put something to you,' Karen said, with a reassuring smile. 'If Mr Watkinson wasn't dead and had staged this whole thing so that he could disappear, is it at all possible that his agent, Andrew Dickens, could be acting as a middle man, passing on his money as and when he needed it?'

Parr frowned. 'I don't understand what you're getting at. Why on earth should Glen want to disappear?'

'Do you know who he left his estate to?' Karen pressed. 'Did he have any family?'

Parr's agitation was growing with every question that was fired. 'I've no idea who he left his money to,' he said, rather loudly. 'Glen left me a small legacy, but I've no idea where the rest of the estate went. This house is up for sale, and when it's sold I shall have to move out.' He huffed. 'This really is none of your business, you know.'

'Maybe not,' Karen conceded. 'But I'd have thought you'd want to know exactly what happened to the man who employed you for all those years.'

'I do know,' Parr spat. 'He was murdered by that Mason fellow who, as we all know, got life for the crime.'

'And then conveniently died a few months into his sentence.'

'Why has that become such a big thing all of a sudden?' His temper was definitely starting to fray. 'If the bloody man had lived for eight or ten years no one would have thought anything about it, and we would all have been left alone.'

Karen frowned. 'What do you mean, you would all have been left alone?'

Parr's cheeks flushed. 'Glen's friends,' he blustered, 'the people who knew him – that's what I meant.'

Matthew wandered across to the desk and glanced down at a stack of papers. They appeared to be a manuscript in proof form. His gaze ran along the lines: *He held her in his strong arms, the fresh scent of her hair in his nostrils, her recently shed tears still wet on his bulging chest.*

'Is this one of Mr Watkinson's books?' he asked.

Parr's head jerked round. 'That's private property, Mr Shelley.' He scurried across to the papers and stuffed them into a drawer. 'You really have no right to be snooping about.'

'I'm sorry,' Matthew said, his face a mask of contrition. 'Are they the proofs of Mr Watkinson's latest book?'

'No, they're not,' Parr told him, angrily. 'If you must know, it's *my* latest book. Oh, you might well look surprised. I was a novelist for thirty years – hardly a bestseller, not even mildly successful, but I had my small following. However, the publishing business has been going through rough times in recent years. Many mid-list writers have been dropped – me, included. That's why I took the job with Glen. He was helping me to rebuild my career.'

'I see.' Matthew's gaze wandered over the book shelves, and there he spotted many titles by Roland Parr. 'So your career had just ended when you took this job, and now it's on the brink of starting up again. That's brilliant timing – one door closes, and another one opens.'

Parr's face was drained of its colour. 'Mr Shelley,' he said, icily, 'I'm beginning to get very annoyed. Glen was helping me to relaunch my career. He'd already pulled a few strings before his death, and it's now been decided that my work is good enough to be published again.' He indicated the door. 'Now, if you've both finished, I'd like you to leave.'

Karen came swiftly to her feet. 'Just one more thing, Mr Parr, then I promise we'll leave you in peace.' She rifled through the pages of her notepad. 'We've been led to believe that Mr Watkinson had trouble with the neighbours when a number of his travelling friends stayed here.'

'That's right,' Parr said, clearly bewildered. 'They camped in the grounds. They were doing no harm at all, but the snobbish neighbours kept complaining.'

'And did Mr Watkinson leave with his friends? Let me see . . .' Karen studied her notes '. . . that would have been a few days before his murder.'

'He did leave with them, yes. He had to direct them to the motorway, but he was back here within a couple of hours.' Parr opened the door and gave them a pointed look. 'Thank you for coming. Now, if you'll kindly allow me to show you out . . .'

They meandered through the huge hall, pausing momentarily to gaze at the fine tapestries that graced the high walls. Roland Parr pulled open the front door, and they had taken one step over the threshold when Matthew turned back.

'One final thing . . .'

Parr shot him a long-suffering look.

'Was Billy Mason a regular visitor to this house?'

'What? Don't be ridiculous,' Parr spluttered. 'I didn't set eyes on Mr Mason until the trial and, to my knowledge, he never came into this house.' He made to close the door but Matthew jammed his foot in the doorway to stop him.

'But you'd have known if he did come here?'

'I wasn't aware of everything that went on in this house. Glen would often tell me to get lost if he didn't want me around.' He stared down at Matthew's foot, and sighed loudly. 'Please, Mr Shelley, I'd hate to get unpleasant, but you are rather overstepping the mark.'

Matthew removed his foot and the door was slammed in his face.

'Well, Shelley, if your theory about Watkinson doing a runner is correct, I'd say Parr is definitely the middle man responsible for handing over the money to his boss.'

'It certainly seems to be shaping up that way, Karen. And once this house is sold Roland Parr will simply vanish, and there'll be no reason for anybody to look for him.' He started to limp down the drive.

'What's the matter with your foot?'

'It's okay, I just caught my corn when I put it in the door.'

She rolled her eyes. 'I should have guessed. Listen, forget your corn for a minute – I think this whole murder business is just one giant scam to keep Watkinson in the big money sales bracket.'

'I think you're right. I reckon it was set up by the publishers and that literary agent, and then it was implemented by the Mob.'

'So, what now?'

'Let's call on the neighbours,' Matthew said, limping ahead. 'Something tells me we need to find those travellers because Watkinson's with them, or somewhere very close by.'

13

The surrounding properties were all five-bedroom detached; quite sumptuous, but small in comparison with Manfield House. Matthew and Karen drew a blank at the first three they tried, finding the doors closing far quicker than they were opened. And a sense of despondency was creeping over them by the time they started up the fourth drive. This time their knock was answered by a petite woman in her sixties, wearing a candy-striped overall and a paisley headscarf. She looked them up and down.

'Before you go into your sales pitch,' she began, tartly, 'I'll have you know I only work here, and I'm not authorised to buy anything or to enter into any commitments.'

Matthew gave the woman a dazzling smile. 'Actually, madam, we're not selling anything, but can I just say what a treat it is to meet someone as friendly as you obviously are.'

She was still regarding them with suspicion, but her icy attitude was thawing fast. 'Well ... they're such a snotty lot, round here,' she said, as if that explained her caustic approach. 'Honest to God, they think that having money buys them class.' She cocked a finger for them to come closer. 'I always say to my Percy, they've got about as much class as an Eccles cake.' She laughed; a sound that would have rivalled a rampant hyena. 'Anyway, what do you want?'

'We're journalists, looking into the Glen Watkinson murder case,' Karen said, pointing towards Manfield House. 'And we'd like to talk to you, if that's okay.'

'I was just about to have a cuppa, so you'd better come in and have one with me.' She was moving to usher them through the door when she seemed to reconsider. 'Here, I'm taking a bit of a chance, aren't I? For all I know, you could be a couple of burglars casing the joint, as it were.'

'We're not, I can assure you,' Karen said, holding out her card.

'I know you're not,' the woman scoffed. 'I wouldn't have

asked you in if I'd really thought that. You've both got honest faces so, come on, follow me.'

She led them into a large kitchen that was fitted out with limed oak units and every state-of-the-art appliance it was possible to own.

'Karen Chandler, freelance journalist,' the woman read from the card. She glanced at Matthew. 'And what's your name?'

'Matthew Shelley. And I'm a private investigator, not a journalist.'

'Sit yourselves down, then, and you can call me Molly.' She bustled across to the sink. 'Mr and Mrs Jeffs have me in to clean the house, do the washing, cook the dinner so as it's on the table for when they get home ... sometimes I say to my Percy, it's a wonder they don't want me to wipe their noses. Only I don't say "noses" to him, but I don't know you two and I always think it's best to be polite.'

They watched her fill three mugs with tea, and Matthew said, 'Did you see much of the great writer when he lived next door?'

She put the mugs on the table in front of them. 'Oh, yes, I did. And a right foul-mouthed hooligan, he was – not the sort I could ever take to. I'll tell you something for nothing – I could never see him writing all that romantic stuff.' She went off for the sugar bowl. 'Mind you, that other bloke who lives there, Roland Parr, now he really can write. I read his books for years, I did. You know what I think? I think he was teaching young Glen how to write. There was a lot of Roland Parr in his books, if you ask me.' She sat down and took a sip of tea. 'I mentioned it to Percy once, but he wouldn't agree. He said all that romantic fiction was rubbish, anyway, and there weren't no difference in any of the books. He said it was all luck, some of them click but that didn't mean their stuff wasn't rubbish – '

'Mrs ... er ... Molly,' Karen interjected, hoping to stem the woman's flow, 'you say you saw a lot of Glen Watkinson when he lived there?'

'Oh yes.' She lowered her voice. 'Look, I know you're not going to drop me in it, so I'll tell you the truth – this job's a doddle, there's not that much work really, so I get plenty of free time.'

'And is there anything else you can tell us about him?' Karen asked, hopefully.

'Like I said, he wasn't a very nice young man, very ill-mannered, really rude to people – liked to shock, I suppose. Do you know, he used to wee all over the bushes when he was in the garden – too bloomin' lazy to get to the toilet. I'm not joking, he'd expose everything, nothing was left to the imagination.' She nudged Karen's elbow, and grinned. 'To be honest, though, I didn't mind all that much. Brought back memories, it did.' She let out an ear-splitting shriek. 'You'll have to pardon me, but I do like a really good chuckle, now and again.'

Matthew obliged her with a laugh. Then, he said, 'Mr Watkinson had some of his traveller friends to stay once, I believe.'

'He did, yes, and a real stir that caused along here, I can tell you. The vet was forever backwards and forwards, what with this lot having kittens all the time.'

Another piercing whoop filled the quiet air, and this time Matthew and Karen dissolved into giggles. Molly was a pleasant change after the evasive types they had so far encountered.

'And when they left, Watkinson went with them – is that right?' Matthew asked.

Molly took a handkerchief from her overall pocket and mopped at her eyes. 'I'll say,' she replied, with a heaving breath. 'It was a Saturday afternoon, and I'd come in to do the ironing. Being Saturday, see, everybody round here was at home, and Glen was hanging on to the side of one of the lorries, giving all of them the two-finger salute and shouting about. His language, though . . . well, I wouldn't like to repeat it.'

Matthew took a sip of tea and considered his mug for a moment. 'Molly,' he said, 'I want you to think very carefully . . . Did you see Glen Watkinson again? I don't just mean on that Saturday – did you ever see him again?'

Her response was immediate. 'No, I didn't, definitely not. And a few days after that I heard on the news he'd been murdered, but I never actually saw him after that Saturday.'

'I know this is asking a lot,' Karen cut in, 'but do you know where Mr Watkinson and his friends were heading when they left that day?'

'I do, as a matter of fact,' she said, nodding eagerly. 'I heard them talking – when the wind's in one direction the sounds carry – I heard them, clear as a bell.'

'And?' Karen coaxed.

'They were going on about things, about people never giving them half a chance. There was a lot of language – still, what's new? – and then one of them said Devon was the place to go. The moors, he said, that was the place to go for some peace. He was a right romantic figure, that one, always wore a red suit.'

'Molly, you're brilliant,' Matthew enthused.

'Glad I could help,' she said, her thin chest puffing with pleasure. 'And I know something else that might interest you ...' They leant forward, their questioning looks urging her to elaborate. 'That gangster bloke they got for the murder, well, he was always at the house, for months before it happened. When news of the murder came out, I said to Percy, when bad lots like them fall out, it always ends in tears.'

Matthew made no claims of possessing great driving skills, which was just as well for he was a lousy driver and quite incapable of getting the best performance out of his car. If he tried for a speed faster than sixty miles an hour thick black smoke would billow from the exhaust and send him into a panic. He was panicking now, and fretting incessantly about missing the exit from the motorway.

'For bloody Christ's sake. How many times do I have to tell you?' Karen studied the map, yet again. 'We're on the M5 which goes straight through to Exeter, where it ends. When you run out of road, Shelley, we'll be in Devon, so stop worrying.'

'I don't like driving long distances, Karen. I get nervous about motorway crashes.'

'We're not going fast enough to hurt anybody,' was her acid retort.

A heavy goods vehicle chose that moment to overtake them, throwing up spray from the wet road and sending it splattering on to the windscreen. Matthew immediately flicked on the wipers and groaned when the nearside one flew off.

'I just knew that was loose,' he muttered to himself.

'Please, God, what have I done to deserve this?' Karen intoned.

A long clear stretch opened up in front of them. 'Okay, I think I'm all right, now,' Matthew said, cheerfully. 'What did Jocelyn Charlton have to say when you reported back to him?'

Karen settled into the seat and stared at her muddy half of the windscreen. Sighing loudly, she said, 'He seemed quite impressed by the progress we've made, so far. He did stress that he'd be unable to publish anything we couldn't prove, but he said he liked the way we were thinking.'

'Do you trust him?' Matthew suddenly asked.

Karen shot him a surprised look. 'Why shouldn't I?'

'I'm not sure. Perhaps it's just me, but I'm only half believing what anybody tells me these days. They all seem to have ulterior motives for everything they say and do.'

'Yes, okay, I'm with you, there, but Charlton's motive is easy. He wants a real scoop for *Profile* magazine, and he also wants the Mob removed from his publishing company.'

'That's one of the things that disturbs me,' Matthew said, with a frown. 'Why would a man of his age go out of his way to upset a crowd of gangsters?'

'Shelley, have you ever read any Sherlock Holmes?'

'No, why?'

'Because you're just like Dr Watson. He's always making stupid remarks.' She gave him a superior look. 'The answer to your question is elementary, my dear Shelley. Jocelyn Charlton doesn't have to worry about reprisals from your so-called crowd of gangsters because he's not in the firing line, in fact, he's keeping well out of it. That's why he's hired us.'

'So that *we* can be in the firing line, you mean?'

'You've got it, Shelley, bravo,' Karen said, clapping her hands. 'Why don't we have the radio on? It'll help to pass the time.'

'Sorry, it doesn't work.'

'Surprise, surprise,' she said, doing a perfect impression of Cilla Black.

'Hey, that was good . . . just like Lulu.'

'Oh, shut up,' she grinned.

'We could sing,' Matthew suggested. 'I tell you what, I'll sing a song and you have to guess who recorded it, and when. That'll help to pass the time.'

81

'How super,' she said, slapping her thighs. 'Or we could do something really exciting, like overtaking a car – now, that would make the time simply fly by.'

'Okay, I'm boring, but I can't help it, I'm afraid.'

Matthew gave a despondent sigh and waited for Karen to make a strong denial, but she said nothing. He gave her a sideways glance.

'You know I told you I was illegitimate . . . Well, there's something else you should know.'

She turned to him, her eyes now wide with interest. 'Oh yes? What is it, then?'

'I used to be married. My wife ran off with somebody else about five years ago.' He gave a half-hearted shrug. 'Anyway, it sort of destroyed my confidence. I find it very hard to feel comfortable with women, now. I always think that if I get too close to one, she'll run out on me.'

Karen studied the wretched look on Matthew's face, and a lump came to her throat. She felt a strong urge to cuddle him, or at least to place a comforting hand on his arm, but she resisted. Instead she sagged against her seat and chewed at her bottom lip.

'I'm sorry, Shelley, I had no idea,' she said. 'And don't take any notice of me, I'm always like this. I suppose it's some sort of defence mechanism. Most men are only after one thing, and then it's bye-bye, Karen.'

She was silent for the next few miles, using the time to contemplate the different aspects of Matthew's character. There was certainly more to him than met the eye. And as each new facet of his personality revealed itself, her fondness for him grew. She wondered what his wife had been like. If she wasn't the motherly type, then Karen imagined a man like Matthew would have sent her climbing the walls. It was odd to think that he'd been married; it made her jealous, somehow.

She was pondering on that fact when Matthew decided to overtake an ancient Skoda in front. His initial manoeuvre was faultless, but when he drew level the Skoda's driver gritted his teeth, slammed down his foot, and juddered away. Matthew, stuck in the middle of the motorway with the loud honking of horns behind him, was forced to pull back on to the slow lane. Karen thought it best to ignore the incident.

'What are we going to do when we get there?' she asked. 'I mean, how do we set about finding our travellers?'

'There must be some permanent caravan sites for travellers in the area. We'll visit some of them and ask around. After all, a man in a red suit shouldn't be too difficult to find.'

'But remember what Molly said, Shelley – these people aren't known for their friendliness. Some of them can be downright hostile, even violent.'

'We'll make out.' The words were boldly stated, but inside Matthew wasn't so confident.

'I want to go to the loo,' Karen announced, as they approached a service station.

Matthew signalled left and crept into the slip lane. Six vehicles back, the indicator of a large Nissan was also signalling left. Inside, the driver smirked.

'Why don't you get out and walk, sunshine,' he muttered. 'Then we'd all get there faster.'

14

The laborious journey came to an end, and when Devon was finally reached they found many sites that could effectively swallow up a chain of travelling caravans. All they needed now was the pluck to enter them.

Near the gates to the first site, they found a teenage couple openly enjoying sex outside one of the caravans. Karen was deeply affronted and promptly dragged an ogling Matthew back to the car. At the second, a bare-knuckle fight was in progress. This time Matthew was the one beating a hasty retreat, with Karen struggling to keep up.

The third looked no less inviting. There were no copulating couples or flying fists, but each of the twenty or so caravans had a barking or baying dog outside its door, and a large group of travellers stood eyeing them suspiciously. The barking reached a crescendo when they climbed out of the car and made their slow approach to the entrance. They hesitated before going in.

Karen said, 'Shouldn't you be delivering some throw-away, devil-may-care line, like Mel Gibson or somebody?'

Matthew's gaze roamed from the snarling dogs, their pink tongues slavering in anticipation, on to the grinning crowd. Even the women looked intimidating, with their wide shoulders and bulging biceps.

'I think I'm getting the wind,' was his urgent response.

'Oh well, in for a penny, in for a pound, as my mother likes to say.'

'Your mother has a lot of sayings,' he grumbled.

They took their first tentative steps, the dust rising in tiny puffs as their shoes dug into the worn sparse turf. Some of the men wolf-whistled and made indecent gestures involving their arms as their greedy eyes followed Karen. The women and children merely stared with open hostility. Over to their right a huge German Shepherd hurled itself in their direction, its teeth bared, a low deep growl forming in its throat. Karen was about to scream when the dog suddenly stopped in mid-air and somersaulted backwards for the end of its long leash had been reached.

'We're looking for a man in a red suit,' Matthew called out in a strangled voice. This was met with loud jeers and catcalls.

Somebody shouted, 'Piss off, before we set the dogs on you.'

When the group moved forward, *en masse*, Karen and Matthew were about to turn tail and run, but were stopped by the swift emergence of a man shouldering his way through the mob.

'Come now, come now,' he chastised. 'Let us show our visitors some respect . . . please.'

It took only a short glance to see that this man was different from the rest. His weathered face was tanned to a deep mahogany; his hair was jet black and tied in a pony-tail. Thick gold loops hung from his ears, and amazingly white teeth gleamed whenever he smiled, which was often.

'Come now,' he said again. The dogs fell silent and the group melted away. He moved with confident strides towards the anxious pair, and said in a firm resonant voice, 'Good evening, my name is Leason Hudson. My people call me Prince.'

Karen took his outstretched hand. 'It's a pleasure to meet you ... Prince,' she said, gratefully. 'And I really mean that.'

'Travelling folk are not what they used to be,' he remarked, with a hint of regret. 'But, worry not, you'll be quite safe, now. Please, walk with me to my caravan.'

He led them to an old wooden wagon that had once been pulled by a horse. Its dark wood still shone, and a tiny but immaculate garden had been created around it.

'Do you live here all the time?' Matthew asked, indicating the flowers.

'I do. I am what you would term a warden. The council pay me to look after the site, keep some degree of order. I'm afraid that's all that is left now for an old travelling man like myself.'

Those teeth flashed again as he opened up the door to the wagon and stood aside for them to enter. The interior was extraordinary – a living remnant of a bygone age. Every inch of space had been utilised, but the accommodation was in no way cramped. Karen gazed with awe at the cheerful chintz, the Nottingham lace, and the colourful design which decorated the dozens of cups, saucers and plates that occupied row upon row of shelving.

'Please excuse the lack of room,' Mr Hudson said. He motioned for them to sit on the long padded seat beneath the window. 'This has been my home for sixty years, and I would not dream of leaving it.'

'I'm not surprised,' Karen said. 'It really is lovely.'

Matthew watched, totally absorbed, as Hudson rolled a cigarette with deft fingers, his tongue running quickly along the gummed edge. With the cigarette lit, Hudson straddled a chair, its back towards him.

'Now, my friends,' he said, blowing smoke, 'tell me what you're looking for, and I'll see if I can help you.'

Karen said, 'We're looking for a man in a red suit,' and then promptly blushed for the sentence sounded so ridiculous.

'And why would you want this man?' Hudson asked. 'Surely not to ask for hints on dress sense?'

'No,' she agreed with a smile. 'I'm a journalist, you see, and I'm doing a series of articles on the murder of a man named Glen Watkinson. Did you know him?'

'I know of him, but I've never met the man.' There was a knock on the door. 'I'm sorry, would you excuse me?'

He moved to the door and opened it up a few inches. They sat and waited while he conducted an urgent whispered discussion with a bearded man. Closing the door he turned, his thumbs hooked into his thick leather belt, his eyes narrowed against the spiralling smoke from the cigarette held between his teeth.

'My friends,' he said, 'did you come here alone?'

They nodded, and shot each other a puzzled look.

'I see.' Hudson resumed his seat and fixed them with a meaningful stare. 'In that case, you are either liars, which I very much doubt, or you are unaware that you have someone watching you.' He paused to crush the remains of the cigarette in a large crystal-cut ashtray. 'A blue car has been spotted. Just one man inside. He seems to be fairly skilled in the art of keeping out of sight while he observes you. This man is known to you?'

'We think he might be with the police, Mr . . . Prince,' Matthew offered.

'But you are not?'

'Most definitely not,' Karen cut in. 'I don't know why that creep's keeping tabs on us, but it's not to help us, that's for sure.'

'I see.' He gazed thoughtfully into the middle distance. 'I have to be very careful here, my friends, because although I have the respect of most of the travellers, I wouldn't have it for long if I started turning over any of their numbers to the police. So, you tell me what this is all about, and then I can make up my mind.'

In hesitant terms, Matthew explained his theory that Watkinson had faked his death in order to disappear.

'And you believe he may be with the man in the red suit because that particular group of travellers stayed with Watkinson prior to the crime being committed?'

Matthew nodded. 'That's how it looks to me.'

Hudson pursed his lips. 'And the people around this Watkinson wouldn't be in any trouble with the law?'

'Aiding and abetting, I suppose,' Matthew candidly replied. 'But I don't know whether the police would pursue that charge.'

86

'You are an honest man – that I like, also.' He patted Matthew's forearm, his gaze unerring. 'I have decided to help you. The group you are looking for have gone on to the moor. They will be moved off, of course, but that will take time. It could be months before they are driven away, especially at this time of year.'

'The moor's a very big place,' Karen pointed out. 'You couldn't tell us exactly where they are, could you?'

'You must head for the centre, a distance of some fifteen to eighteen miles, and then leave the road. They are camped some three miles due west, on high ground. But, be careful, they will have look-out points.'

'What do you know about them?' Matthew asked.

Hudson gave a tight smile. 'You see how things work here . . .' He waved a hand towards the scene beyond the window. 'Almost anyone can be accepted into the travelling fraternity, no questions asked. But the group you're after, they are bad medicine, as the ancient Indians would have said. So, I would approach with caution. Also, they have someone with them who is not a traveller. He dresses like one, but that is all.'

Matthew looked thoughtful. 'Prince, if a man was away from this sort of life for about six years, would he have trouble adjusting to it again?'

'If he'd lived in a big house and enjoyed the life of a bestselling author, you mean? Yes, I think he would. A traveller's life is cramped, and lacking in many of the finer things.' He smiled. 'You are more perceptive than you look, my friend.'

'Thank God for that,' Karen muttered under her breath.

Matthew shot her a withering glance. He said to Hudson, 'You believe these people have look-out points – why is that? They can't be too bothered about the wardens on the moor.'

'I agree, but they are frightened about something – terrified, might be closer to it. My friends, if they feel they are being cornered, they could become very dangerous indeed.'

'So,' Karen said on a long breath, 'it looks like we've found our group of travellers.'

'And now all you have to do is get close to them,' Hudson said, with a note of caution. 'Close enough to find out what you need to know.' He crossed to a cabinet above the sink and took out a pair of binoculars in a black leather case. 'Take these, they may prove to be useful. They may allow you to observe without getting too close. And remember . . . be very careful.'

The moon had risen, and the grounds of Manfield House were bathed in an ethereal glow that threw strange shadows among the mighty oaks. Inside the house a single light burned, its brightness spilling from the study window where Roland Parr was crouched over the telephone.

'The completion date for the house sale is in ten days' time,' he murmured, hurriedly, 'but I want to be away from here long before then.'

He listened for a moment, his brow creased, his long fingers curled around the receiver.

'But, I . . . No, *you* listen . . . Look, Andrew, I know we're in this together. I've got the book and I'm looking for you to negotiate the deal. What? Yes, which we split fifty/fifty – I've given you my word, haven't I? – but I want to get away, just lose myself somewhere. At the moment, thank Christ, you're representing a client whose identity they don't know. If they find out I've got the book, I'm in real trouble.'

An urgent reply issued from the earpiece.

'That's as maybe,' Parr growled, 'but it doesn't make me feel any more secure. Things stay as they are for the time being – you're not to know where the manuscript is because that's my only safeguard – and I'll give you my new address as soon as I have one.' He slammed down the receiver.

15

'We've done about fifteen miles,' Matthew said, nodding towards the dial on the dashboard. 'So we'd better start looking for high ground on our left.'

Already a chill was creeping across the inhospitable moor, and

Karen shivered as she peered into the gloom beyond the side window.

'There's a number of tors, but I can't see any high ground,' she told him. 'Oh, hold on, hold on . . . yes, there is, but it's still away in the distance.'

Matthew slowed the car and pulled it off the road. 'We're on foot from now on, I'm afraid.'

Karen bit back a stiff retort and clambered out on to a bed of coarse bracken. Gone were the smart suit and high-heeled shoes. She was wearing heavy duty jeans, a thick sweater, and a blue anorak with fur-lined hood, but still the cold seemed to penetrate her very bones.

'I don't like to complain, Shelley . . .'

'No?'

'No,' she snapped. 'Look, do you think this is a good idea? Wouldn't it have been better to stay at a guest house and watch the travellers by day?'

'We need to get as near as we can under cover of darkness, so we can dig in,' was his impatient reply. 'And in any case, we can't just watch them by day. What if they do a moonlight flit?' He threw a rucksack across his back. 'Keep close to me, and don't worry, I was a leading light in the Cubs.'

As she watched him stride ahead, Karen fought to dispel a feeling of despondency that was fast sweeping over her. Slowly, she began to follow, and her breath was coming in ragged gasps by the time they approached the high ground.

'This should do it,' Matthew declared, stopping by a large depression in the peaty earth.

Karen fell to her knees and took in a series of deep breaths. 'Thank you, God,' she muttered.

Matthew set about pulling dead brushwood around the spot to hide it and then he turned to her, his face rosy with exhilaration, even in the dwindling light.

'Sleeping bags out of the rucksack, Karen, and let's settle in.'

'Dib, dib, dib,' she mouthed, helping him off with the pack and unzipping it. 'Okay, what do we do now?'

'You get some sleep, and I'll watch the camp. You see that red glow? That's their fire.' He passed her an insulated bag. 'There's a flask of hot coffee in there. Choosing high ground for a camp, Karen, means they can see anybody approaching, but it also means they're very easy to spot.' He focused the binoculars and studied the hill. 'As far as I can tell, they've got about six vans up there. Come the morning, we should have a clearer view.'

She passed him a cup of coffee. 'How long will we have to stay here?'

'Not too long, I shouldn't think. As soon as we know Watkinson's up there, we'll wait until dark and then go to the nearest police station.

Karen drained her coffee which was cooling by the second, and crawled into the thick quilted sleeping bag. She glanced to where Matthew was still watching the camp and realised that he was actually enjoying himself. He's in a minority of one, she thought, glumly, as she moved to find a comfortable position.

However, the long walk had tired her and soon all sounds were becoming distant, fading further and further away. She burrowed deep into the sleeping bag and drifted towards sleep.

Suddenly she was wide awake. Something had disturbed her. But, what? Sitting bolt upright, she called, 'Shelley,' in a hoarse whisper.

'Yes?' he grunted in reply.

'What about the toilet arrangements?'

Karen was still shivering when she came awake. Gingerly moving her stiff limbs, she forced herself into a sitting position and let out a loud and prolonged yawn. Matthew glanced over his shoulder and grinned.

'They have got look-outs,' he told her. 'There're two guys scanning the moors through binoculars. I keep catching the sun's glint on their lenses.'

Despite the awful conditions, Karen felt a surge of excitement and scrambled out of the sleeping bag.

'That must mean we're really on to something,' she enthused. 'Shelley, I have to admit you were right, after all.'

He inclined his head. 'Nice of you to say so. Now, I'll watch the camp while you keep an eye open for flying pigs.'

Karen chuckled while she unpacked the primus stove and filled their small kettle with water.

'I'll make us some tea,' she said. 'And then I'll do us some bacon sandwiches.'

All of a sudden she was filled with contentment. Even the biting wind that had come with the dawn could not quell her euphoric mood. The bacon sizzling in the pan made her drool, and its taste was far better than when eaten between four walls. The tea scalded her mouth, but she gulped it down greedily.

'I like it here,' she said.

Matthew halted his attack on his sandwich and gave her a wary glance. 'That's an odd thing to say.'

'It's how I feel,' she responded merrily, pushing wisps of hair out of her eyes.

'It's called freedom,' Matthew said, grinning, 'but don't get too used to it. Once we've got what we came here for, it's back to civilisation as fast as we can go.' He pointed a finger. 'You, Miss Chandler, are sitting on the biggest story you're ever likely to have.'

She watched him devour his breakfast. The bacon sandwich was the first meal she'd ever cooked for him, and Karen was filled with a ridiculous amount of satisfaction because he was enjoying it so much.

'Shelley?'

'Hmmm?'

She scrambled to his side. 'Do you still see your foster parents?'

He gave a humourless laugh. 'Which ones? I had dozens.'

'Dozens?' Karen asked, shocked.

'Okay, not dozens, but a fair few. And, no, I don't see any of them.' He sucked a piece of bacon from his teeth and settled down beside her. 'None of them were what you'd call caring, especially the men. From the age of five I had a succession of macho men as father figures. They were always aggressive, never allowed anyone to mess them about. And, do you know something, Karen, as I got older I could see they were like that because they were frightened of life. They all adopted the same tough act, hoping that everyone would be scared and leave them alone.' He shook his head ruefully. 'I didn't want to be like that. Like most people on this planet, I'm basically frightened. I'd like to think I'd be a hero, if it ever came to it – you know, do something that would win me respect – but I don't want to be some sort of fraud, always trying to convince people that I'm something I'm not.' He gave her a sheepish smile. 'I go on a bit, don't I?'

'No,' she said softly, 'I don't think you go on, at all. And I understand exactly what you mean.'

'So, your parents wouldn't think I was mental, then?'

'Oh, definitely,' she said, laughing, 'so you can't be that bad.'

She flashed him a smile, then wormed her way to the rim of the depression and grabbed the binoculars. She had peered through them for less than a minute, when she turned.

'Hey, Shelley,' she said, with a frown, 'they all seem to be looking this way.' Karen returned her attention to the camp while Matthew crawled to her side. 'The man in the red suit's there,' she told him. 'And there's somebody in one of the vans – he's just a shadow at the window, but the others keep waving for him to get back.' She lowered the binoculars and met his gaze. 'Do you think they know we're here?'

Matthew trained the binoculars on the hill. 'Looks like it,' he said, heavily. 'And they're probably all about to come charging down any minute.'

An hour passed, then another, and still the travellers made no move towards them.

'Perhaps they just thought they saw something, and it panicked them,' Karen suggested. 'They seem quite at ease, now.'

Through the eye of the binoculars, Matthew watched thick columns of smoke climbing from their camp fire.

'Hmm, a little too at ease,' he murmured, worriedly. 'I mean, if you were trying to drop out of sight, would you build a fire that size? And that guy hasn't left the caravan, and I haven't seen him at the window for a while.'

'What do we do?'

'We wait. And in the meantime, I could do with some sleep.'

*

Matthew slept until late afternoon, and dusk was creeping across the moor by the time he joined Karen at the observation ridge. She had spent much of the time watching the travellers.

'Any movement?' he asked.

'None. The man's still in the van, and he hasn't left it once in all the time I've been watching. There's one thing I've noticed though, Shelley, they don't seem to be keeping a look-out, any more.'

'Even so, we'd better make some tea now, Karen, because if we leave it any later they'll see the glow from the stove.'

She smiled. 'Already done, boss. I've filled the flask.'

Matthew looked on, duly impressed, as she poured the steaming tea. While the mugs thawed their chilled fingers, they nibbled on chocolate biscuits in that twilight world so far removed from reality. Soon, an inky-black darkness descended, and somewhere in the distance could be heard the muffled sound of an engine firing into life.

'What was that?' There was alarm in Matthew's voice as he dashed to the rim of the dug-out. 'Sod it, they've gone,' he exclaimed. 'They must have coasted the vehicles down the far side of the hill and then started the engines.'

'What next, then, Shelley? Do we go back to the car and follow them?'

'Karen, that car has a job to stay in one piece on the road. If we take it on to this rough ground it'll fall to bits.' He let out a dismal sigh. 'In any case, we don't know which way they're going. They could double back and head for the road.'

'Okay, Mastermind, what *can* we do?'

'Let's get round to the other side of the hill. Maybe we can see what direction they took.'

They made slow progress over ground that was riddled with pot-holes and dense bush. And neither of them relished the eerie silence, which was now so intense it seemed to wrap itself around them and assult their eardrums. Circling the hill took far longer than they expected but thirty minutes later Matthew was on his knees, studying the tyre tracks.

'I think they went that way,' he said, pointing straight ahead. 'But the ground's so hard, these tracks are going to be difficult to follow.'

'Matthew,' Karen hissed. 'Matthew . . .'

But Matthew didn't hear her. 'I think we'd better go back to the road and wait for morning.'

'Matthew,' she shrieked. 'I think we're in real trouble, here.'

'Do you know, that's the first time you've ever called me . . .'

The words froze on his lips, for he had glanced up and could now see the circle of travellers all around them, their arms folded and ominous smiles playing on their lips. The man in the red suit stepped forward.

'Well, well . . . what have we got here? A bird and a ponce.' He let out a loud laugh. 'And we've spent all day thinking it was the big bad wolf, come for our hides.' As if on cue, the others chuckled and moved in closer.

'We're only camping on the moor,' Matthew stammered, straightening up. 'We've no idea who you are.'

'No? We know who you are, all right.' He stabbed a nicotine-stained finger at Karen. 'You're a journalist and your friend's the lap-dog. Now, I'm telling you to keep your noses out of our business.'

'Who's your friend?' Karen asked, in a tone that was none too steady. 'The one you're hiding?'

'None of your business – like I said.'

'Is it Glen Watkinson? Is that who you're hiding?' The man merely smirked in reply, and Karen grew bolder. 'You say you know who we are . . . but do you really?' She raised an eyebrow. 'I know who the big bad wolf is. How can you be so sure we're not working for him?'

In the gloom she sensed, rather than saw, the colour drain from the man's face.

'You work for some magazine,' he blustered.

'Outdated information,' she said. 'So why don't you just hand your friend over, and we'll forget we ever saw you.'

Over to their left, a huge bear of a man suddenly became agitated. He said, 'Don't let a bleedin' bird talk to you like that, Stew.'

'Yes, come on, Stew,' Karen coaxed, motioning for him to step closer. 'The rest of our people are following on our tail, so give us what we want.'

'Tell her Glen's dead,' somebody shouted.

'Shut it,' Stew barked. He turned back to Karen, his hands raised in defeat. 'We weren't hiding Glen – that's the honest truth. It was somebody who had nothing to do with the murder case. But he's gone now. We sneaked him out as soon as it got dark.'

'Then you'd better tell us who he is,' she said.

The man hesitated, glanced from Matthew to Karen. 'Wait a minute,' he said. 'The Organisation know who we'd got. They've been looking for us for weeks. That's why we've been hiding out.' He shot them an accusing look. 'You're not working for the Mob.'

Karen swallowed hard. 'Shelley,' she whispered urgently. 'I've just put both feet slap bang in the middle of it. Get ready to run.'

'I'm very ready,' he whispered back.

'Right, lady . . .' In a flash, Stew had taken a forward step and grabbed the back of Karen's hair.

'Leave her alone,' Matthew protested.

'Shut it,' the man warned. 'Now, lady, who sent you after us? And you'd better start talking, right now, because it'd take a hell of a time to find two bodies out here.'

His face was close to hers, his warm, tobacco-tainted breath fanning over her features.

'Okay, okay, I'll tell you.'

The moment the grip on her hair loosened, Karen brought her knee up between his legs and let out a cry of sheer delight when she connected with his testicles. The man gave an agonised howl and collapsed at her feet. Quickly, Karen grabbed the lapels of his red jacket and shoved him away. He collided heavily with other members of his gang and Matthew watched with astonishment as they went sprawling into a heap.

Karen adopted a fighting pose. 'Come on, you bastards, do you want some more of it?'

'Karen, run,' Matthew urged. 'Forget the John Wayne bit, let's just get out of here.'

She didn't have to be told twice. They turned on their heels and sprinted, their heavy shoes beating a tattoo on the hard ground. Behind them, they could hear shouting and the sound of pounding feet.

The travellers were making ground, with Stew hobbling along

behind, when something happened that stopped them in their tracks. One by one they came to a skidding halt and stared ahead at the horizon, Matthew and Karen forgotten. For there, against the night sky, stood the silhouette of a powerfully built man with a sawn-off shotgun.

'Stew . . . Stew, look,' the bear-man babbled.

'I see him,' he said, coming to a painful stop. 'Now, there's somebody who *is* from the Organisation. Quick, we'd better get back to the vans and then split up. There's no reason for them to come after us, now – we've paid our dues to Glen.'

Matthew and Karen kept running until they feared their lungs would burst. Only then did they fall on to all fours, fighting for breath.

'I think we've lost them,' Matthew panted.

Karen glanced over her shoulder. 'You're right, but I'd still like to get back to the car as soon as we can move.'

'With you, there.' He grinned. 'By the way, I'm impressed. You certainly shook that lot up. I don't think old Red Suit knew what hit him.'

'When I get mad, Shelley, I get mad.' She paused for a while, her breath returning to normal. 'At least we've established who they're frightened of – the Organisation.'

'Do you think it was Watkinson with them?'

'I wouldn't think so. I saw their faces when we mentioned his name – they just looked bemused.' She struggled to her feet. 'Come on, let's make a move.'

Matthew eased himself upright and felt his forehead. 'I hope I don't catch a cold. I'm bathed in sweat, and with the chill in this wind . . .'

'Shelley, just for once try acting like a man,' Karen huffed.

'But I catch a chill very easily,' he said, trudging behind. 'And they usually go straight to my chest.'

16

They drove back to Handwell in silence, both lost in their own thoughts while the car slowly ate up the miles. At Bristol they went through a police speed trap without being stopped, blissfully unaware that an hour before the mystery man from the travellers' camp had seen the signs just in time and brought the speed of his Rover down to the required forty miles an hour.

However, the driver of a Nissan Primera, in hot pursuit, had not enjoyed the same luck and was pulled over for doing sixty. The delay caused him to lose the Rover, and by the time the police allowed him to continue his journey, he was not a happy man.

'Can we go in the front door this time?' Karen asked, cheerfully.

'That should be novel,' Matthew said. 'But I'd still better park a few streets away.'

The walk back to his digs was relaxing. The night air smelt of the nearby river, a tangy dark aroma that tickled their nostrils as they chatted. They had almost reached the steps to Matthew's front door when two men stepped out of the shadows to confront them.

'Hello, Mr Shelley – remember us? James and Nick? We paid you a visit a short time ago.'

'James and Nick,' Matthew echoed. 'Yes, I do remember you.'

'Another friendly visit,' James said, patting Matthew's shoulder. 'It's been brought to our attention you've not been following our advice.'

'Look, you pair of shits – ' Karen began.

'Don't start,' James snarled, stabbing a finger at her chest.

Something in his tone sent shivers along her spine and Karen found herself rooted to the spot.

'That's more like it.' He reached down for Matthew's hand. 'Now, I'm going to have to give you a slap on the wrist, Mr

Shelley. Today on Dartmoor you messed something up, you caused us some trouble.' He brought the flat of his hand down lightly on Matthew's arm. 'And that always upsets me.'

Matthew was trying to think of a fitting response when the man grabbed handfuls of his anorak and smashed a rock-hard forehead into his face.

'So, don't do it again,' he said, head-butting him for a second time.

Matthew uttered a little squeal and staggered back against the wall. Blood was spurting from his nose and soaking into his clothes. James backed away, that charming smile once again on his face.

'This is the last friendly warning you two get. Next time things get really rough.' He eyed Karen's body. 'And I could enjoy myself with you, pretty woman.' With that, the men walked away, strolling casually as if they were taking the evening air.

'Oh, my God,' Karen cried. 'Are you all right, Shelley?'

He was holding a hand to his nose, attempting to stem the flow of blood that was oozing between his trembling fingers. He groaned.

'Of course I'm not all right. I think I'm bleeding to death.'

'Let's get you inside.' Her voice was edged with concern.

'Hold on a minute, I'd better put a handkerchief over my nose. If I get blood on Mrs Perkins' carpet, I'll have to pay the cleaning bill.'

Matthew fumbled around in his pockets, pulling out old supermarket receipts, pens, peppermints, anything but a handkerchief. He let out a cry of alarm as his gaze fell upon the widening pool of red on the doorstep.

'Oh God, how much blood have we got in our bodies, Karen? I think mine's nearly all gone.'

A new day dawned, and with it came another side to Matthew's character for Karen to study at close quarters. Overnight, his nose had swollen to twice its normal size and was now developing a faint purple tint. And although the flow of blood had stopped hours ago, he was still walking about with his head held back. It would seem that Matthew Shelley was not the type of man to easily shrug off his injuries.

'Try to forget it,' Karen advised, while she poured the coffee. 'Mind over matter, that sort of thing. Mum always says most things are only in the mind.'

'I'm beginning to hate your mother,' he muttered under his breath.

'Pardon?' She sugared the coffees.

'I said I'll have two aspirin with mine. I've got to get rid of this pain, Karen, it's driving me mad.'

A large part of her wanted to shake him until his brain rattled, wanted to yell at him to grow up. But she did neither, for his nose *had* taken a terrible bashing and it *did* look awfully painful. She watched him shuffling around in circles, his face turned towards the ceiling.

'Shelley, I've been thinking that maybe it's time we baled out of this. I don't know whether you realise, but twice yesterday we could have been killed.'

'I've thought of nothing else,' he said, fingering the swelling. 'In fact, I very nearly was killed.' He took the aspirins she was holding out and washed them down with coffee. 'I suppose you're talking sense, though. We're just not equipped for this caper – those boys play too rough. Trouble is, I'd like to know what really happened to Glen Watkinson.'

She threw him a surprised look. 'Are you saying you want to carry on?'

'I think I am, but I can't see any way we can. That lot could top us if we don't stop poking around.'

'I feel the same way.' She sipped her coffee. 'But we could outwit them, Shelley, you're cleverer than you look.'

'Oh, thanks very much.'

'I meant it as a compliment. Mum always says, an ounce of brain is worth a ton of brawn.'

'Are you sure she knows what she's talking about?' Matthew asked, still prodding gingerly at his nose.

Karen moved to his chair and placed her arms around his neck. 'You really are different – do you know that?'

'Yes, I do.' He heaved a miserable sigh.

'No, I mean, most men who'd gone through what you did last night would be strutting about this morning, saying, just give me five minutes up an alley with that pair ... five minutes, that's all I need ...'

'Five minutes?' Matthew said, appalled. 'But he nearly killed me inside thirty seconds.'

Karen grinned and gave his shoulder a comforting pat. 'We could stay somewhere else, you know. And if we're really careful, they might not find us.'

'You're thinking along the same lines as I am,' he said, brightening a little. 'From there we could carry on with the investigation. But we'd have to watch our backs ...'

'My mother always told me never to look over my shoulder.'

Matthew spun around to face her. 'Karen, does your mother ever say anything other than clichés?'

He missed her spirited reply; he was more concerned with the determined fist that was hammering away at his door. Straight away, he rushed to the window and hauled it open.

'Okay, I've had enough – down the fire escape, quick. I'm damned if I'm tangling with those two goons again.'

'Mr Shelley, can I see you for a couple of minutes, please?' It was Mrs Perkins.

They both gave sighs of relief, and then Matthew threw himself into panic mode. 'In the cupboard,' he said, pushing Karen ahead. 'If she sees you, she'll know you stayed the night.'

Later, at the office, Matthew was still complaining about the pain and still walking with his head tilted back.

'You'll have to check through the post, Karen. I daren't look down in case the bleeding starts again.'

She picked up the pile of envelopes and flicked through it. 'Looks like they're all bills,' she said, tearing them open. 'Yes, final demands for the gas, electricity, council tax, and water rates.'

'Are any of them threatening court action?'

She sorted through again. 'No, doesn't look like it.'

'Bin them, then.' He eased himself behind the desk. 'Oh, if only this pain would stop. Please, God, make it stop.'

'Right, Shelley, I'm going to ring our benefactor, Mr Charlton. If we've got to stay somewhere else, I don't see why he shouldn't pay for it.'

'It's worth a try.'

'Leave it to me.' She tapped out the number and waited for the connection to be made. 'Ah, Mr Charlton, it's Karen Chandler, here. I just thought I'd update you.'

'Hello, my dear.' He chortled. 'Well, you certainly seem to have stirred up a hornets' nest.'

'I know, and we're getting stung.' She told him about the events on the moor, and the nasty incident outside Matthew's digs.

'Oh dear, oh dear, I trust Mr Shelley is all right, now?'

'Oh yes, he's not one to complain . . .' She swallowed a giggle. 'The thing is, Mr Charlton, at the moment we feel that our lives are under threat and we're a bit worried about it.'

'I did foresee this situation, my dear, and, luckily, I've planned for it. I don't know what you'll think of my plan . . .'

'Run it past me.'

He paused. 'It would entail a certain loss of face on your part. I don't know whether that would be acceptable . . .?'

'Run it past me,' she said, again. The phrase had a nice ring to it.

'You would need to contact Judith Ward and agree to do the articles exactly as she wanted – '

'Oh, I don't know about that, Mr Charlton, the woman gets right up my nose. Every time I see her, I get the urge to stick two fingers up to her . . . preferably in her panda-eyes.'

'It would guarantee your safety,' he said, his tone persuasive. 'And I really do think you're making splendid progress. Think how much sweeter it would be, Miss Chandler, if she thought you were toeing the line and then you blew the whole thing apart.'

She could see his point. 'But we'd still have to investigate the case, and they'd know what was going on, so we'd be back at square one, surely?'

A mischievous chuckle travelled down the line, and Karen could imagine the man's blue eyes sparkling with devilment.

'Ah, but the investigation could wait for a while. If and when

101

you need protection, I could find you alternative accommodation. I own a lot of property, both here and in the surrounding areas.'

Brilliant. Rent-free digs, and she didn't even have to ask. 'I'd have to think about it,' she said, trying hard to conceal her excitement. 'Anyway, what's this hornets' nest we've stirred up?'

'I'm extremely pleased with what you're doing,' Charlton enthused. 'I don't know the identity of the man you chased off the moor, but I do know that what you did delighted Judith and Giles Abbot immensely.'

'Oh?' Suspicion surfaced rapidly in Karen's mind. 'How do you know that?'

'Because I arranged for an internal phone tap and I overheard their conversation. They were being ultra careful, no names were mentioned, but they seemed to think that this man could supply them with what they wanted. And as you had driven him out of hiding, he was now ready to talk a deal. Abbot suggested they should get together, and he arranged for Judith to meet with the man.'

'But no time or place was mentioned?'

'None. As I said, they were being very careful. It would be up to you and Mr Shelley to watch and follow Judith.'

Karen cast a quick glance at Matthew. He gave her a questioning look back and then winced, for it pulled at the tautness of his injuries.

'Mr Charlton,' she said, firmly, 'all this is costing money, you know.'

'But I've already paid you both a thousand pounds,' he said, indignation loud in his tone.

'No, you paid *me* a thousand pounds,' she hurriedly corrected him. 'Mr Shelley is a private investigator with a business to run, overheads, et cetera. He can't afford to work for me full-time unless I can pay him on a regular basis.'

'I could advance you another thousand.' The offer was grudgingly made.

'Make it two, and you've got yourself a deal.'

That sly chuckle came again. 'You strike a hard bargain, my dear. No doubt you've calculated that I'm desperate to get this matter sorted out, once and for all. But Mr Shelley isn't the only one with a business to run – I too have to keep tight control over my financial dealings, and therefore I would have to insist that the two thousand comes off any final payment made to you. After all, you're employing Mr Shelley, not I.'

It was Karen's turn to laugh. 'And you say I strike a tough bargain. Okay, I'll go along with that.'

'That's good, my dear, I'll have the cheque with you as soon as possible.'

'It's a pleasure doing business with you, Mr Charlton. I'll be in touch.' She replaced the receiver and stood grinning at it.

The promise of money was a far more effective painkiller than the aspirin. Matthew's face was stretched into a wide grin, and he was punching the air repeatedly.

'Two grand? Oh, Karen, you're great, you really are. You'll have to come and work for me permanently.'

'I'm seriously thinking about doing just that, partner. If we could knock this business into shape, the sky would be the limit.' She gave him a rueful look. 'Somehow I don't think journalism is for me, Shelley.'

She told him what Charlton had said. 'So, it looks like I'm off to the office of the charming Judith Ward for a meal of humble pie.'

'Do you think you can stomach that?' Matthew asked warily.

'Keep your fingers crossed, it could go either way.' She gathered up her things and stuffed them into her shoulder bag. 'Listen, when the money comes through we'll get mobile phones – right? Let's drag this agency into the nineties. And I'm sorry to nag, but don't you think you should make the payments on the car?'

'Hardly worth it. It's almost knackered, anyway, so why pay off God knows how many hundreds of pounds just to end up with something worth twenty-five quid for scrap?'

'But, Shelley, if they do repossess it we'll have no form of transport.'

He shot her a pained look. 'You really must learn to trust me, Karen. When the money starts rolling in, we'll replace it. Till then, I've got plenty of friends working on the market who'll lend me a car.'

'Okay, I'll trust you,' she said, heading for the door. 'Just so long as we don't end up with a three-wheeler like Del Boy's.'

Two hours later Karen was back. Matthew sat transfixed while she stormed through the door and over to the far wall where she threw down the carrier bag she was holding and struck out repeatedly with her open palms.

'That snotty, bloody cow . . .' Each word was punctuated by a blow to the wall. 'You should have heard her. Of course, Karen, we'd be glad to have you back, but you realise you must do exactly what you're told this time.' She turned to Matthew, her face like thunder. 'And I had to say . . .' She stopped, mid-sentence, her mouth gaping open in amazement. 'Shelley, what the hell have you done to your hair?'

'I've had it cut,' he said, proudly. 'I thought, if we've got to follow Judith, I'd better make myself look less conspicuous.' He ran self-conscious fingers through his new short back and sides. 'And I wish you hadn't asked me what I'd done to it – the hairdresser's just spent half an hour asking me what I'd done to my nose.'

'I think it's a brilliant idea. Actually, you look great, it really suits you. And as I'm going with you, perhaps I'd better change my appearance in some way, as well.'

'Dark glasses?' Matthew suggested. 'And perhaps gel your hair and comb it straight back off your forehead?'

'Dunno, I'll have to think about it.' She fetched the carrier bag. 'Look, Shelley, we are now the proud owners of two mobile phones.'

'You look great, Karen.'

'No, I don't.'

'But, you do, honest.'

'Shelley, I look like I've dipped my head in a tub of lard. And these sun-glasses are much too big. Look, they keep sliding down my nose.'

Karen had tried the gel idea, and although the scraped-back style in no way detracted from her good looks, she had not yet adjusted to the change and was convinced she looked awful. She sat well down in the passenger seat, her mouth a brooding line. They were parked in a corner of the underground car-park beneath the *Profile* offices where they had a clear view of Judith Ward's gleaming Jaguar.

'I wonder if they'll meet up tonight?' Matthew mused. 'You know, my money's still on Watkinson being the mystery man.'

'I'm not so sure,' Karen said, turning slightly and dislodging the sun-glasses. With an irritable tut-tut she pushed them back into position. 'If it is him, why would he come back here?'

'Think it through. We've flushed him out, so he'll probably feel safer here with the people who're protecting him. He'll reason they're the only ones able to find him somewhere secure to stay, and he'll probably think they'll frighten us off his scent.'

Karen gave a derisory snort. 'Much as you like that theory, Shelley, I don't go along with it.' Suddenly, she gripped his arm. 'Hold on, look, there's Judith.'

'Okay, get down, in case she looks over here.'

Peering above the rim of the dashboard they saw her hurry to the Jaguar and slide into the driver's seat. The sound of the perfectly tuned engine hardly carried across the car-park.

'Start the car, Shelley, quickly, or we'll lose her.'

Matthew turned the key, but the engine failed to catch, and they could only watch helplessly as Judith backed the Jaguar out of its parking space and slipped into first gear. He tried the key again and held it while the engine fired and roared into life, but then it spluttered and died. Judith seemed to look in their direction but no sign of recognition showed on her face and the Jaguar continued to glide towards the exit.

'Don't just sit there, Shelley, get it started. She's already on the ramp. If she gets into the traffic, we'll lose her.'

'I'm doing my best,' he snapped. 'All this is making my nose hurt.'

Holding his breath Matthew turned the ignition. Yet again the engine kicked into life and then began to die. Desperate, now, he jabbed the accelerator to the floor and kept it there. The car shuddered and shook, thick black smoke pouring from its exhaust.

'It's started,' he said excitedly.

'Just get it out of the car-park,' Karen shouted above the din.

The Jaguar was still at the top of the ramp, slowly edging its way into the late evening traffic. Behind it, Matthew was having to rev his engine repeatedly to keep it going. He was making such a noise that Judith glanced back. Karen swiftly ducked and Matthew pretended to be searching furiously through the pocket on his door. When he looked up, Judith was easing her car into a gap in the traffic. Matthew kept close to her tail, pulling out into the path of an oncoming Metro. The driver braked sharply and leant on the horn.

'For God's sake,' Karen yelled, 'what are you doing?'

'I can't stop till the engine's warmed up,' he said, as if speaking to a child. 'If it stalls now, I'll never get it started again.' He stabbed an accusing finger at her upper arm. 'You have a distinct tendency to panic, Karen.'

17

Roland Parr passed from room to room, reliving his memories of the last six years. During those years he had come to love Manfield House. For the first time in his life he had found somewhere that was good for his writing, a place where creative freedom abounded.

'And all taken away in a few short weeks,' he muttered, scornfully. 'By human greed.'

He was standing at the doorway to the study, pain showing clearly on his face, when someone leant heavily on the doorbell.

'What the hell . . . ?'

Parr glanced at his wrist-watch. It was getting late, and he wasn't expecting anyone. Mumbling crossly under his breath, he shuffled along the hall and slid back the heavy bolts. The door swung inwards and Parr's face fell.

'Oh God, no . . . not you.'

He tried in vain to slam the door, but the man in the porch kept his weight fully against it.

'Listen to me, Roland,' he almost begged, 'I'm meeting Judith

Ward near here, and afterwards I'll need somewhere to lie low.'

'Well, you can't stay with me,' Parr blustered. 'This'll be one of the first places they'll come looking for you.'

The man's eyes narrowed. 'Don't ever forget, Roland, that I'm one of the few people who knows the truth about the book. It's a deal that could still be worth millions to us, so you'd better let me in.'

Parr was attempting to stand his ground, but one look at the man's determined expression caused his defiance to crumble. With great reluctance, he stepped back and pulled the door wide.

A cash-point machine in the town's main street was to be Judith Ward's first stop. Matthew managed to find a parking space four cars back from the Jaguar, and he kept the engine running while Judith drew money from the hole in the wall. She hurried back to the car, her wary gaze flitting left to right, and as she stooped to open the driver's door her eyes seemed to be directly on them, but she scrambled in without an acknowledgement.

'She must have seen us,' Karen murmured.

'Could have done, but she didn't seem to recognise us,' Matthew said, pulling out as the Jaguar sped away. 'I only hope she's not heading for open country, Karen. If she gets into a seventy speed limit, we're never going to keep up.'

It seemed that his fears were about to be realised when Judith took the ring road. Pushing the car to its pathetic limit, Matthew managed to get the needle up to sixty miles an hour. Unfortunately, the temperature gauge was also rising, and its needle hovered just this side of the red danger zone.

'We're losing her,' he groaned.

With sinking stomachs, they watched the tail lights of the Jaguar disappear into the distance. But then its left-hand indicator started to flash.

'Shelley . . . look. She's turning into the slip road.'

Matthew nursed the car along. He had no real hope of catching up – once off the slip road the Jaguar would still outrun them – but he continued with a dogged persistence, only to find that the roundabout at the top was emtpy.

'She's gone.' Anger and despondency showed in his voice as they made another circuit. 'We've lost her.'

'No, we haven't,' Karen called out, excitedly. 'See? Over there, in the supermarket car-park.'

He looked to where she was pointing and saw the red Jaguar parked on the tarmac. 'She must have gone into the store.'

'To meet our man?' Karen pondered. 'It'd be a good place to go unnoticed, right in the middle of a crowd.'

'Hmm, possible, I suppose. Still, we won't know until we get in there.'

Matthew fell silent and concentrated on finding a space. He eventually squeezed between a Micra and an Escort and gratefully turned off the engine. So intent were they on getting inside the superstore that neither of them noticed a truck pulling into the car-park and heading for their car.

The automatic doors opened up before them, and they crossed the air-conditioned foyer with its dry-cleaning counter and children's rides.

'We'll split up,' Matthew said in a hushed tone.

'Not a good idea,' Karen countered. 'What if I find her, then follow her out, and you're still in here?'

'You win, come on.'

They wandered along the row of tills, hurriedly searching the sea of faces for a glimpse of Judith Ward. Failing to find her, they almost ran along the tops of the aisles, peering frantically into the crowds.

'She's not in here,' Karen declared, breathlessly. 'Perhaps the man picked her up in the car-park.'

Matthew was about to reply when a harassed mother pushed her shopping trolley into the backs of his legs. With an indignant, 'Ouch', he jumped aside and stood on one leg, rubbing hard at his ankle.

'You shouldn't stop like that, without warning,' the woman said, tartly. 'It's people like you who cause accidents.'

'And you should look where you're going,' was his angry reply. 'Look at that, my ankle's swelling up, already.'

'It'll match your nose, then, won't it?' the woman called over her shoulder.

'Balls, balls, balls,' he mumbled, tentatively testing his foot on the floor.

Karen took one last look around. 'Shelley, we'd better get back to the car.'

'But I'm in pain, here. I don't know if I can walk.'

'Oh, stop making such a fuss,' she said, strutting off towards the exit. Matthew limped behind her, muttering under his breath.

After the oppressive warmth of the supermarket, the night air rapidly chilled them as they made their way across the car-park. Suddenly, Karen came to an abrupt stop.

'Shelley,' she hissed, 'there're two guys messing about with your car.'

'Oh, Jesus, they're trying to open the driver's door ... They're going to nick it. Karen, perhaps we'd better leave them alone, just in case they get nasty.'

'Hey, you,' Karen shrieked at the top of her voice. 'Get your bloody hands off that car.'

Matthew watched in horror as she sprinted towards the furtive figures. Still mouthing expletives, he hobbled off in pursuit.

'What do you think you're doing?' Karen screamed at the men.

'We're repossessing the car because the payments haven't been made,' one of the men hurled back. He was a Mr Universe type, dressed in jeans and a sleeveless black T-shirt.

'You can't do that,' she said, wrestling him away from the door handle. 'Where's your paperwork?'

The man shook himself free of her clutches and marched off to his pick-up truck, returning with a clipboard he had taken from the passenger seat. He held it under Karen's nose.

'There you are – all complete and legal. Now, go and be silly somewhere else.'

Karen studied the papers, her bravado rapidly dwindling. 'You've got an attitude problem,' she said, needing to have the last word.

'Tough shit. Now, get out of my way. We've been following you two all day, and we're not leaving without the car.' He pushed her to one side.

'Get your hands off me. How *dare* you.'

'Don't act like a prat, love.'

Karen's eyes grew wide with indignation, and she stood before the man with hands on hips while Matthew threw his gaze towards the heavens, his lips moving in silent prayer.

'Who are you calling a prat?' Karen demanded.

'Bugger off,' he said, turning back to the car.

'You make me,' Karen dared, shoving him against it.

His face registered shock as he smashed into the bodywork, his paperwork flying in all directions. 'You're out of your tree, love.'

Realising that she was lining up her shoulder bag, ready to take aim, Matthew grabbed her from behind. 'Leave it, Karen,' he said, sharply, 'Now, stop it.'

'I'll have him . . .'

While he kept her in a bear-hug, the startled man bent to retrieve his papers.

'Karen, listen to me,' Matthew shouted in her ear. 'Judith Ward's on the supermarket's free bus. I've just seen her get on and go upstairs.'

She immediately stopped struggling and looked to where the bus was parked outside the main entrance.

'Judith must be leaving her car here and using the bus to make sure she's not being followed,' he said. 'We can sit downstairs, and she won't even know we're there.'

Karen stole one last baleful glance at the man, and then strode away.

'Well, don't just stand there, Shelley,' she called, briskly. 'We need to get on that bus.'

They found the bus full of shoppers and managed to lose themselves at the back. At each drop-off point they held their breath and waited for Judith to emerge from the upper deck. But after four stops they were still waiting, and worrying, too, for the passengers around them were quickly thinning out.

'We'll be the only ones left at this rate,' Karen whispered. 'And what would we do, then?'

'Shush . . . listen,' Matthew said. 'Is that her?'

Sure enough, above the conversational buzz that surrounded

them, they heard the metallic click of high heels on the stairs. And then Judith was before them, her elegant, doll-like appearance totally out of place among the cluster of frazzled housewives.

Matthew and Karen hid their faces, but there was no need, for the women in front of them were leaving their seats and shuffling towards the door. In any case, Judith was peering intently out of the driver's window, allowing them to edge their way towards the front, unseen. At the stop, Judith jumped off the moment the doors swished open, and she was hurrying along the poorly lit side street by the time the bus pulled away.

'We'd better keep a good distance behind her,' Matthew said. 'If she sees us now, we've had it.'

'I think we're already there, Shelley. Look, she's going into that pub.'

'Great.' He shot her an excited grin. 'Karen, I think we're about to meet Glen Watkinson.'

The pub held mostly young people, and loud music blared from the juke box while pinball machines whined and beeped in the corners. Through a low haze of cigarette smoke Matthew led Karen across the crowded bar, all the time scrutinising the huddled groups in search of Judith. The noise prohibited normal chat so Matthew simply pointed to a door at the far end of the room and motioned for Karen to head for it. At the door they spilled out into a large hallway with other doors leading off. It was quieter now; all that could be heard was the clink of glasses and the low drone of conversation.

'Which door?' Karen mouthed.

'We'd better work our way along,' was Matthew's hushed reply. 'I'm just hoping she didn't go in the front and straight out the back, just to cover her trail.'

'Shelley, she's in there,' Karen said, gripping his arm. 'Look through that hatch.'

He stooped slightly and peered through. Judith, installed at a corner table, was engaged in a whispered but undoubtedly fractious conversation with a man who was sitting with his back towards them. While Matthew watched she leant across the table, her finger stabbing aggressively at his chest, and subjected him to a spirited tongue-lashing. Then, without warning, they got to their feet.

'They're coming out,' Matthew whispered. 'Now, we've got to get a look at the guy, but they mustn't spot us.'

They back-tracked along the passage and came to a halt by a machine attached to the wall.

'I'll get some cigarettes,' he said, feeding coins into the slot.

Judith was the first to emerge, but she stopped in the doorway so the man remained hidden. They were still arguing violently.

'You're upsetting a lot of people,' she was saying.

'But I don't know where it is, I swear to God I don't . . .'

And then they saw him. He was around mid-forties, with light brown hair worn long over his ears and a smooth but pasty complexion. His suit was expensive and well-tailored. His hands were held out towards Judith, as if begging her trust or support or conviction.

'If I had any idea,' he continued in a tremulous tone, 'don't you think I'd tell you?'

'You'd better explain it to the powers that be,' Judith replied. And then she turned smartly and hastened to the outer door.

With one eye still on the man who was now racing after her, Matthew pulled the knob on the machine and a packet dropped into the tray.

'Well, that's not Glen Watkinson,' he said, clearly disappointed.

'Definitely not,' Karen agreed. 'And they're not cigarettes, either.' She pointed to the tray. 'You've just bought yourself six cherry-flavoured condoms, Shelley.'

18

Loud knocking ploughed its way through Matthew's dreams of unlimited funds with not a creditor in sight, and he greeted the morning with a churlish snort. He turned over in the sleeping bag and stared up at Karen, still snoring quietly in his bed.

'Hey, Karen,' he called in a low whisper. 'There's somebody at the door.'

She stirred, and swore softly. 'Why don't you open it, then?' she murmured, through a wide yawn. 'Now they've taken the car back, you don't owe anybody money.'

'Oh . . . all right.' He unzipped the bag and padded to the door feeling rather vulnerable in just his red boxer shorts. 'Who is it?' he called. Hiding from bailiffs for so long had made him cautious.

'Police,' came the booming reply. 'Open this door, or we'll have to knock it down.'

Matthew let out a squeal of alarm and turned his pleading eyes to Karen.

'Don't look so worried,' she said, calmly. 'It's only the local fuzz playing at *The Bill*.'

'You answer it . . . please?'

She sighed and climbed from the bed, struggling into her white bathrobe on her way to the door.

'Hang on,' she said to the police. 'And if you dare to smash it down, then you'll have to pay to get it replaced.'

A series of loud knocks shook the thin plywood, and its handle rattled violently while Karen reached resignedly for the lock.

'Hurry up,' the officer said. 'We haven't got all day.'

Karen opened the door and stood before the two plain-clothed detectives with arms folded, determined not to be undermined. They were the pair who had been so unhelpful at the police station when she had asked to see the Watkinson pathologist's report.

'What do you want?' she demanded to know.

The officers exchanged a look which held much amusement. 'You're not Matthew Shelley.'

'Well done,' she said, applauding wildly. 'Whatever people say about the police, at least you two are in the right job. Let's see some identification.'

'Don't be silly, love, you know who we are.'

'I saw you at the station, it's true, but you were both so lacking in charisma, you could have been cardboard cut-outs, for all I knew.'

The detectives had expected an altogether more deferential reception and both were openly fuming while they dug in their pockets for warrant cards. Karen studied the cards carefully.

'Okay, they seem to be in order.' She turned her icy gaze to their faces. 'Now, what do you want?'

'Just step aside, and let us in,' said the bulkier of the two.

'DS Spencer,' Karen said, smiling sweetly. 'Have you got a warrant? Because if you haven't, you're not setting foot in this room.'

Spencer's face flushed. 'You're getting up my nose, love.'

'Oh, really? And I'm getting fed up with your lot pushing us about, so think again, boys.'

Matthew was hurriedly pulling on his clothes and cringing at Karen's haughty tone. He appeared beside her, his expression apologetic.

'Karen,' he said, his watchful gaze fixed on the detectives, 'I don't think this is the best course of action . . .'

'Ah, Shelley,' Spencer said. 'Mackmin wants you and your girlfriend down the nick for questioning – now.'

Karen watched, open-mouthed, while Matthew moved to collect his anorak like an obedient pet.

The detective sniggered. 'What happened to your nose?'

'Somebody smashed it in.'

Spencer nudged the other officer. 'Does that happen a lot?'

'Only if they catch me.'

'Shelley,' Karen exclaimed, 'you're not going to let them push you about . . .?'

'Come on, love, chop, chop – '

'Don't you chop, chop, me, Spencer, I know my rights.'

The officer leant forward, his aggressive sneer not far from Karen's face. 'Get your clothes on – now. You're about to spend a few days with us.'

Karen's eyebrows rose. 'Are you arresting us?'

'No, we're taking you down the nick for questioning.'

'So, you're merely asking us to help you with your enquiries?'

'Leave it, Karen,' Matthew said. 'Mackmin's going to nail me to the wall if we mess him about.'

'Shelley, he can only nail you to the wall if you let him.' She glared at the detectives. 'The trouble is, sergeant, I haven't yet heard you ask for our help.'

'We could nick you,' Spencer threatened.

Karen gave a shrug. 'And take the chance of being done yourself for wrongful arrest? I don't think so.'

The detective swallowed hard; he wasn't used to women getting the better of him. Still, his chief inspector wanted them at the station post-haste and so he had better play along, however much it went against the grain. He tried a smile.

'Miss Chandler, Mr Shelley, I wonder if you'd come to the station to assist us with our enquiries?'

'But, of course,' Karen said. 'We'd be only too happy to help, wouldn't we, Shelley? If you'd be kind enough to wait there while I get dressed . . .' The door was slammed in their faces.

Matthew glanced at his watch. It was 10.45 a.m. He had been sitting in the interview room for over two hours. He knew Chief Inspector Mackmin would keep him waiting, would want him to worry, but he'd expected to have just the blank-faced uniformed officer positioned at the door for company. Instead, DS Spencer and his fresh-faced sidekick, DC Cooper, were there, too, both lounging about in chairs beside the tape recorder. Karen had been taken to a separate room directly on arrival.

Spencer's penetrating gaze never left their reluctant guest, and all the while a taunting smile played on his thin lips and showed in his eyes. Matthew had already developed a strong dislike for the man. He had seen his type before: arrogant, brash, full of himself. And yet Matthew sensed an underlying lack of confidence. It manifested itself in the man's low hair parting mere centimetres above his right ear, in the thin grey strands combed across his crown to disguise advancing baldness, and in the close-clipped beard he was forever fiddling with, its function simply to prove that the sergeant was capable of growing hair somewhere. Cooper was younger, more conventional, but he too possessed the swaggering, look-at-me body language that was unique to plain-clothed policemen.

Matthew pushed to one side his mounting distaste for the detectives and tried to call to mind any misdeeds that he and Karen might have committed to land themselves in this predicament. Not even Mackmin would dare to drag them into the station without good cause – would he? Shifting his position in the buttock-numbing plastic chair, Matthew heaved a resigned sigh and settled down to wait.

In the adjoining interview room Karen, tired of letting out exasperated sighs that only fell on deaf ears, was now making more verbal complaints with which to register her resentment.

'How much longer am I going to be kept here?' she asked, and not for the first time.

The WPC, standing by the door, let out an impatient breath. 'I've told you, Chief Inspector Mackmin will interview you as soon as he's free.'

Karen studied the woman's bored expression. 'Do you know how long I've been here? Two whole hours. And nobody's bothered to offer me a drink or anything to eat. I do have rights, you know.'

'I can send for a cup of tea or coffee,' was the officer's weary reply.

'I'll have tea. Oh, and you can get me some paper, an envelope, and a stamp, so I can write a letter of complaint to my MP.'

The WPC exhaled sharply. 'Look, Chief Inspector Mackmin is a tough copper – '

'And I'm a tough lady,' Karen hurled back.

'A lot think they're hard when they come in here,' the officer said, hiding a smile, 'but they've usually changed their minds by the time they leave.'

'I won't.' Karen cast a disgruntled look at the opposite wall and decided to change tack. 'What's your name, anyway?'

'WPC Marlow.'

'Oh, cut the crap, WPC Marlow. I mean, what's your first name?'

'It's Jane. Now just behave, will you? I'm not enjoying this any more than you are.'

'Maybe not, but at least you're getting paid to stand there.' She let a few seconds tick by, and then said, 'What's all this about, Jane?'

The officer shook her head. 'I can't tell you, it's more than my job's worth. But I do know you're in for a long wait, they're interviewing your boyfriend first.'

'Oh yes? Because they think he'll bend under pressure?'

'They may feel he's more likely to co-operate,' Marlow replied, diplomatically. 'You're not making this easy on yourself, you know.'

'I suppose not,' Karen grudgingly replied, 'but I do have the right to know why I've been brought in, and I also have the right to walk out unless I get some answers.'

'Karen, let me give you a tip,' Marlow said, hurriedly. 'Mackmin regards himself as a law unto himself. Now, if I were you I'd just go along with this, because if you don't it'll become a matter of, you will or else . . .'

Karen regarded the woman with open disbelief. 'Are you saying he'll manufacture evidence against Shelley and me?'

'I've said too much already,' Marlow stammered.

'Jane, is Mackmin on the take? Is there somebody paying him to get the results they want?'

Karen persisted for several minutes, but no reply was forthcoming. Instead, the WPC maintained a stony silence and stared straight ahead at the plain white wall.

The door to the interview room flew open.

'Right . . . out,' Mackmin barked to the uniformed constable stationed at the door. Surprise flickered briefly in the man's eyes but then, with a servile meekness, he turned on his heel and left the room.

'Ah, Mr Shelley . . .' Mackmin kicked the door shut and stood with his back against it. 'I would hardly have known you, what with that false nose and your short haircut. Trying to change your appearance, were you?'

The detectives tittered and Matthew's throat went dry. All of a sudden he felt as if the walls were closing in on him.

'Yes . . . I mean, no. Oh, God . . .' He stared up at the ceiling, realising only too well how the chief inspector could twist what he had said.

'Yes? No? You're not making yourself very clear, Mr Shelley.

Having trouble making up your mind?' Mackmin crossed to the table, his sheer bulk intimidating. 'Oh, by the way, the lawyers have just finished carving up my pension – fifty per cent to the bitch, and the other fifty to me.' He pulled out a chair and sat down. 'So, I'm not a very happy man, Mr Shelley. In fact, I could become very depressed, should you decide to mess me about.'

Matthew tried to meet the man's steely gaze but it was far too menacing, so he stared instead at the burn marks on the metal ashtray in the centre of the table.

'Right, Mr Shelley, for our first run through, I'm going to dispense with the tape recorder.'

DC Cooper shot his superior a questioning glance. Even DS Spencer appeared to be a little uncomfortable.

'You've no right to do that,' Matthew said, boldly. 'Any more than you had a right to send the constable out.'

Mackmin's sullen mouth twisted into a sardonic smile. 'I'm only trying to help you, Mr Shelley. I mean . . . yes-no, in answer to a question? You could get yourself into a lot of trouble like that. No, I think we should run through your story first and then tape it.' He sat back and studied Matthew for a few moments, and then launched into his interrogation. 'You and that journalist were on Dartmoor, two days ago. What were you doing there?'

'Looking for someone we've been asked to find.'

'And who might that be?'

Matthew hesitated. He was unwilling to lie, but the truth at times could sound so absurd. 'Glen Watkinson,' he said, at last.

'Glen Watkinson?' Mackmin's hearty laugh sounded doubly loud in the confined space. 'You're confusing me here, Mr Shelley – you see, that man is dead. True, there wasn't enough left of him to positively identify, but he is dead. Who asked you to find him?'

'I'm working for Karen Chandler,' Matthew said in a rush. 'She's doing a series of articles – '

'Balls,' Mackmin exclaimed. 'Little Miss Charm had already been sacked from *Profile* magazine by the time you got to Dartmoor. Although, I do believe she's now been taken back on the understanding that she does what she's told. And that's a state of affairs I can't see lasting very long.'

Matthew glanced up. 'How do you know that?'

'I'm asking the questions, Mr Shelley. Who asked you to find him?'

Matthew almost mentioned Jocelyn Charlton, the name was on the tip of his tongue but he bit it back and forced himself to meet Mackmin's eyes.

'Nobody's paying us,' he said in an even tone. 'We were hoping to sell the story to the highest bidder.'

Yet again Mackmin let forth his robust laugh, but then he smashed his fist on to the table, making Matthew recoil.

'You came into some money, Mr Shelley. We know that because you paid your debts off. Pity you didn't make some payments on your car – you wouldn't be sitting here now, if you had. Never mind, you'll probably both end up with fifteen years inside, so you'll be able to regret it at your leisure.'

'Chief inspector,' Matthew said with a sigh. 'What are we supposed to have done?'

'You chased somebody off the moor. You know that, and so do we.'

'We knew one of your men was following us.'

Mackmin shook his head. 'I had no officers on the moor.'

Matthew's confused glance flitted between the three men. 'But – '

'But, nothing,' Mackmin yelled. 'None of my people were on the moor.' He rubbed at his temples, attempting to stay calm. In a more controlled tone, he said, 'It's been established, Mr Shelley, that you ran this man off the moor – the Devon police talked to the group of travellers he was staying with. We also know that the man came back to Handwell and arranged a meeting with Judith Ward, from *Profile* magazine, for last night.'

The chief inspector rose to his feet and took to pacing the room. 'We have proof that you and your friend followed Miss Ward – you did cause something of a fracas when your car was repossessed, and we have plenty of witnesses who saw you in that supermarket car-park. Then you followed Ward to the White Elephant, where she'd arranged the meet . . .' He abruptly stopped his pacing, and returned to his seat. 'Do you deny that you were in the White Elephant, Mr Shelley?'

'Yes,' Matthew blurted. 'You have no proof . . .'

'Oh, but I do. The landlord clearly remembers the two of you.

He deliberately kept an eye on you because of your suspicious behaviour – his words, not mine.'

'Where's all this leading?'

'I'll tell you.' Mackmin took from his inside pocket an envelope from which he extracted a photograph. 'Do you recognise this man, Mr Shelley?'

Matthew took a quick glance at the photograph, and nodded. 'That's the man who was with Judith Ward at the White Elephant.'

'And that's also the man you've been chasing all over the country,' Mackmin confided. 'Now, let me show you more.'

A second photograph was put before Matthew. This one was altogether different, and his stomach gave a sickening roll as he stared at it, long and hard. It was a picture of the same man, only now his blood-covered jaw sagged alarmingly, and his eyes were open but unseeing.

'Dead,' Mackmin confirmed. 'Not murdered, as such. He was taken to an empty house on the Heath Estate, where he was tortured in an upstairs room. The man was found with burns all over his body, probably caused by an electrical current; there was extensive bruising to the genital area; a number of his fingernails had been torn off . . . Not nice, is it, Mr Shelley?'

Matthew swallowed what little saliva he had, and gave silent thanks when the photograph was returned to the envelope.

'It would seem,' the chief inspector continued, 'that at some time during his ordeal he managed to break free and, in desperation, hurled himself through the first-floor window. His neck and spine were broken on impact with the pavement.'

Mackmin fell silent, and Matthew took in his quizzical gaze with mounting confusion.

'But I don't know anything about this,' he blustered, his face white with shock.

'Don't you? You did hound this man. You and your journalist friend seem to be obsessed with the idea that Glen Watkinson is still alive. I put it to you, Mr Shelley, that you kidnapped this man and tortured him in the hope that he would tell you where Watkinson was.'

'You're mad,' Matthew yelled. 'I wouldn't do anything like that. You're trying to fit me up . . .'

'I'm only doing my job,' Mackmin said, shrugging.

'But I don't even know who the man is,' Matthew said, his voice rising to a shrill pitch. 'I don't even know who he is.'

'Was,' Mackmin reminded him. 'Was, Mr Shelley. His remains are lying in the morgue right now, and I'm going to have you for putting him there.'

'But I didn't know him,' Matthew argued, strongly. 'And you can't prove that I did.'

Mackmin gave a slight smile. 'I'll have a good try. At the very least I'll prove that you knew who he was. What with your interest in this case, it would have been impossible for you not to have known Andrew Dickens ... Watkinson's literary agent, and the man who apparently went missing.'

19

Karen was extremely bored by the time DCI Mackmin finally entered the room with DS Spencer.

'Your friend's coughed,' Mackmin informed her.

She skimmed her eyes over the pair, then returned her gaze to the table top. 'It must be the number of cigarettes you smoke. He's got a weak chest.'

'I mean, he talked, Miss Chandler, he told us what we wanted to know.'

'Thank God for that.' She gave an exaggerated yawn. 'That must mean I'm free to leave.'

'I'd prefer you to stay seated,' Mackmin growled. He placed his open palms on the table and leant towards her. 'Do you know why you're here, Miss Chandler?'

'Oh, yes, chief inspector, I know exactly why I'm here,' she said, angrily. 'I'm here because some time ago Shelley worked for your wife, gathering evidence to help her divorce you. Now, somewhere in that cavity where your brain should be, you've got the idea that it was all his fault.' She gave him the full force of her hostile glare. 'But you're wrong, chief inspector, it was your fault. If only you'd kept your zip done up you'd still be married, and your bank balance would be intact.'

Mackmin was shaking with rage. He grabbed the back of a chair, and it looked for a moment as if he might hurl it across the room. Over by the door, WPC Marlow turned away to conceal a grin.

'Now, you just listen to me,' he said, through gritted teeth. 'Shelley's in there, now, and it's only a matter of time before he cracks.'

Karen shook her head, her expression adamant. 'You're misjudging him, as most people do. He might be insecure and lacking in confidence, but he's still worth ten of you, and he won't be confessing to anything he hasn't done.'

Mackmin's eyes bulged in their sockets. 'I'll break you,' he quietly promised.

'Oh, go and play with yourself,' she muttered, scornfully. 'And you'd better believe that I'm not saying a word until there's a solicitor present. I'm entitled to that, so I'm requesting it.' She huffed. 'I shouldn't even be here without being told what it's all about. So, you, chief inspector, and Spencer, there – and you, as well, Jane – had all better take note of what I'm saying. If I'm denied a brief, I'm going to play merry hell, and your jobs could be caught up in it.'

Mackmin stood at the door, his huge hands bunched into fists. 'Let her make a phone call.' He turned to Karen. 'I'll make sure you're here for a very long time, Miss Chandler. I can hold you for thirty-six hours. After that, I can go to the magistrates and request a further thirty-six.' He sneered. 'Add all that up, and it comes to a nice little stay.'

'Huh, you don't seem very confident that you'll be charging us with anything,' Karen threw at him, quite unperturbed. 'Somebody might start asking questions about that.'

DS Spencer made his way back to the interview room where Matthew was being kept.

'I'm sorry about all this, mate,' he said, checking the corridor before closing the door. 'The guv'nor's hard on everybody, but he really seems to have singled you out.'

'Aren't I the lucky one?' Matthew said, pulling a face. 'Is Karen all right?'

'Holding her own,' Spencer assured him. 'Because of her you'll be getting a brief. So he should make sure everything's done by the rules from now on.' He perched on the edge of the table. 'Listen, we'll be wanting some of your things for forensic, but don't agree to anything until you've talked to your solicitor about it – okay?'

'Thanks, I appreciate it.' He gave the man a tired smile. 'Tell me, sergeant, were any of your officers on Dartmoor?'

'Nobody from this nick was there.' Spencer frowned. 'That guy you say was following you – did you get a look at him?'

'I didn't, unfortunately. I know he drove a blue Nissan, though – a Primera, I think it was – but I haven't got a registration number.'

'Sorry, mate, doesn't ring any bells. What makes you think he was from the police, anyway?'

'Just something somebody said,' Matthew murmured, as he stared into the middle distance. He brought his attention back to the sergeant. 'Do you think Mackmin's reacting like this because he's got something to hide?'

'Like what?'

Matthew shrugged. 'He could be taking bribes. It has been known.'

'But situations like that usually involve more than one officer. If we wanted to turn a blind eye to drugs, say, it wouldn't be any good if it was just the guv'nor doing it – officers below him would have to be in on it, as well, and that'd mean greasing palms.'

'And that's not happening here?'

'Well, nobody's greased mine, or even offered to. No, mate, I'd have to say you're barking up the wrong tree.' He moved closer and dropped his voice. 'I'd say it's more likely that Mackmin doesn't want the Watkinson case looked into because, if you or anybody else did turn something up, it'd reflect badly on him. Upstairs would question whether he was doing his job properly.'

'I don't suppose I've improved my chances by helping his wife to divorce him,' Matthew muttered, gloomily.

Spencer chuckled. 'You can say that again. He's a vindictive man, is the guv'nor, and for the foreseeable future he'll be leaning on you every chance he gets.' The sergeant made for the door. 'Anyway, how about lunch? Do you want us to send out for a Chinese or a vindaloo?'

Mackmin was as good as his word. They were held at the police station for three days, sleeping and eating in the cells, and spending many of the daylight hours under questioning.

Their solicitor, a Mr Gordon Roach, told them that although all evidence against them was circumstantial, the police were within their rights to carry out forensic tests in view of the fact that they had watched and followed Andrew Dickens on a number of occasions. Various items of clothing were taken from Matthew's digs, and the time-consuming forensic procedures were started.

The three days were up, almost to the minute, when they were finally told they were free to leave. Matthew was pale and subdued, but Karen had lost none of her bounce.

'Thank your guv'nor for the free board and lodgings,' she said, as she swanned past DS Spencer. 'It's saved us a bomb.'

Spencer pulled a face. 'No need to get at us, love. We're on your side, really.'

'So, why am I worried?' she threw over her shoulder.

Outside, they sat on the wide steps of the police station and relished the feel of the icy wind cutting through their clothes.

'Cheer up,' Karen said, playfully digging Matthew in the ribs. 'We're out, now.'

'I know,' he replied, with a faint smile. 'But I was so depressed in there. I had visions of being locked away for life.'

She gazed at him fondly. 'Shelley, you've got to learn how to hide your feelings. Everything shows on your face, in your voice . . . Don't let the bastards know they're getting to you.'

'You're right, I know you are.' He gazed along the street, his thoughts tumbling over themselves. 'Karen, why do you think Andrew Dickens was tortured?'

She considered the question for a moment. 'Probably because

somebody wanted information that he either didn't have or wasn't willing to part with.'

'But what could he have known?' Matthew turned to her and frowned. 'You know, Karen, I'm beginning to think this whole business may be far more complex than we first thought. Andrew Dickens is the second person to have died . . .'

He suddenly got to his feet and wandered down the steps. Karen watched his retreating back while a warmth spread in her middle.

'I can't quite decide what I feel for you, Matthew Shelley,' she murmured to herself, 'but sometimes I feel like giving all this up just to protect you.' She struggled to her feet and, with one last look at the station building, she shouted, 'Hold on, Shelley, wait for me.'

When news of Andrew Dickens's demise was made public, Roland Parr reacted very badly. The fact that the man had been tortured made his flesh crawl. He could never withstand such an ordeal, he knew he couldn't. He was already preparing to leave Manfield House, but now his movements were injected with an almost manic urgency.

Parr threw open a suitcase and hurled into it as many belongings as it could carry. Then, he collected together his passport and bank books, and drove to the cottage by the sea. Nobody would find him there because nobody knew about it. The cottage belonged to his sister. She used it for holidays and therefore it was empty for most of the year. It was the perfect place in which a man could drop out of sight.

He was still worrying, still ruminating over recent events, when the familiar thatched roof and stone walls were illuminated in his car's headlights. What had Andrew told them in response to their torturous deeds? Had he confessed all, or did their secret die with him?

Matthew and Karen were heading for the bus stop. On the way a Silver Cloud Rolls Royce pulled up at the kerb beside them.

125

While they ogled the vehicle, a man in a grey chauffeur's uniform climbed from behind the wheel.

'Would you like to get in? Mr Charlton wishes to see you.' He opened the rear door.

'Wait a minute,' Karen said. 'How do we know you're from Mr Charlton?'

'Madam, if you'd care to look in the back of the car, you'll see that Mr Charlton is already in there.'

She peered into the plush interior, and the owner of the publishing house smiled back at her. They climbed in beside him, savouring the scent of luxury, the feel of soft leather cushioning their bodies.

'I had a team of top class lawyers standing by, in case you were charged,' Charlton told them, as the car glided effortlessly along.

'Thanks,' Karen said, 'but it was Shelley's earlier misdemeanours that got us dragged in there.'

'Is that how you see it, Mr Shelley?'

'No, I don't. Mackmin's involved in all this, somehow. I think the whole point of taking us in was to try and frighten us ... which is what everybody seems to be doing, lately.'

'I'd go along with that,' Charlton conceded. 'It seems to me that you're getting too close for comfort, as far as some people are concerned – or they think you are. And that's why I've decided to install you in one of my properties. It's a penthouse apartment, and the building is warden controlled. No one, apart from residents, gets in or out. So, while you're there, you'll be safe. Out on the street . . . well, I can't guarantee it.'

'We'll cope,' was Karen's spirited reply. 'Mr Charlton, have you any idea why Andrew Dickens was tortured before he died?'

'He obviously had something they wanted. I've given it a lot of thought, and the only thing I've come up with is that Dickens, as Glen's agent, was the person most likely to have his manuscripts.'

'You mean he would have had Watkinson's unpublished novels?' Karen queried.

'That's right. The publishers wouldn't see a new book until they were ready to buy it. Now, just suppose that Andrew Dickens became greedy and wanted more than his ten per cent fee before he handed over any new work. He may have seen it as good business sense, negotiating a bigger share for himself. Perhaps he thought that by vanishing for a while he could up the price even more. Unfortunately, he underestimated the people he was dealing with, and by the time he realised, it was too late.'

'And now, with Dickens dead, nobody knows where the manuscripts are,' Matthew mused. 'I bet there's a lot of people panicking, right now.'

The old man rocked with mirth. 'Oh, yes, Mr Shelley, you could say that. The whole of my publishing house is in a state of disarray.'

Matthew gave Charlton a sideways glance. 'But, doesn't that worry you?'

'Not a bit. If Giles Abbot can't produce the next Watkinson novel, then he'll have to explain why, and that's a situation I would truly relish.'

Karen had been listening intently, and allowing the smooth motion of the vehicle to focus her mind. 'If the publishers paid to have Watkinson killed,' she said, 'and are now paying the Organisation to find the missing books, wouldn't you know? I mean, it is your money.'

'Miss Chandler, I've had accountants going through the books for weeks, and they haven't found the slightest irregularity. No, I don't believe my people are paying the Organisation – to my mind, it's the other way around. I believe the Mob were creaming money from Glen, and then they decided they wanted the lot. So, it was bye-bye, Mr Watkinson.'

'But how would they get the lot?' Karen persisted. 'He must have left his money to somebody.'

'There are plenty of dishonest lawyers and accountants working for these gangsters, and they would easily find ways to flout the law. These people know all the tricks.'

But Karen was still not convinced. 'The police would know, surely? Isn't it a fact that when a wealthy person is found murdered, one of the first things they check is the name or names of those inheriting the victim's money?'

'Police officers can be dishonest.' Charlton shot her a challenging look. 'Is the picture beginning to fit together?'

20

Roland Parr made himself a corned beef sandwich. Too nervous to stay still for long, he went through the motions of eating while roaming around the cottage. He had very little appetite and the food seemed to stick in his throat, but he needed to keep up his strength in case of emergency.

When the snack was finished, he made his way back to the kitchen and deposited the plate in the sink. For a few moments he stood beneath the low beamed ceiling and stared out of the window at a grey, heaving sea that battered against the cliffs on which the cottage was built. Memories of happier, more carefree days came to mind, and they brought with them a sadness Parr found hard to shrug off. But he must not dwell on the past – that was gone. And if he wanted a future, he must always stay one step ahead.

He climbed the narrow stairs and unpacked his suitcase in the main bedroom. When shirts and trousers, underwear and socks had been neatly laid out in the chest of drawers, he gazed down at the one item that was left in the suitcase – a bulky brown padded envelope.

'Where in God's name can I hide it?' he muttered to himself.

The cottage would be of little use if they were to find him – he was aware of that. He was aware also that his only chance of staying alive was to retain possession of the manuscript. And that he must do at all costs. But where could he hide it?

The penthouse flat took their breath away. Its lounge-diner was large and airy, with deep pile carpet and walls of pastel yellow. The furniture was ultra-modern and absolutely wonderful, or so Karen thought. Matthew, with his more reserved tastes, thought it was pretentious rubbish. The kitchen reminded Karen of an advertisement in an up-market glossy magazine and she walked around it, touching surfaces, with a silly wide grin on her face.

From every window they had an incredible view of the town; the dots of faraway street lamps and the expressway lights looked like one giant canvas of Christmas fairy lanterns.

'Will you take a look at the bathroom,' Karen called excitedly. 'We've got a sunken bath, and floor to ceiling tiles. I mean, it's . . . God, it's fantastic.'

Matthew appeared at her shoulder, and gave a low whistle. 'This is what I call a flat.'

She turned to him, grinning. 'There're two bedrooms, Shelley, so your honour can remain intact.'

He flinched. 'And what's that supposed to mean?' But before she could respond he had turned smartly and walked away.

'Damn, damn, damn,' Karen muttered. 'Why can't I keep my bloody mouth shut?' She followed him into the lounge. 'Sorry, partner, it was a joke, that's all.'

'Forget it.' He gave her an apologetic look. 'I reckon my thin skin's disintegrated after three days with Mackmin taking the piss.'

'So, what do we do next?' she asked, steering them on to a safer course. 'I think we can now safely assume they were Watkinson's remains in that crushed car.'

'I don't accept it.' Matthew was resolute, and seemed ready to expand on that statement, but then changed his mind. 'Maybe we're looking in the wrong place, Karen. I feel if we could find out why Billy Mason confessed to a crime he didn't commit, everything else would fall into place.'

'And how do we do that?'

'Search me.' He wandered across to the window. 'This case has really got to me, you know, and I won't be able to rest until I get to the bottom of it.'

'Well, partner, whatever you decide to do, you can count on me.'

Karen was reluctant to leave the flat, next morning, for two reasons. Firstly, she was very much enjoying the surroundings; they were a definite improvement on Matthew's digs. And secondly, she was to see Judith Ward at *Profile*, and was apprehensive about the reception she would receive. After all, Judith now knew that they had followed her about – spied on her, in fact. The woman's attitude was frosty, at best, so how would she react to that betrayal of trust? Another thing, Karen very much doubted whether she could kowtow to the woman for very much longer. An explosion was due, and she guessed it would come sooner rather than later.

After she had gone, Matthew moped about and kept his caffeine level topped up with endless cups of tea. He was finding the elegant surroundings rather unsettling, and yearned instead for the organised chaos of his bedsit. He took another swig of tea and attempted to put his thoughts into some sort of order.

'Billy Mason,' he said, aloud. 'I just wish you could talk to me. I'm trying to clear your name, here, and I could do with a bit of help. What, or who, were you protecting? It wasn't your wife, that's for sure. She's almost as tough as you obviously were.' Once again, he filled the china cup, missing his mug with Superman on it. 'Another woman, perhaps? A mistress? Someone they could get at you through?' He lounged against the cabinet, sipping the stewed tea. 'Now, where would I start looking?'

Brilliant sunshine fell on the raging sea, and at the window of the cottage Roland Parr was pondering that his position, as well as the view, seemed much brighter that morning. Not a soul knew where he was and he found the thought refreshing, exhilarating, even. In a few days' time, he could be out of the country and negotiating the worth of the manuscript from a far warmer climate.

Directly after breakfast, Parr drove to the nearby village to stock up with groceries. And although he managed a smile as he steered the car along the narrow lanes, a worrying thought kept nagging at his mind.

He had to get rid of the manuscript. He was a fool to have kept it with him. If those pages got into the wrong hands, he would have nothing left to bargain with. A safe deposit box? A left luggage locker? They were possibilities, certainly. And maybe he should lower his asking price from six million to three. If he did, they might see it as a let-off.

But whatever he decided upon he must not panic, as he had

done at Manfield House. Decisions made in haste were invariably disastrous. All he had to do was keep a clear head and everything would work out fine.

Roland Parr eased his car along the deserted village high street, and was humming a tune as he parked in front of the village store.

Matthew decided to start at the pub where Billy Mason had supposedly met Glen Watkinson on the night of the murder.

He found the Queen's Arms in the older part of Handwell. It was a proper man's pub; no plush seating or atmospheric lighting could be found within those venerable walls.

The bar was empty of customers. The landlord, with shaven head and barrel chest, was swilling glasses behind the counter. An amiable smile softened his grim features when Matthew approached.

'And what can I get for you, sir?'

'A pint of lager, please.'

The landlord dried his hands on a towel and Matthew watched, fascinated, as his massive biceps flexed with the movement.

'You look like you've been in a war,' the man said, touching his own nose.

Matthew shrugged it off with a laugh. 'It looks a lot better than it did a couple of days ago.'

'Walk into a wall, did you?'

'I had a slight tie-in with the Organisation.'

The landlord's eyebrows rose, and he viewed Matthew quizzically. 'Here, I know you, don't I?' He threw aside the towel and pulled a pint. 'You're Matthew Shelley. I saw your picture in the local rag.'

'That's right.'

'Nice to meet you. I'm Ron.' He set the pint glass on the counter and held out a hand that looked like a side of ham.

'Pleased to meet you,' Matthew said.

Ron grasped his hand in a vice-like grip and shook it warmly. 'That pint's on the house. You know, you and your girlfriend are quite the local heroes.'

Matthew quickly reclaimed his fingers and tried to massage some sensation back into them. 'How's that?' he asked in the deepest voice he could muster.

'Being taken in for questioning by Mackmin's heavy mob, and leading the "Billy Mason Was Innocent" campaign, for starters.'

'Cheers for this.' Matthew put the pint to his lips and took a long drink. Placing it back on the counter, he said, 'Did you know Billy well?'

'Like this we was,' Ron said, clasping his hands together. 'Proper gent was Billy – an honourable man. Not like today's villains – a load of wrong uns, they are, if you ask me.' He caught Matthew's puzzled frown. 'I know that don't make much sense, but what I mean is, Billy had ethics, a code of living, call it what you will. You might not have agreed with it, but you could respect the man. You wouldn't have found him snatching old ladies' handbags, and God help anybody who did when he was about.'

'Do you think he murdered Glen Watkinson?'

Ron gave a snort. 'Billy wouldn't have been seen dead killing some poncey author.' He considered his words and then grinned. 'There I go again – I do come out with 'em, don't I? But, no, that wasn't Billy's style.'

Matthew took a long pull at the lager and glanced around the bar. 'Does the Organisation bother you much?'

'No, not now. They don't go in for protection nowadays, they're more subtle than that. It's all undercover stuff. Of course, some of their gooks push the little people about, the traders, the pimps . . .' He pulled himself up to his full height. 'But they don't give me no bother.' He pointed a finger. 'Which one did that to your nose?'

Matthew leant nearer to the man. 'Two guys named James and Nick.'

'Them two are real nutters,' Ron said, pursing his lips. 'And you're still on the case after a set-to with that pair?'

Matthew winked. 'How can I put this so it doesn't sound like bragging . . . ? I'll just say that neither of those guys is clamouring for a rematch – do you get my drift?'

Ron's eyes widened. 'If you saw that pair off I'd better buy you another pint. Drink up.'

Matthew sensed that now would be an inappropriate time to explain about his weak bladder, so he swallowed what was left of the lager. Stifling a burp, he passed across the glass.

'Of course, it's that bastard Mackmin I have to watch,' Ron confided. 'He ain't what he seems, that one.'

'Oh? Why do you have to watch him?'

'My licence, see. The police, they could really put the mockers on that, if they wanted to.' He placed the fresh pint on the bar and Matthew stared at it with dread.

'Does Mackmin bother you much?'

'No,' Ron said, with a swift shake of the head. 'I keep my nose clean in that quarter. But he thinks he can get away with murder, that one. Him and his two detectives have leant on quite a few people to keep quiet about the Watkinson case.'

'Me, for one,' Matthew replied, ruefully, as he tackled the second pint. 'Ron, would you know whether Billy had any girlfriends?'

'Oh yes, Billy had plenty of women, but he never let his love life get in the way of his marriage. He took his vows very seriously, did Billy.'

Matthew frowned; he was finding the man's way of putting things sometimes hard to fathom. 'Do you mean he never got deeply involved with anybody other than his wife?'

Ron grinned. 'Only between the sheets. Women worshipped him, of course, but I doubt if he knew the names of most of the birds he went with.'

'So, nobody could have put any pressure on him in that direction?'

Ron looked blank. 'How do you mean, pressure?'

'You know, do this or we'll injure your girlfriend, that sort of thing.'

'What? No way,' Ron exclaimed. 'They haven't invented the man that could've forced Billy to do anything he didn't want to.'

'But that's exactly what they did do. He confessed to the murder, didn't he? If he was innocent – as we both know he was – why would he do that?'

Ron scratched his shaven scalp. 'I can see what you're getting at – I never thought about it like that before. Well, this is a turn-up for the books.'

Matthew dropped his voice to a conspiratorial whisper. 'We spoke to a man who knew Billy in prison, and when he asked about the murder, Billy said they'd found his weak spot.'

'His weak spot?' Ron was flummoxed. There was nothing weak about the Billy Mason he knew.

Matthew pressed on. 'I want you to think back, Ron, and think hard because this is very important. Was there anybody or anything in Billy's life that someone could have used to make him act against his own wishes?'

Ron's fleshy features puckered thoughtfully as he cast his mind back. While he waited, Matthew had another go at his pint. If he could just finish half of it, he could perhaps leave the rest.

'Things are starting to slot into place,' said a triumphant Ron. 'Billy was a strange mixture, see, a right hard geezer, but at the same time he had a real soft spot for the underdog. I remember one night – must have been about four years back – there was a lad used to come in who was a bit thick. Well, the regulars kept getting on to him – all good-natured stuff, it was, nothing nasty . . . But this particular night we had a crowd of right yobs in, and they made a beeline for this lad. They were giving him hell, pinching his drinks and fags, snatching his wallet and throwing it about while the poor sod tried to get it back. Anyway, Billy just walked over to them, grabbed the wallet and gave it back to the lad. Then he took his own wallet out – the look on his face could have stopped a clock, I ain't joking – and he asked the yobs if they'd like to try it with him.' He laughed. 'Billy didn't get any takers, I can tell you that much – '

'Ron,' Matthew quickly interjected. 'I can't quite see the relevance of all this.'

'Hold on, I'm getting there, I had to explain about Billy first. He didn't have no kids from his marriage, see – probably because he couldn't stand them – but he had a lad by one of his other women, and the kid wasn't all there.' Ron lifted one of his huge hands and made a circle at his temple.

'Mentally retarded?' Matthew asked.

'That's probably what they call it now, but around here in them days they were called thickos.' Ron gave a shrug. 'His Mum was a right slag, she didn't want nothing to do with him,

134

so Billy had him put in a private home. And all those years he paid to keep him there.'

'How old is the boy, now?'

'I reckon he must be about eighteen.'

'And did Billy see much of him?'

'Oh yeah, visited him every week, he did. That was the reason he came to Handwell every Wednesday. The lad's in that fancy place just outside town.'

A rush of excitement sent adrenalin coursing through Matthew's veins. Could this be the breakthrough he needed?

'Billy saw him every week, Ron? Are you sure?'

He gave a definite nod. 'Without fail. Mind you, at one point it didn't seem like a very good idea. Well, I mean, them retarded people come in for a lot of stick. But old Billy had a saying – if they spit in your face, spit right back in theirs. Trouble was, he drummed it into the lad, and by the time he was about sixteen he'd picked up a couple of cautions for assault. Nothing serious, but there was some that said Billy was a bad influence.'

'Bingo,' Matthew murmured into his glass.

'Drink up,' Ron urged. 'I like a man who can hold his beer.'

21

Matthew arrived back at the flat, highly excited, and desperate to use the lavatory.

'Shelley?' Karen's voice rang out from the hall.

'I'm in the loo,' he called back. 'Just give me a minute.'

She was pacing up and down when he finally opened the door. 'I'm going to kill Judith Ward,' she fumed. 'With extreme care, and infinite satisfaction.'

'Hello, Shelley, where have you been?' he muttered, pointedly.

'Do you know what she had the cheek to say to me?'

'No, but, Karen, I've got some great news – '

Her anger was in full sway, however; she wanted her say first, and so she ignored him. 'I'll tell you what she said . . . God, I'm so annoyed. She said she'll let me off for following her the other night because she doesn't think it was my fault. She says you're a bad influence on me. Can you believe that? *You're* a bad influence on *me*.' She stormed off into the lounge, and Matthew quickly followed.

'Karen, listen for a minute, I've found out that Billy Mason had a son. He's mentally retarded, and he's living in the Claremont Nursing Home, just outside town. Don't you see? He's the lever they used to get Mason to confess.'

Karen had taken up an indignant stance by the window. 'That woman thinks she can do just what she likes with me,' she told her reflection in the glass. 'I felt like saying, take your job, you patronising bitch, and stick it up your . . .' She stopped suddenly and turned around. 'Shelley, did you say Billy Mason had a mentally retarded son?'

'Yes, and that's how they – '

'But, that's it,' she said, snapping her fingers. 'They used the boy to get Billy to confess.'

Matthew let out a sharp breath. 'That's what I've been trying – '

'Now, all we've got to do is find out where he is.'

'But I've already told you, he's in a home on the outskirts of town.' He tutted. 'Oh, wait a minute, I've got to go to the loo again.'

'What's the matter with you? You've only just been.'

'I had to drink four pints of lager,' he explained crossly, 'and I can't hold it in.' He dashed into the bathroom. Karen waited by the door.

'Shelley, I bet they were threatening to hurt the boy if Billy didn't do exactly what he was told.'

'The thought had crossed my mind,' he said.

Chief Inspector Mackmin aimed a snarl at DS Spencer and stabbed out his cigarette in an already overflowing ashtray.

'That Shelley is getting a little too close for comfort. He's been sniffing around, and now he knows about Mason's kid.'

'I've heard, guv.' Spencer sat before the desk, his own cigarette clamped between his teeth. 'Not much we can do about it, though.'

'I want him taken out,' Mackmin growled. 'If we don't get rid of him, he'll balls up this whole thing.'

'Guv . . .' Spencer leant forward, his tone tentative. 'There's a limit to how far we can go with this. If people start asking questions – '

'I know, I know.' The chief inspector lit another cigarette and tossed the lighter on the desk. 'To think that a fucking idiot like Matthew Shelley – '

'He's not that much of an idiot,' Spencer cut in. 'He asked me if you were on the take. Believe me, guv, that guy seems to know instinctively when things aren't quite right.'

'If we could pull him in for something – anything – just get him out of the way.'

Spencer bent forward to knock ash off his cigarette. 'Not that simple, though, is it, guv? We can't start charging him with crimes he hasn't committed.'

'You're right, of course.' Mackmin sat back and blew smoke towards the ceiling. 'I don't suppose we can make it difficult for him to see Steven Mason . . .'

'I shouldn't think so,' Spencer said. 'Not unless we want perverting the course of justice levelled at us. And that would bring the whole deck of cards crashing down.'

Mackmin made a face. 'Wouldn't it just?'

An hour had passed, and although Matthew was pretty certain his bladder had settled down, he wasn't taking any chances.

'Maybe we'd better hang on for a while longer,' he suggested, eyeing the door to the bathroom.

Karen gave an exaggerated sigh. 'Shelley, you only had four pints, and you must have passed at least eight since then.'

'I've got a weak bladder.'

'Do you know, you've told me that every time you've headed for the loo.'

He made a grab for his jacket. 'Okay, then, if you're going to keep on complaining, we'll start off for the Claremont, now.'

'That's it,' she said, punching him lightly on the shoulder. 'Tough it out, big boy.'

He made for the door. 'I just hope there's some public toilets between here and the home.'

'Bushes,' Karen said, with a glint in her eye. 'That's the answer to your problem – plenty of bushes.'

A security guard stopped them at the gates.

'Good afternoon, sir . . . madam . . .' He politely touched the peak of his cap. 'Can I help you at all?'

Karen said, 'We're here to see Steven Mason. I did ring earlier. We have an appointment with Dr Masters.'

'Excuse me for a moment.' The guard reached inside his small wooden hut and produced a clipboard. 'Could I have your names, please?'

'Karen Chandler and Matthew Shelley.'

He quickly scanned the list. 'That seems to be in order. If you'd like to follow the path up to the main block . . .' He pointed along the wide tarmac drive. 'It's quite a way. Most visitors come by car.'

'We're trying to give them up,' Matthew replied, dolefully. 'Anyway, thanks for your help.'

Quite a way turned out to be an accurate description. The main block was well over a mile trek, and it took them twenty-five minutes to reach it. Eventually, they rounded the top of the drive and got their first clear view of the large sandstone building. Weak sunlight was reflecting from its countless windows, giving it the appearance of a huge mirror. In front of its main entrance, shuffling impatiently on the spot, was a short, squat man in a white coat. When they appeared he rushed towards them, his hand outstretched.

'Miss Chandler? Mr Shelley?' he asked, hopefully.

'That's right,' a breathless Karen replied.

'Good. I'm Dr Masters.' His handshake was firm but friendly. 'When the gatehouse informed me that you were here, I expected you in a few minutes.' He gave them an amiable smile. 'It's been a long wait.'

'We walked up,' Matthew told him.

'Ah, I see.' His smile slipped a little. 'Now look, before we go inside, I'd like to ask you a few questions. Firstly, why do you want to see Steven?'

'I'm a journalist,' Karen said, 'and I'm doing a series of articles about Steven's late father. Mr Shelley is helping me.'

'I see.' The doctor scratched his head in a pensive fashion. 'You'll know, then, that Steven's father died recently, and that he was in prison at the time.'

She nodded.

'Your coming here has created a bit of a problem for me,' Masters continued. 'Steven has clammed up where his father is concerned, simply refuses to talk about him. He's been like that ever since Mr Mason was charged with that awful murder. I've tried everything, but I can't get him to open up. I don't want you to upset him.'

'I can't see the problem,' Matthew said. 'We'll be going in from the angle that his father didn't commit the murder and we're trying to clear his name.'

The doctor was thoughtful again. 'I would like him to start talking, it's true. Before the murder charge Steven was such a happy-go-lucky boy.'

'Please let us see him,' Karen urged. 'Maybe we can get him to talk. I mean, we're not doctors or the police – maybe he'll feel more relaxed with us.'

Masters made an immediate decision. 'All right, come inside.' He led them to the front entrance. 'I take it you won't object to my sitting in on the interview?'

'Oh, I'd much rather you didn't, you might inhibit Steven,' Karen said. She gave the doctor a persuasive smile. 'But we'll be taping the whole interview, so perhaps you'd like a copy of it.'

'Very well.' He held open the door for them. 'But before you see him, I'd like to have a chat about Steven. If you'd care to come into my office . . .'

He ushered them swiftly along lengthy corridors, unbroken in their uniformity except for the occasional table on which stood vases of freshly cut flowers. He came to a halt by a door and gave a wan smile before opening it.

'My office,' he said. 'Please, do come in.'

One entire wall was lined with books, mostly medical journals and psychological studies. The only furniture was a desk and three chairs – one behind the desk, two in front – and a table which was home to a coffee machine. Masters took his seat and motioned for them to sit.

Karen considered the doctor carefully. He seemed very edgy, hyperactive; and he fiddled constantly with a pencil, holding it between the fingertips of both hands and revolving it repeatedly. Karen found the action almost hypnotic. She blinked rapidly and focused instead on the doctor's intelligent features.

'Has Steven been here all his life?' she asked, opening up her notepad.

'He's been in care for most of his life, certainly. He was an unwanted child, as you undoubtedly know.'

'But his father did visit him regularly?' Matthew said.

'Oh yes, every week, without fail. I was using the term "unwanted" in the sense that neither of his parents, because of the circumstances, was able to provide a home for him. But Billy Mason thought the world of the boy, and that love was returned.'

'I was told that Mason paid for Steven's care, here,' Matthew said. 'Is that right?'

Masters allowed the pencil to drop from his grip, and it joined the jumble of papers on his cluttered desk. 'I'm afraid I can't discuss financial arrangements,' he said, suddenly aloof. 'All I can say is that a trust fund was set up to provide for Steven's care.'

'Was the trust fund set up by Billy Mason?' Matthew persisted. 'We'd really appreciate the information, doctor, it's important to our case.'

Masters hesitated briefly, the pencil once again spinning within his agitated fingers. 'All right, if it's that important . . . off the record, you understand. Yes, the trust fund was set up years ago by Steven's late father.'

'What's Steven like?' Karen asked. 'I mean, how do we handle him?'

'Like an adult, is the answer to that. Steven is a bright boy, but he operates on feelings most of the time. If he takes to you, he'll co-operate fully. If not . . .' A broad smile transformed the doctor's puckered mouth. 'Well, let's just say he's not above throwing a tantrum from time to time.'

Matthew said, 'I understand he has a couple of cautions for violence.'

'True, but the offences were very minor.' He gave a heartfelt sigh. 'I'm afraid there are some out there who enjoy baiting the mentally challenged. Steven doesn't take kindly to such behaviour, although I must admit he shows far more control, nowadays.' The doctor rose from his seat and slipped the pencil into his breast pocket. 'Well, if that's all, I'll go and tell Steven you're here. But I must warn you, it'll be his choice whether he sees you or not. Please wait here.'

22

The large room was pleasant, airy, and below a window that looked out on to the extensive grounds was a single bed, its covers neatly tucked beneath the mattress. Steven Mason was sitting on that bed, his hands folded in his lap.

While Dr Masters made the introductions, Matthew glanced around. Never before had he seen such a tidy room; not a thing was out of place. Every surface was covered with possessions and souvenirs that were obviously special to the boy; and each had been given its own space, its own small piece of his world.

Steven was a Down's child, a possibility never considered by either Matthew or Karen. He was shorter than the average eighteen-year-old but was powerfully built, with broad shoulders and strong, healthy limbs. He viewed them, now, through bright suspicious eyes that were half-hidden by heavy lids. As soon as the doctor had left, Karen switched on her tiny tape recorder and positioned it on the window sill. She gave the boy a smile.

'You don't mind us recording the interview, I hope?'

'Nothing to me,' he replied, with a sullen movement of the shoulders. 'I won't be saying anything I don't want to.'

Matthew wandered across to a wall unit that was home to a collection of model cars. He counted twenty in all.

'I like these, Steven,' he said. 'I used to collect them myself, years ago.'

The boy made no reply, but he kept a close eye on the cars in case Matthew actually touched one.

'Steven, we'd like to talk to you about your father,' Karen said, pulling up a chair.

'Dad's dead, so there's nothing to talk about.'

The words were spoken softly with an endearing lisp, and all the while Steven's gaze rested on the tiny cars. Karen moved her chair up close to the bed and tried to make eye contact with the boy.

'We were hoping you'd tell us about him,' she murmured, quietly. 'We're trying to clear his name. Do you know what that means?'

Steven's hands became fists on his lap, and Karen made an involuntary backward movement in the chair. After a moment, she tried again.

'Steven, we're trying to help your dad. Would you like that?'

He leant towards her, and spat out an aggressive, 'No.'

'Oh, that's a pity,' she said, in that same soft tone. 'We were hoping you would.'

'No,' he said, again.

She shot a wary glance at Matthew, and then said, 'Did you ever meet any of your dad's friends, Steven?'

'Stop treating me like a baby,' he yelled, his fists now pummelling the bed.

'Then stop behaving like one,' Karen snapped back.

Suddenly the pummelling stopped, and Steven surprised them with a mischievous grin. 'My dad would've liked you. He liked anybody who bit back.'

Karen stared at him, open-mouthed. 'Hey, kid, are you putting me through some sort of test to decide whether you like me enough to talk to me?'

'Something like that.' His grin widened.

'You cheeky so-and-so,' she said, laughing. 'And are you going to talk? You won't have to answer any questions you don't like, and you can tell us to push off when you've had enough. Have we got a deal?'

Steven nodded vigorously, that grin still on his face. 'We've got a deal.'

'Great. Now, first of all, we need to know whether you met any of your dad's friends.'

'Yes, I met some.'

'And were any of them famous, you know, like writers, or something like that?'

'Oh, yes ... Roland,' he said, excitedly. 'He wasn't famous, but he wrote stories.'

'Roland Parr? You met Roland Parr, Steven?'

'Yes, Roland Parr. He wrote stories.'

Over by the toy cars Matthew was itching to question Steven. But the boy seemed to like Karen, and he thought it unwise to disturb the rapport that was swiftly building between them.

Keeping her tone impartial, Karen said, 'Did you ever meet a man called Glen Watkinson?'

And then their affinity was gone; in the space of a second, the good vibes were shattered. Steven turned his face to the wall, and said, 'I don't want to talk about him.'

Karen looked at Matthew, her expression asking for guidance. He motioned for her to go on.

'You've heard of Glen Watkinson, then, Steven? Did you ever meet him?'

'I said I don't want to talk about him.' His voice had risen to a wail, and he covered his head with his arms.

'All right, then, that's okay.' Karen gently turned him to face her. 'I said you won't have to answer questions you don't like, and I meant it.' She slowly pulled his arms to his sides. 'Still friends ... eh?'

Steven nodded and returned his hands to his lap. Karen sat down again and tried to recapture that fragile harmony they'd had.

'Tell me about your dad. What was he like?'

The boy's mood softened. 'He was great. He came to see me every week, and sometimes he'd take me out.'

'Did he ever bring you model cars?' She nodded towards the wall unit. 'For your collection?'

'Sometimes. And he used to give me money, lots of money.'

143

Karen cleared her throat. 'Now, Steven, I'm going to ask you some questions, and I want you to answer them like an adult. Okay?'

His wary eyes searched her face and Karen instantly regretted that latter remark, but she decided to push ahead.

'Have you ever been in trouble with the police?'

Of all the reactions she might have anticipated, the one before her was the least expected. Steven was bouncing about on the bed in an absolute fury, repeatedly crying, 'Wasn't my fault . . . wasn't my fault. It wasn't my fault . . .'

'Hey, hey, I'm sure it wasn't,' she soothed. 'Why don't you tell me about it?'

The boy eventually became still and stared into the middle distance, his normally bright eyes now dull.

'Everybody thinks if you look like me, you must be stupid,' he said, after a while. 'But I feel things, just like you do. I'm no different from you.'

'I know, I know . . .' Karen patted his arm, and when he made no move to push her away, she let her hand rest there. 'What happened, Steven? Did some people make fun of you?'

'Calling me a loony . . .' His hands became fists again. 'I didn't like it.'

'And you got mad?'

'Pushing me about . . . pushing me. Calling me a loony . . .'

'So you hit them?'

'Yes.' He flexed his powerful shoulders. 'Then they stopped laughing.'

Karen smiled. 'I'll let you into a secret, shall I? I get mad sometimes, and when I do I always lash out, just like you did.'

'And do the police get you?'

She shook her head. 'They haven't caught me, yet. Did your dad approve of what you did?'

Steven brought a hand to his mouth and let out a guilty giggle. 'I think he did. But he said I must never do anything like it again because I'd get into more trouble, and he didn't want that to happen.'

'You loved your dad, didn't you?'

'Yes.' He turned to her. 'Dad was the only person in the world who cared about me.'

Karen's gaze lingered long on the boy whose mother was a slut and whose carers were paid for their time. And she reflected that there was good in everyone, even a hardened criminal like Billy Mason. Suddenly the quest to quash his conviction seemed all the more important.

'Do you think he killed Glen Watkinson, Steven?'

But the shutters were well and truly down this time. He climbed from the bed, his expression hostile.

'Four o'clock, it's tea. They serve tea at four o'clock.'

'I'm sorry, but I've got to know,' she said, getting quickly to her feet. 'We don't believe he did it, you see, and we want to find out what really happened.'

'Tea's at four o'clock. They serve it at four.'

Karen made a grab for his arm, but he pushed her aside as if she weighed nothing.

'Talk to me, Steven, I'm trying to help.'

He was standing by his model cars, gently rocking with feet apart, his arms pulled in tightly at his sides. 'I don't want to talk about it. Go away, I don't want to remember. Don't make me remember . . . please.'

Dr Masters listened to the recording with a quiet intensity, moving only to scribble brief notes on a foolscap pad.

'You certainly got further than I did,' he said to Karen. 'But there's definitely something he's still trying to block out.'

'Yet you say I got further than you . . .'

'Definitely. When I tried he refused to say anything at all.' He stared down at the tape recorder. 'Your questioning obviously disturbed him, hence that slightly violent reaction.'

'I suppose he would remember . . . ? He couldn't have actually closed his mind to events, could he?'

'He remembers,' Masters assured her. 'What you were getting there was suppressed guilt.'

Karen retrieved her shoulder bag and stood up. 'I'd like to see him again, doctor, if that's all right with you. I think I might get through to him.'

'He certainly likes you, no doubt about it.' The doctor cast Matthew a fleeting glance. 'But I would suggest that you see him

145

alone next time, Miss Chandler. Oh, and bring some cigarettes – our Steven is a closet smoker.'

The walk back along the drive was downhill and therefore easier. During it, Karen put through a call on her mobile telephone to Jocelyn Charlton.

'A son?' he said. 'Now, that is interesting. And you think the boy was used as a lever against Mason?'

'Undoubtedly, but there's more to it than that. I think Steven witnessed something, and he's now trying to blot it out of his memory. Anyway, I'm going to have some more sessions with him, and I'm pretty sure they could lead to a revelation.'

Matthew gave her a sideways glance. There was a smugness about her now that he didn't like. And he liked even less his feelings of resentment that had surfaced in Steven's room and which were even now distorting his view of their professional relationship.

'There, Shelley,' Karen said, slipping the phone into her bag. 'I do believe I've pleased the man who's paying the wages.' She noticed the sullen line of his mouth. 'What's wrong with you?'

'I don't like what's happening here, that's all. *You* questioned Steven, *you've* pleased the man paying the wages ... I did most of the investigating, remember.'

'I never said you hadn't,' she answered, taken aback. 'What's brought all this on?'

He dug his hands deep into the pockets of his anorak, and shrugged. 'I don't know ... It's almost as if you don't need me any more.'

Karen slipped her arm through his and gave him a squeeze. 'Oh, come on, Shelley, I didn't mean it to sound like that. Steven relates to me for some reason – even Dr Masters saw that.' She squeezed his arm again. 'Tell you what, I'll treat you to a Chinese out of the money Charlton paid me.'

Matthew came to a sudden stop and jerked his arm from her grip. Rounding on her, he said, 'Charlton paid *us*, Karen. He paid *us*.'

'Absolutely correct,' she said, her anger spilling over. 'And we split the money in half, didn't we? You've got the money

Charlton paid you, and I've got the money Charlton paid me.' She marched on ahead. 'So, if you want that Chinese, to be paid for with *my* money, you'd better keep up. And stop being so bloody hypersensitive.'

23

The Temple Of The Rising Sun didn't quite live up to its name. The tables were too closely packed, making intimate conversation impossible; and the piped oriental music was repetitious and began to brain-wash after a time. But the food was cheap; and that was the main reason why Matthew and Karen chose to eat there.

'These beansprouts aren't very crisp,' Karen remarked, chasing the food around with her fork. 'And this spring chicken has a definite taste of autumn about it.'

Matthew was tucking in heartily. 'Mine's all right,' he said. 'You should have had the duck.'

She motioned to the waiter, a diminutive man whose tired white shirt had seen too many washes. He skirted between the tables, his broad smile aimed at Karen.

'My meal's overcooked,' she said loudly.

The waiter merely spread his hands and gave a helpless shrug.

'I can't eat it,' she said, slowly enunciating each syllable. 'The chicken is too dry.'

Again, he shrugged. 'No English ... very sorry.' He backed away from their table with a series of low bows.

'Well, bloody hell ... If they expect me to eat this crap, they can think again.'

Matthew eyed her plate. 'If you don't want it, I think I can make room.'

Karen continued to complain vehemently while Matthew cleaned both plates, and by the time he had finished she was ready for a confrontation. The waiter paled somewhat when he saw her edging towards him but, under orders to stay by the till, he was forced to stand his ground. Karen put her bill and the exact money on the counter. The waiter checked the money twice.

'That's all you're getting,' she told him. 'I'm not paying the service charge.'

A bitter argument ensued, during which it was obvious to all that the waiter had a firm grasp of the English language. The other diners, sitting like battery hens in their cramped rows, looked on with amusement at the impromptu floor show. And there was even a smattering of applause when Matthew finally managed to drag Karen towards the door. Out on the pavement, she took in a number of deep breaths.

'Sometimes, Shelley, I think people go out of their way to be awkward with me,' she said hotly.

He gave a diplomatic cough. 'I think I'd better get you to the bus station.' They started along the deserted high street. 'Do you know, Karen, before cars – I mean, before the majority of people owned cars – they went everywhere on public transport. Out to work, to the pictures in the evening . . .'

'Really?' She shot him an amused glance. 'That's totally fascinating, Shelley.'

'Oh, yes,' he said, warming to the subject. 'Fifty years ago, this road would have been packed with buses.'

'Gosh, that must have been some sight.'

Matthew caught the sarcasm in her tone. He grinned. 'I took a course at night school once on the art of conversation. They taught us how to pick a topical subject and talk about it until the person we were with responded. Then, hey presto, we'd got a conversation going.'

'And did it work?'

'I didn't see an immediate increase in my number of friends, I must admit.'

Karen laughed, and slipped her arm through his. 'You're mental, Shelley, you really are.'

Matthew enjoyed the feel of her body close to his; and he liked the casual way she held his arm. Karen might be too domineering at times, too eager to take control, but she was open and honest, and she made him feel comfortable. He felt they were becoming closer all the time, and it pleased him. She was good to have around.

At the bus terminal, a dreadful place with orange overhead lights and high walls that made words echo, they found an old drunk lying in a shelter, singing 'Land of Hope and Glory'. And there was a group of youngsters playing a noisy game of football with a soft drink can.

Matthew guided Karen to the number twenty-one bay. And there they stood, each with a wary eye on the drunk who had taken to marching about with an imaginary flag held aloft. Urgent footsteps sounded behind them, but they felt no need to turn around; it was no doubt someone late for a bus.

'Good evening, folks.' The voice was only inches away from Matthew's left ear. 'No need to wait, like the rest of the herd. We'll give you a lift.'

Matthew felt icy fingers walking along his spine. The voice was all too familiar. He spun around, flight already uppermost in his mind, but the evil grin that was ever present on James's face rooted him to the spot. Karen let fly a string of abuse, and her shoulder bag was about to follow suit when the thug took from his pocket a long, narrow flick knife. He held it before her, deliberately close, and released the blade. Karen found herself staring at its savage tip that had stopped just short of her face.

'Lady,' James rasped, 'I'd strongly advise you to keep your mouth shut, and do what you're told.'

The harsh orange lights reflected from the blade. Karen swallowed hard.

'That's better . . . much better. What you do now is, you walk out of the depot with me. All friends together – right? There's a car waiting.'

With his left hand tightly gripping Karen's arm and his right, plus the knife, in the small of Matthew's back, James led them ever closer to the street. All around them buses made slow, ungainly progress out of the bays, leaving the air heavy with diesel fumes.

Karen's high heels clickety-clicking on the tarmac roused the drunk from his reverie, and Matthew fervently prayed that the man would suddenly rise up and attack, or that the kids playing football would collide with them. Anything to cause a diversion, to give them a chance of escape. But they reached the car – a blue Nissan, Matthew noted – without incident. James nodded to Nick in the driver's seat, and the rear doors flew open.

'In you get,' he said. 'And I wouldn't do anything silly, if I was you . . .' He wielded the knife. 'You might get more than you bargained for.'

They were miles away from the well-lit town centre when the car slowed to a stop.

'Okay,' James said. 'I'm going to have to blindfold you. Look on it as waiting for a surprise.'

Matthew stiffened when a strip of soft black material was placed over his eyes, and total darkness replaced the shadowy side street. He could feel Karen's leg pushing against his; it was trembling. The air inside the car was heavy with the stink of stale tobacco, and as they pulled away Matthew heard the click of cigarette lighters. Deprived of sight, he found his mind focusing on the movement of the vehicle which, coupled with the smell of cigarettes, brought a terrible sickness to his stomach as the car travelled over surfaces that were rapidly becoming uneven.

After what could have been ten minutes or twenty, the car once again glided to a halt. A door was opened and cold air rushed in.

'Out,' James said, harshly.

Highly disoriented they stumbled from the car. There, beside it, they were subjected to a body search. Nick must have left the car, too, for Matthew could hear Karen's whimpered protests at the rough treatment, while his own clothing was pulled and probed by James. Their mobile phones were taken and tossed away, the sounds as they hit the ground disproportionately loud in the silence of the night.

'Walk.' James dug a fist into the middle of Matthew's back and almost sent him sprawling.

Soon they were moving forward into an icy wind that stung their cheeks and bit at their ears. Then, abruptly, it was gone and Matthew sensed buildings of some sort. He heard a key turn in a lock, the low creak of a door swinging open, Nick's menacing 'Move', as Karen lagged behind.

James pushed Matthew over the threshold, his elbow connecting painfully with the door jamb as he strove to keep on his feet. He was hustled to his left and then bundled up a stairwell. Karen, hindered by her high heels, was having trouble negotiating the steep flight, but Nick's barbed threats saw her safely to the top.

They stopped. Another door was opened, and Matthew was shoved from behind. He pitched forward and fell, hit a hard floor, the breath jarring in his middle. Karen landed close by. She swore and let out a short scream of terror.

'Night-night.' James's mocking voice bounced off the walls. 'See you in the morning.'

The door closed, and the key turned in its lock. Matthew dragged damp-smelling air deep into his lungs and pulled himself to a sitting position.

'Shelley?' The word was carried out on a quivering breath. 'Shelley, have you taken your blindfold off?'

'No . . . why?'

'Just do it. Just do it, now.'

He tried to pull it down over his nose but it was on too tight. Intense cold, and more than a little fear, brought a clumsiness to his fingers and he grappled with the knot for what seemed like minutes, but was probably only seconds. With the blindfold gone Matthew blinked rapidly, desperate now to focus on Karen. But the room was in total darkness. He could see no more without the blindfold than he could before it was off.

'What the . . . ?'

'Shelley, I can't see anything. Where are we?'

'Christ only knows.' He looked in the direction of her voice. 'Are you okay?'

'No.' She was perilously close to tears. 'Where I've landed, there's a hole in the floorboards, and my arm's gone straight through it.' She gave a wild sob. 'There's nothing underneath us, Shelley, I can feel the cold wind on my hand.'

'Right, just keep calm.' The firmness of his voice surprised him. 'Now, the floor over here is solid. So, just work your way over, Karen. Follow the sound of my voice.'

'I can't . . . I can't,' she babbled. 'I'm too frightened to move. I can't do it.'

'Do it – now,' he shouted. 'Just for once, do as I say.'

'But there could be other holes,' she screamed back. 'I can't move.'

'Okay, Karen, I know you're scared, but it'll be all right.' He kept his voice light and hoped she wouldn't catch the fear in it. 'Listen, work your way slowly towards me. Concentrate on my voice and head for it. Before each move, feel what's in front of you. Come on . . . come to me.'

Matthew heard the rustle of her skirt, the grating sound of her long fingernails on the bare boards. She was making headway, very slowly, but she was getting nearer.

'You're doing great, Karen. Keep coming, that's it, just keep coming.'

Soon she was so close, Matthew could feel her warm breath on the palm of his outstretched hand. He made a grab for her, and she lunged the last few feet. With a low-pitched groan she crumpled into his arms and clung to him, trembling violently.

'Where are we, Shelley?'

'I wish to God I knew. We're obviously in some sort of building. If there're windows, they must be well covered with something. But with the state of this floor we'd better not move about too much. We'll have to wait for daylight – we'll be able to see something, then.'

Karen was shivering and within his arms she felt frozen to the touch. Matthew tightened his hold.

'Are you cold?' he asked. 'Do you want my anorak?'

'I'm too scared to be cold.' She rested her head against his chest, and was instantly comforted by the strong, regular beat of his heart. 'Talk to me, partner, use those famous conversational skills.'

Matthew searched his mind, and eventually said, 'How are you on Yorkshire pudding?'

'Not very good,' she said, managing a smile. 'What's that got to do with anything?'

'Not a lot. It's just that once, when I was fostered out, I stayed with this couple, and the woman made the best Yorkshire puddings in the world. I'm not kidding, my mouth waters just thinking about them. She used to pour the batter mixture round the joint in the meat tin. And when it was cooked, the part touching the meat was a sort of purple colour and it had all the meat juices in it. It was all sloppy and tasted fantastic.' He peered down at her in the dark. 'Are you sure you don't know how to cook it?'

''Fraid so,' she replied in a tiny voice.

'That's a pity.' He gave her a reassuring hug. 'I've always said if I could find another woman who could make Yorkshire puddings like that, I'd marry her.'

'Oh, Shelley,' she suddenly sobbed. 'I'm so bloody frightened.'

So am I, he thought.

24

The night passed slowly. Darkness had a way of stretching time, of making it seem like the dawn would never come. It was in that unbearable state of limbo that Matthew held Karen for hour upon hour, his arms numb from lack of use. Outside, the weather had worsened, and a howling wind sent heavy rain lashing against the walls of their prison. It was a comforting sound, however; better that, than to have to endure darkness *and* silence.

Just as they were beginning to fear that the earth had spun from its axis, leaving them with perpetual night, dawn lightened the eastern sky and brought with it the distant hum of traffic that greeted each new day. Very little daylight found its way to where they sat, but they could at least make out the damage to the floor and the position of the doors. There were two, side by side.

They appeared to be in a bedroom of a dwelling house. The room was quite large and entirely empty. Extensive damp had forced the paper from its walls, and it now hung in decaying strips. The hole through which Karen had almost fallen was clearly visible, as were others around the room, gaping voids where the floor had been smashed. The reason for the total blackness of the previous night was now apparent: all of the three windows had been boarded up. Planks of wood criss-crossed the openings, the gaps between each letting in those precious shafts of light.

They got to their feet and stretched, their joints stiff from hours of inactivity. Now that she could see again, much of Karen's fear had gone. She took in their surroundings with a look of deep scorn and, skirting around the holes in the floor, made for the pair of doors on their right.

'Welcome to the Ritz,' she said, lightly.

'Be careful,' Matthew warned. 'Those two bastards could well be out there.'

Ignoring him, Karen pushed tentatively on the handles of the two doors. 'They're both locked, Shelley.' She stood back and considered them. 'If we could work out which one leads to the landing, maybe we could smash it down.'

'Karen, you're not listening,' Matthew said, sharply. 'Those two gorillas could be outside and anyway, if they're not, I'm not sure these floor boards would stand any strain. If we start throwing ourselves at doors, we could easily find ourselves on the ground floor.'

'What do you suggest, then?'

Matthew moved towards her, testing his weight before each step. At the doors, he peered through the keyholes. 'Can't see a thing. It must be as gloomy out there as it is in here. If only we knew which door we came through.'

'Hang on a minute, Shelley,' Karen said, almost cheerfully. 'When he pushed me, I ended up near that hole. Now, I know I went in a straight line, so it must be that one.' She pointed to the door on the left.

'Right.' Matthew knelt down in front of it. 'Have you got any wire, anything like that?'

'Oh, yes,' he heard her mutter, as she groped in her shoulder bag. 'I always carry a roll of wire around. There's no telling when it'll come in handy.'

'This isn't the time for sarcasm,' he threw over his shoulder. 'A hair grip will do.'

'I think I've got one, somewhere. Oh, yes.' She passed it across and crouched by his shoulder while he bent one end of the grip into a tiny 'O' shape. 'Have you ever done this before, Shelley?'

'No, but I saw somebody do it in a film.' He studied his

handiwork. 'I think it was Tom Cruise . . . or *was* it? Did you see that film about the fall of—'

'Shelley, will you shut up and bloody well get us out of here?'

Without thinking, Karen stamped an impatient foot. The rickety floorboards shook, and they heard large chunks of plaster fall from the ceiling below them. They exchanged a fearful glance, each aware that the pent-up tension twisting the pit of their stomach was being felt just as acutely by the other.

Matthew turned back to the keyhole. Striving to keep his hand steady he inserted the grip, turning and wriggling it around while Karen peered over his shoulder.

'Damn it,' he muttered, again and again, when it failed to connect with anything.

Another few moments went by and then he felt it slip over the pin that would have gone into the key, had he been using one. He had to summon up all of his restraint to stifle a triumphant whoop. But, in any case, the whoop would have died when he turned the grip; there was resistance for a second or two, but then it turned in his fingers and nothing happened. He grunted with frustration.

'I've found the pin,' he told her, 'but the grip won't hold long enough to turn it.'

'Hold on, Shelley, I bought some Superglue the other day to mend my shoe. Yes, here it is. If we cover the end of the grip with it, do you think it'll stick to the pin?'

'Worth a try,' he said, eagerly. 'Good thinking.'

When the glue was applied to the end of the grip, Matthew pushed it into the keyhole, holding his breath and praying that he would find the pin at the first attempt. Then he felt it slip in.

'Yes,' he intoned on a rush of breath. Only a second elapsed before the two surfaces were bonded solidly together. 'Pray, Karen.'

After the briefest hesitation, Matthew tried to turn it, but the grip dug into his fingertips and refused to budge.

'Let me try,' Karen said.

'Wait a minute.'

He took in a calming breath and turned the grip again. The exertion made the colour rise in his cheeks, and he was about to give up when it began to turn. Metal grated with the slight shift, and then it came to a standstill. He stepped up his effort, growling with the strain, and the pin finally clicked all the way back.

'I've done it.'

'Oh, well done,' Karen said, hugging his shoulders.

'Now, we'd better be careful—'

'Never mind all that, Shelley, let's just do it.'

'Okay, you sit that side of the door,' he said, pushing her towards it. 'I'll open up and take a peep outside.'

Karen squatted while Matthew did the same on his side. She watched as he reached for the handle. It made a protesting squeal when he pulled it down. Biting his lower lip, he eased the door open and stared through the narrow crack. A moment later he slammed it shut and sank back against the wall, sighing heavily.

'Well?' Karen asked.

He turned his disappointed gaze her way. 'It's the toilet.'

Roland Parr was enjoying his walk along the beach. In the pale half-light of dawn the grey sea reared up and advanced with a mighty roar, only to recede on a sibilant whisper. Seagulls circled overhead, squawking loudly and then diving into the heaving mass in search of breakfast. He surveyed the scene for many moments, enraptured by the raw energy conjured up by gale force winds and that inhospitable sea.

But Roland Parr's anxieties pulled him back to the present. He was behaving like a holiday-maker, standing there, enjoying his surroundings. Such nonsense had to stop at once. He must not let his guard slip for a single second. Far too much was at stake.

Silently berating himself, Parr continued his walk to the village. Soon the sand gave way to steps leading into the harbour, and the cobbles of a narrow street were beneath his brogue shoes. Only one in the line of shops was lit up. Tom Harris – Newsagents and General Store. He approached it at a leisurely pace and found that, despite his earlier caution, he was rather savouring the prospect of the morning paper and a full English breakfast.

The tiny bell above the shop door tinkled airily as he walked in. The shopkeeper glanced up.

'Well, good morning to you, Mr Parr.' His weathered face broke into a smile. 'The *Telegraph* is it?'

'Yes, thanks, Tom.' He took some coins from his pocket and handed them across. 'It's a very bracing wind out there, today. Goes right through you.'

'You wait till the winter,' Tom warned. 'There's them that don't want to leave their fires come January.'

'I can believe you,' Parr said, as he scanned the front page headlines.

'Oh, by the way,' Tom said, handing Parr his change, 'I had somebody in asking after you yesterday.'

Parr glanced up sharply. 'Who was that?'

'Didn't leave a name. City gent, he was, smart suit and all that. Said he was looking for you 'cause of a business matter and he wondered if you were staying at the cottage. I didn't tell him, of course, knowing you didn't want a soul to know you were here, wanting to get away from the rat-race, like you do. So I scratched my head, like, and said I couldn't remember the last time Mr Parr was down this way, must be all of five years, now.'

'Thanks, Tom, I'm grateful.'

Parr scurried from the shop, his heart pounding against his ribcage. On the beach he no longer felt in awe of the elements, in fact the sea was no more than a back drop. He was suddenly vulnerable, alone, like a naked runner in the sights of a gun with no place to hide. He should have known they would find him. With their network they could find anybody.

25

'It's the loo?' Karen ranted, throwing open the door. 'We've just spent fifteen minutes picking the lock of the bloody loo?'

'Your choice of door,' Matthew reminded her.

'I'm well aware of that, Shelley, but thanks for pointing it out.' She sank to her knees. 'So, now what do we do? The hairgrip's bonded to the pin in the lock and I haven't got another one.'

Matthew was forming an answer when a low rumbling began

beyond the boarded-up windows. It swiftly grew louder and was accompanied by a sort of whistling hiss. He stood transfixed, his mouth gaping open, while he looked towards Karen who was staring with wide-eyed horror in the direction of the noise. They had both identified the sounds, and nothing they could do would prevent the inevitable from happening.

Within the time it took to pull in a breath a mighty object had smashed into the wall. Part of the ceiling came crashing down, showering them with white dust. Karen screamed, and tucking her chin into her chest, she protected her head with her arms while the house shook and shuddered. Again, that horrendous boom assailed their ears, and their bodies were rigid as they waited for the impact. This time one of the boarded windows imploded, sending large splinters of wood and bricks hurtling across the space. Galvanised into action Matthew grabbed Karen's arm, but fear had stolen her reasoning.

'No, leave me,' she whimpered, fighting him off.

Matthew spun her round and shook her shoulders with a brutal urgency. 'Karen,' he yelled, 'if we don't get out of here right now, we're dead. Do you understand me? We're dead. Will you follow me?'

Her expression was blank, but she gave a brief nod and reached for his hand. Matthew found his desperation evaporating before the growing will to survive. Raising his foot he took deliberate aim and smashed his heel into the door, slightly above the lock. Again and again he did this until the hinges began to creak and groan and the door collapsed on to the landing.

'Follow me, Karen . . . quickly.'

He started for the stairs, pausing at the top just long enough to check that she was behind him. For a third time the house jarred and shook. Thick clouds of dust billowed out from the room they had just left, blinding them temporarily and making them cough and choke. Beneath their feet the staircase shifted continually, throwing them from side to side, their bodies smashing against the walls.

They stumbled and slid to the bottom and Matthew immediately reached for the outer door, relief washing over him when it opened. He staggered from the ruins of the house, pulling Karen behind him. His vision was impaired because of the dust, but he could just make out hard yellow hats above startled faces. In front of the house stood a huge red crane with a metal ball suspended from a chain which was even now tearing into the upper floor. Then, and only then, did his bladder threaten to overflow.

All thoughts of crispy bacon and fried eggs had been pushed from Parr's mind. His throat was too dry to contemplate food. He tried to wash away that dryness with cup after cup of instant coffee, but at the same time added to it by chain-smoking. He had been in the cottage for about an hour. Glancing at the bolted front door with the chair wedged beneath its handle he attempted to take stock of the situation. With a fresh cigarette between his teeth Parr approached the door and took away the chair.

They wouldn't come for him yet; that wasn't how they worked. They would leave him to fret for a while but would let him know, in a dozen different ways, that they were about. They would want this over without further bloodshed – he was certain of that – and definitely without anything that remotely smacked of murder. No longer were they thick-headed megalo-maniacs who thought they were above the law. The 1960s had taught them that much. In those days they'd had the local police in their back pockets. But they had gone too far, behaved too outrageously, caused a public outcry that had led to an investi-gation by other, more impartial officers from neighbouring forces.

Parr reasoned that they would want to make him sweat – and, by God, he was sweating already – then simply walk in and take the manuscript without the slightest fuss. But he had no intention of letting them. There was money due to him, and he intended to collect it.

Andrew Dickens had acted like the naïve fool that he was, making his demands without first taking measures to ensure his own safety. Parr was determined not to make the same mistake. An insurance policy meticulously planned, that was what he needed. To out-fight them was beyond his capabilities, but to out-think them was not.

Matthew had vague recollections of standing outside the half-demolished house on the Heath Estate. He could remember feeling very proud of his bravery. He'd shown real bottle – one of the men had said so. But then the metal ball had smashed into what was left of the house, cutting through the weakened structure as easily as a knife through butter, and thoughts of what might have been quickly filtered into his feeble consciousness. His head had started to spin, round and round like a top, all sounds fading into the distance. And then he was falling . . .

Matthew opened his eyes to find a blaze of light above him. He was debating whether to follow it into the next world when he realised it was a fluorescent light strip on the ceiling.

'Where am I?' he murmured, trying to sit up.

Cool hands restrained him. 'Don't you try to move, now. You're in hospital, safe and sound. We think you must have fainted and hit your head on the pavement.'

Fainted? That hardly fitted in with the image of a hero. Pushing aside the hands, Matthew brought himself up to a sitting position.

'I don't think I did faint. I took a lot of knocks on the head, you know – bricks, plaster . . . I reckon they must have knocked me out.'

'You're probably right,' the doctor said, with a hint of a smile. 'But the good news is, there's nothing broken.'

'Karen . . . where is she?' he asked urgently, pulling back the sheets.

'She's fine, so you just stay where you are. As a matter of fact, the police are talking to her at this very moment.'

'The police?' Matthew almost fainted a second time. 'Is it Mackmin?'

'The chief inspector, yes.'

Mackmin was being deliberately tough on Karen. He had pulled up a chair beside the bed while DS Spencer stood at the foot. DC

Cooper, his young features made blank by boredom, was leaning against the door. Karen briefly wondered why the three men were always together. Detectives usually worked in pairs, surely?

Mackmin yawned repeatedly while she told them all that had happened, and the moment she finished he let out a sarcastic laugh.

'James and Nick, you say?'

'That's their names,' she replied, her tone defensive. 'I should imagine they're well known in this dump you call a town.'

'James and Nick,' Mackmin said again. He turned to his detectives. 'Do either of you know them?'

Spencer grinned. 'Never heard of them, guv.' Cooper simply shook his head, his gloomy expression unwavering.

'There you go, we've never heard of James and Nick.' Mackmin turned back to Karen. 'Now, I want you to pay attention, Miss Chandler, because I'm going to tell you what happened. You and Shelley were looking for somewhere to spend the night because he'd been thrown out of his flat for not paying the rent. Seems you picked the wrong place to doss.'

'How dare you insinuate that I would *doss* anywhere,' Karen spluttered. 'I've told you what happened, and I'm sticking to my story because it happens to be the truth.'

Mackmin moved forward, his face close to hers. 'I've just told you what happened, and that's how your statement will read . . . word for word.'

'Go to hell, chief inspector.'

He gave her a warning look and headed for the door, motioning for Spencer to follow. DC Cooper stood aside and cringed when the door slammed shut.

'I said, go to hell,' Karen shouted after them.

Cooper approached the bed. 'Sorry about that,' he muttered, taking out his notebook.

'I'm not going to say that in my statement,' she stubbornly told him. 'I'm going to tell the truth.'

He settled into the chair left by Mackmin. 'I'm no happier about all this than you are,' he said, avoiding her eyes.

'Then do something about it,' she said, banging impotent fists on the bed covers.

161

'What we'd normally do,' Cooper said, ignoring the outburst, 'is drag this James and Nick in for questioning. They'd take an open piss at us for an hour, then their brief would spring them and we'd be left with the paperwork.'

'Are you telling me,' she said, with a quiet anger, 'that this is happening because you don't want to do the bloody paperwork?'

He shook his head rapidly. 'I'm saying that's what we should be doing, and I don't like what's happening here.'

Karen stared at the constable. 'You think there's something iffy about Mackmin, don't you?'

Cooper quickly averted his gaze. 'He oversteps the mark, sometimes.'

'I think it's more than that. You're uncomfortable about what he's asking you to do. So, why don't you report him?'

'It's not as easy as that,' he replied, running restless fingers through his hair.

Sensing she had him on the run, Karen pursued the point. 'You know Mackmin's not on the level, don't you, constable?'

Cooper crossed to the window, as if that very act would distance him from her questions. 'I don't know anything. I suspect a lot, but I don't have any proof.' He turned to her, his mouth a bitter line. 'Have you any idea what would happen if I did report this? There'd be an internal enquiry and they, the powers that be, would look into it, find nothing amiss, and I'd be finished in the police force.'

'But James and Nick ... they must be known to you. Why don't you pick them up for questioning?'

His laugh was hollow. 'The problem is, Miss Chandler, you don't have any surnames. Mackmin would cover his own arse, make a few enquiries at the bus station. But he'd come up with nothing and, well, end of story.'

'But we were very nearly killed,' Karen pouted, tears shining on her lashes. 'Doesn't anybody care about that?'

'I care, but my hands are tied at the moment.' Cooper moved to the edge of the bed. 'Shelley was tailor-made to be set up for this. He's always being pulled over by uniformed – and we all know the reason for that, don't we? He's always in debt, always

162

owing rent to his landlady, so it's quite logical he might have to doss one night in a derelict building.'

Karen chewed on her bottom lip as she considered his words. 'I'll have to make a false statement, then?'

'Shelley will. He's probably allowing Mackmin to choose the wording as we speak.'

The thought that this officer, himself too weak to do the right thing, was dismissing Matthew so easily suddenly made Karen angry.

'Shelley isn't as big a jerk as you lot think, you know.'

Cooper nodded his agreement. 'He's the one Mackmin's really worried about, to be honest. I've heard him talking to Spencer. They reckon Shelley'll go all the way with this unless he's stopped. I wouldn't put it past Mackmin to fit him up.'

'Fit him up?' Karen echoed, horrified.

'Give him a couple of years inside for something he didn't commit, just to get him out of the way.'

'He couldn't do that.' But while Karen picked at the hem of the sheet, she guessed that maybe he could.

Cooper shrugged. 'He can do just about anything he wants at the moment. Mackmin's an expert at covering his trail.'

'It's terrifying to think that you can't turn to the police when you're in trouble. Do you know, constable, this whole thing's making me feel like we're the criminals, Shelley and me.'

'I can understand that.' He shot a guarded look towards the door. 'But you *can* turn to the police. It's all a matter of which officer to approach.' He winked and took a card from his inside pocket. 'Ring this number and you'll get straight through to me at the nick.' He scribbled something on the back. 'And this is my home number.'

Karen took the card and studied it. 'How do I know I can trust you? Say you're only trying to gain my confidence, so I'll tell you what we're doing at the time we're doing it?'

Cooper snorted. 'I want to laugh at that, and I would if this wasn't such a serious matter.' He hesitated. 'Just think ... Mackmin's always one step ahead of you – don't ask me how, he just is – so the last thing he'd need is one of his own people spying on you.'

Karen gave him a resigned smile. 'Okay, you win, I'll let you have the statement.'

It was another two days before they were allowed to leave the hospital. On the second day Mackmin brought in their mobile telephones that had been discovered at the scene of the derelict house. Karen hotly declared that the presence of the phones went a little way to proving their story, but Mackmin simply paraded that snide grin of his and sauntered out of her room.

She was still furious about the encounter when they emerged from the hospital into weak sunshine. Matthew, true to form, was hobbling and wearing his usual pained expression.

'What now?' he said, struggling to keep abreast.

'I don't know, partner, but by the look of you I'd say a good rest would be in order.'

'Oh yes?' He forgot his limp for a moment and went striding off in front. 'You're trying to get rid of me again. I'm right, aren't I?'

'Of course I'm not.' She hesitated. 'It's just that . . . well, if you must know, I want another talk with Steven Mason.'

'Great, so you are trying to get rid of me. Well, thanks very much, Karen, I owe you one.'

It was difficult to march off in a huff when you could hardly walk, but Matthew tried his best. And while Karen stared at his retreating back she wondered whether he had enough money for the bus fare.

26

Karen sat with her back to the wall, considering Steven Mason. Every so often he would raise his distrustful gaze and then quickly glance away. The cigarette packet was between them on the table.

'Why don't you have another one?' she gently coaxed. 'Go on, I bought them for you.'

Steven's fleshy fingers snaked across the table and curled around the packet. 'We're not supposed to smoke in here,' he said, extracting a cigarette.

'I won't tell on you, I promise.'

She flicked the lighter and held it out. Steven lit the cigarette and settled back in his chair, smoke trailing from his mouth and nostrils.

'Tell me about your dad,' Karen urged.

He lifted his shoulders. It was an impatient gesture. 'I told you last time, there's nothing more to tell.'

'I think there is, Steven. I think you're hiding something.' He remained silent. 'What are you hiding? Please tell me.'

'Things . . .' He drew on the cigarette.

'What things?'

'Things I don't want to remember.' He flicked ash on the floor and worked it into the carpet with the toe of his shoe. 'It's easy to hide things when you're like me. Everybody thinks you're stupid, and after a time they leave you alone.'

'But you're not stupid, are you, Steven? You're a very clever young man.'

He ackowledged that sentiment with a wide grin, and said in a hushed tone, 'I had to promise my dad I'd never tell anybody.'

Karen leant forward, her face on a level with his. 'Why didn't he want you to say anything?'

'He said . . .'

Karen waited. 'He said what?'

'Dad said he knew a lot about certain people, and if he did what they said then they wouldn't get to him.' Steven suddenly giggled, but his eyes remained sad. 'He used to say if he couldn't dance on their graves, he'd at least be there to welcome them in hell.' His giggle became a laugh and he took a drag of the cigarette in order to stifle it.

'And that amused you?' Karen asked, frowning.

Steven hung his head. 'I always laugh when I'm frightened. It's just the way I am.'

'You're not frightened now, I hope, You needn't be frightened of me.'

'I'm all right now, but I was scared when Dad said it. He

wasn't shouting, he was really quiet, but I knew he was angry because I could hear it in his voice.'

Karen looked towards the display of model cars. 'Did any other men come to visit you?'

Steven stubbed out the cigarette and used it to push the other butts around in the ash. He was deliberately ignoring her.

'Please answer me, Steven. You can trust me, you know you can. Did anybody else come here to visit you?'

'Don't know.'

She caught his wrist and forced him to look at her. 'You do know, Steven. Did any of your father's friends ever come to see you?'

Pulling away from her, Steven clamped his hands over his ears and chanted, 'Don't know, don't know, don't know . . .'

Karen sat back against the wall and watched him. After a while he took his hands away from his ears and slid them over his eyes. Then, moments later, he opened his fingers and peeped through them.

'I'm still here,' she said, with a heavy sigh. 'And that act's not fooling me one little bit.'

Suddenly his hands flopped on to the table, making Karen jump. His heavy-lidded eyes surveyed her with acute annoyance.

'It's something else I don't want to remember,' he said.

'Right, it's gloves off time.' She pointed a stern finger. 'Did you know your dad was ill?'

Steven's eyes brimmed. 'He told me he was dying.'

'Did you ever meet a man called Glen Watkinson?'

He blinked at the speed of the question and a tear escaped down his cheek.

'Yes,' he murmured, grudgingly. 'Dad used to take me to the big house where Glen lived.'

'And did you like the man?'

Steven shook his head so violently that he almost toppled from his seat. 'No . . . no, I didn't, I hated him. He used to say horrible things to me every time Dad was out of the room – and sometimes even when he was in the room.'

Karen's blood was pounding at her temples. She was so close to a breakthrough, she mustn't blow it, now.

'Steven . . .?' He turned away, his shoulders hunched. 'Steven,

166

look at me ... Do you think your Dad killed that man because of how he treated you?'

'No!' The word came out as a wail, and Steven's hands were once again at his ears to block out the sound of her voice. He turned to her, his eyes bright with terror. 'I *know* Dad didn't kill Glen.'

Karen could feel her own heartbeat, could hear her shallow intake of breath that came with nervousness. She hesitated.

'Steven, did you kill Glen Watkinson?'

He seemed to flinch, and then he pushed the cigarette packet to the edge of the table so that it fell into her lap.

'I don't want to talk to you any more,' he said quietly. 'I want you to go. I want you to go now.'

The tape of the interview had come to an end minutes ago but Dr Masters still stared at the tape recorder, lost in his own thoughts.

'You should have gone into mental health care,' he told Karen grimly. 'You certainly have a flair for handling Steven.'

She said, earnestly, 'You do see what I'm getting at ...?'

'With great clarity.' He let out a long breath. 'I suppose you'll want another session with him?'

'If you'll allow it, doctor. I feel I'm so near to the truth now, I can't stop.'

Masters raised an enquiring eyebrow. 'Even if it means hurting Steven?'

Karen considered her answer carefully. 'Doctor – oh, this is so dificult ... Surely it's not a matter of what we personally might want to conceal. If certain things come to light, you have a duty –'

'You don't have to remind me of my duty,' he muttered harshly. 'That's the only reason I'm allowing you to see Steven again. But I must warn you, I shall be advising him to say as little as possible.'

'Pity the tape recorder isn't on,' she said, with a humourless smile. 'Come on, doctor, you know as well as I do that Steven's got something weighing on his mind. Until we find out what it is, until he's able to exorcise the ghost, he's never going to be the way he was. Whatever it is, it'll fester and distort his mind, not to mention his personality.'

Masters sighed. 'I know you're right, but I do so hope you're wrong with regard to what Steven's actually done. I would dearly love to see you come a cropper on that score.'

'I think we know where we stand.' She rose to her feet. 'I'll be back in two days' time.'

The doctor glanced up at her. Was that contempt she saw on his face?

'Maybe this will give offence,' he said, heavily, 'but I won't be looking forward to your visit.'

Karen couldn't wait to share her news with Matthew, but she got back to the flat to find he was still nursing his grudge. He sat at the kitchen table, cantankerous and tight-lipped. Karen pretended not to notice and filled him in on the details of the interview while she made coffee.

'You're playing with fire,' was his gruff reply. 'You're setting that poor sod up so you can get a good story.'

'Balls, Shelley, it's as plain as the nose on your face.'

'What is?' he goaded. 'Steven killed Watkinson because he didn't like him? And his father, knowing he only had so long to live, confessed to the crime to protect his son?'

'Yes. And if that is what happened, how the hell am I setting him up?'

Karen turned back to the coffee mugs. She was furious, and hurt, too. How dare he accuse her of using Steven? She would no more do that than she would take short cuts to get her story. Her theory was the right one, only he was too cross at being sidelined to admit it. Matthew wandered over to the units and watched as she angrily stirred the coffee.

'It's too simple,' he said.

She cast him a scathing glance and took the mugs across to the table. 'Too bad, that's how it's shaping up. Just because you don't like it, doesn't mean it's wrong.'

He leant against the worktop and studied her seething back. 'What about the literary agent who was tortured before he threw himself out of that window? Did Steven do that, as well?'

Suddenly, Karen rounded on him. 'What exactly do you want from me, Shelley?'

'I'll tell you,' he shouted. 'For once in your life I'd like you to stop and think, instead of just assuming you're always right.'

'I resent that. I think it's getting up your nose, the fact that I cracked the case before you did.'

He let that remark go; it didn't justify a response. They fell silent, Karen at the table, Matthew at the units, the space between them heavy with recrimination.

'Charlton phoned while you were out,' he said, returning to his chair. 'He said we can stay here for as long as we want. And he's still interested in the end result of our investigation, but in the meantime he doesn't want us to contact him. Seems he's received threats from the Organisation, they've told him to mind his own business and they advise us to do the same.'

Karen stared thoughtfully into her coffee mug. 'I wonder how they found out he'd hired us?'

Matthew gave a shrug. 'How do they find anything out? Charlton's worried about how easily mobile phones can be tapped into.' He headed for the door.

'Shelley, where are you going? You haven't touched your coffee.'

'It's okay, I don't want it,' he threw over his shoulder. 'I think I'll pop into the office and pick up the latest batch of bills. Who knows? Somebody might even have sent some money.'

Karen hurried out of the kitchen and found him in the hall, pulling on his anorak. 'But, Shelley, we've still got some of the money Charlton paid to us.'

He gave her the briefest of glances, his expression stony. 'You can keep the lot, Karen. After all, you're the one doing all the work.' He slammed the door as he left.

27

Sometimes, when a safe hiding place was needed, the one in front of your very nose was the least obvious. With that thought in mind, Roland Parr searched his pockets and belongings for the business card Matthew had given to him that day at Manfield House. He eventually found it, but gave a loud groan when he saw that the telephone number had been blanked out with a thick black felt-tipped pen.

Parr sat on the window seat in the bedroom at the cottage and let out a weary breath. Directory Enquiries was his only hope, now. He hurried down to the living-room, where the telephone was housed, and dialled the number.

'Directory Enquiries. Which town, please?'

'Handwell,' Parr said, his fingers crossed.

'Right, sir, and what name is it?'

'Shelley. Matthew Shelley.'

Seconds later an electronic voice gave the number. Parr quickly jotted it down. He dropped the receiver back in its cradle and sat looking at the piece of paper.

'You're the only hope I've got, Mr Shelley,' he said aloud. 'That book's worth three million pounds to me, and I think you might just be the one to keep it safe until I can collect it. After all, you're the last person they'd expect to have it.'

He stretched across to the window and peered over the deserted cliff top. They were out there somewhere, watching, waiting, certain that he would crack. Parr was aware that they had visited the village several times, making discreet enquiries of his whereabouts.

They knew where he was, all right; those questions softly murmured into a shopkeeper's ear were designed to frighten him into making a mistake. But he wouldn't. He'd show them what they were up against.

Time, now, was of the essence. Parr glanced at his watch and picked up the telephone receiver to dial Matthew's number. He listened to the ringing tone, counted the number of rings. Nine, ten ... When the number reached twenty and there was still no answer, Parr flung down the receiver and tried to keep steady his jittery nerves.

Matthew had been gone for a couple of hours, and Karen was still silently fuming about his attitude. Over recent weeks, she had come to believe that Matthew was someone with whom she could have a good working relationship. But he was as bad as the rest, over-critical and jealous when she did her job well. Why couldn't he see that she was right? The puzzle was almost solved as far as she was concerned. There were just a few loose ends left to be tied up.

The urgent buzz of the telephone cut through the quiet and startled Karen out of her reflective mood. However, she was fully composed by the time she lifted the receiver.

'Hello?'

She half expected the menacing tone of James, or the shrill voice of Judith Ward. Instead, a man said, 'Karen?' in a hushed, guarded manner.

'Yes. Who is this?'

'It's Alec ... DC Cooper.' There was a slight pause. 'Look, I haven't got long ... Could you meet me at the Moorscroft Coffee Shop in, say, half an hour?'

'Yes, okay.'

There were voices in the background, and Karen was about to ask Cooper where he was phoning from when the line went dead.

Matthew collected the stack of mail from behind his office door and sank heavily into his chair to start opening it. Minutes later he had one cheque for two hundred pounds – the balance from a divorce case – plus last notices before court from the water authority and the council tax office. And it would seem that he was in danger of losing his typewriter, according to the brusque

171

letter from the office equipment and stationery shop. Matthew glanced at his faithful Olivetti and made a face. He'd forgotten all about that agreement.

Screwing up all of it except the cheque, he aimed the bundle at the wastepaper basket, missing by a good yard. Then, he settled back in his chair, hands behind his head.

'Well, Matthew, how's life treating you?' he asked himself. 'Not so springfield, my old son, not so springfield,' he replied, with a large dose of irony.

The Moorcroft Coffee Shop was a good choice of venue. It was hidden away in a side street, well off the beaten track. Most of its trade came at lunchtime when ready-made sandwiches were sold to the staff of a nearby DSS office.

Alec Cooper was already there when Karen arrived. He was sitting at a table at the rear of the shop, and he looked very nervous. Cooper pointed to the two cups on the table in front of him to let her know he'd bought the coffee. Karen picked her way between the empty tables, while tinny piped music played in the background.

Cooper stood up when she reached the table. 'Thanks for coming, Karen.' He glanced towards the door. 'I'm taking a bit of a chance, actually.'

Karen pulled out a chair and made herself comfortable, dropping her shoulder bag beside her feet while Cooper sat down again.

'It sounded urgent on the phone,' she said.

'It is. What's Shelley doing?'

'He's gone to the office. Why?'

'It's just that Mackmin's been ranting and raving about him. There's been a development . . .' He lowered his voice. 'Glen Watkinson's former secretary's gone missing.'

'What, Roland Parr? Are you looking for him?'

He shook his head and took a sip of coffee.

'But, why not?'

'Because he left Manfield House when it was sold. It's a legitimate reason, so we've got no call to go out looking for him. He's a free agent, after all.' He gave a hollow laugh. 'When he turns up dead, we'll go and collect the body.'

Karen frowned. 'Do you think that's likely? That he'll turn up dead, I mean?'

'It's on the cards, in my opinion.' Cooper picked up his spoon and stirred his coffee, deliberately avoiding her eyes. 'What are you and Shelley doing at the moment?'

Karen was very tempted to tell him about Steven Mason, but she held back, unwilling to trust him fully.

'We're not doing much, to tell you the truth. Judith Ward's promised me a series of articles along the lines of "Billy Mason was guilty – Okay", and I need the money, so . . .'

But Cooper shook his head. 'I've an idea things have gone too far for that, what with Andrew Dickens turning up dead on that pavement . . . Now Parr's gone missing, and if anything happens to him, those asking the questions will be asking even more.'

Karen studied his face. 'So you're saying the truth will out.'

'Something like that.' He looked around the empty shop. 'Anyway, I'd better be off. I just wanted to make sure you were all right.'

Karen so wanted to trust him, to feel she had someone there to back up her theories. But again she held back.

'Oh, don't worry about me, DC Cooper,' she said, with a smile. 'I'm not so springfield.'

He gave her a puzzled look. 'You're not so what?'

She laughed. 'It doesn't matter. I'm doing all right . . . really. There's just somebody I can't get off my mind.'

With fingers that trembled slightly, Roland Parr reached for the telephone receiver. He had promised himself he would wait for a full five minutes before trying Matthew's number again. Only three and a half had passed, but his nerves were fast getting the better of him. His stomach turned as he tapped out the last digit.

'Answer it this time, Mr Shelley . . . please.'

'That somebody being Matthew Shelley – yes?' Cooper said.

Karen nodded.

The constable returned to his seat and fixed her with an inquisitive stare. 'Is there anything you're not telling me, Karen?'

'Maybe. But you must understand how hard it is for me to trust you. Mackmin's your superior officer – how do I know that anything I say won't be taken straight back to him?'

'You can't know, and there's nothing I can do about it. I can only tell you I'm not a bent copper.' He looked her straight in the eye. 'Karen, you've got to believe that my only interest in all this is to see that justice is done, for want of a better phrase.' He hesitated, as if expecting her to open up. When she didn't, he rose briskly to his feet. 'I won't bother you again, Karen, but if you need me, just get in touch.'

She reached out and touched his arm. 'Look, Alec, I'm sorry if I've offended you . . .'

'You haven't,' he said, with a bleak smile. 'But I'd better warn you – if you are up to something, Mackmin's going to come down on Shelley like a ton of bricks.'

Karen chewed worriedly on her lower lip. 'I've been interviewing Steven Mason,' she blurted.

Cooper whistled softly and sat down. 'I think you're on the right track, but Mackmin's not going to like it.'

'Does that matter?'

'Does Shelley go along with the direction you're taking?' Cooper asked, ignoring her question.

She shook her head, and sighed heavily. 'He thinks it's too simple a solution.'

'Get rid of him,' Cooper urged, 'before Mackmin fits him up with something.'

Karen's jaw dropped. 'But I can't just ditch him, Alec, we've been through a lot together.'

'Do it. Unless you want to visit him once a month in one of Her Majesty's prisons.'

'But why Shelley?' Karen asked, close to tears. 'Why doesn't Mackmin come after me?'

'Come on, Karen, you know the answer to that. Shelley's easily frightened, and you're not. Besides, what could Mackmin fit you up for? You're a journalist – he'd never get away with it. Whereas, Shelley, with the best will in the world, is nothing but a tosser.'

'No, he's not,' Karen responded, heatedly. 'And you yourself said he's the one Mackmin's worried about.'

Cooper shrugged. 'He may well be, that's the reason I want him off the case. And, if nobody's paying him, that's exactly what's going to happen.' Cooper grasped her hand and gave it a gentle squeeze. 'I'm sorry if I've upset you, Karen. I have Shelley's best interests at heart, I really do, and I don't want to see the guy get hurt if it can be avoided.'

Matthew had locked the office door and was half-way down the stairs when his office telephone started ringing. Tutting loudly, he fumbled in his pockets for the key.

'Oh, what the hell,' he muttered. 'It's probably somebody ringing to demand money.' He carried on down the stairs.

28

Karen pressed the start button on the tape recorder and cast a surreptitious glance towards Steven. He was sitting on his bed, back straight, hands on his lap. She noted his sullen attitude, his uncooperative expression, and wondered what Dr Masters had said to him in the two days since her last visit.

She cleared her throat. 'How have you been, Steven?'

'Don't know.' He turned away from her and gave the opposite wall the full force of his petulant glare. 'Don't care, either.'

'You don't care how you are?' she said, trying a laugh.

Steven shook his head; the gesture was clumsy and leaden. 'I don't care about you,' he said, still focused on the wall. 'Dr Masters says you're a nosy cow.'

Karen had to smile at his frankness. 'And what do you think?'

'Don't know. Don't care, either.' He pulled his feet up on to the bed and propped his chin on his knees. 'Dad said if this ever happened, I was to keep my mouth shut so they wouldn't be able to do anything to me.'

'That's what your dad said, eh? I see.' She wandered over to his model cars and did a quick count. 'How many cars have you got, Steven?'

'Twenty-one.'

'Have you always had twenty-one?'

The boy looked at Karen for quite a while, saying nothing, his brain working fast behind that broad, heavy forehead. Finally, he said, 'My dad came to see me just before he told the police he'd killed Glen. He said he was doing it for me.'

Over by the cars, Karen's pulse was racing but she tried to stay matter-of-fact. 'He did it to protect you?'

'Suppose so,' he said, hugging his knees tightly. 'He told me to forget all about him. He said I'd always be looked after, and I'd got the rest of my life to think about.'

'But you haven't forgotten him, Steven. How could you? You loved your dad.' She let out a long breath. 'But you're not getting on with your life, either, are you? You're worried about something, and it's stopping you from going on. Why don't you tell me what's bothering you?'

'Nothing's bothering me,' he said, angrily. 'Nothing's bothering me.' He studied his watch.

'Steven, did you – '

'It's twelve o'clock, time for my walk.' He jumped from the bed.

'You can do that later,' Karen said, barring his way. 'Did you – '

'I said, it's time for my walk.'

Karen bristled at his sharp tone, at his hands bunched into fists at his sides. She was taller than Steven, but there was no doubt that she would easily be overpowered by his strength should a struggle ensue. She stood her ground, nevertheless.

'Please tell me what's bothering you, Steven.'

'It's time for my walk.' His voice had taken on an edge of panic, and his fists were flexing rapidly.

'Tell me,' she said, sharply.

He began to shudder, and his face paled. 'I want to go,' he wailed.

But still she stood in his path. 'Talk to me, and then we'll both go for a walk.'

Steven glanced around wildly, then ran to the wall unit and swept his model cars aside with an anguished cry. He watched them clatter around the room before slowly turning to Karen, his face contorted with pain.

'It was my fault my dad went to prison,' he screamed, advancing on her.

She shrank back, fearing an attack. But Steven simply ran past and flung open the door. While she listened to her own rapid breathing, Karen heard his rubber-soled shoes slap-slapping along the corridor.

Dr Masters knew his duty. As soon as he heard the contents of the tape he telephoned the police, and from that moment on his main concern was for the treatment and welfare of his patient.

When Chief Inspector Mackmin arrived with DS Spencer, they listened with long faces to the contents of the tapes.

'We'll have to take him in for questioning,' Mackmin said, when the third interview had finished.

'He must have someone there while you question him,' Masters insisted.

'His rights will be observed. A social worker will be present at all times to make sure they are.' Mackmin sounded peeved and Karen wondered why.

'He must have meal breaks, tea breaks, plenty of rest – '

'I've told you, doctor, his rights will be observed to the letter,' Mackmin snapped. 'Now, let's go and collect him.' He glared at Karen as they left the room.

Roland Parr tried Matthew's number continually, but to no avail. His bags were packed and loaded in the car, airline ticket booked, but he still had the manuscript and no idea where to hide it.

He knew he would have to take a chance. If he could get to Spain and contact them from there, they would talk. A few million pounds would seem like chicken feed for that little work of art. And even they wouldn't dare to pursue him on to foreign soil. No, from there he could talk deal with them, and they would have to listen. But if they caught him with the manuscript before he boarded the plane, then . . . Parr mentally drew a finger across his throat.

There was nothing else for it, he would have to take a chance on Matthew Shelley. He would send the manuscript to his office with a covering letter explaining that he needed to hire the investigator's services. He would instruct Shelley to lodge the manuscript in a safe deposit box and then wait for further instructions. A cheque for one thousand pounds as a down payment would doubtless ensure that the man would comply with his request.

There was an element of risk, of course, but it was a chance he would have to take. There was one rather large problem, though. How on earth could he get to the post office if he was all the time being watched?

After two hours of questioning Steven Mason finally broke down and confessed to the murder of Glen Watkinson. DC Cooper called Karen at Charlton's flat with the news.

She held on to the telephone flex as if it were a lifeline. She had expected to be pleased, having played such a major role in the affair, but all she felt was a cold numbness.

'Karen, are you still there?'

'Yes, sorry, Alec. I knew he'd own up, but it's still come as a bit of a shock.' She brushed her hair off her forehead, suddenly hot. 'Is Steven okay? Did Mackmin treat him all right?'

'He's fine. There was a social worker with him all the time, a Mrs Waite. She made sure Mackmin didn't overstep the mark, believe me.'

'So, why, Alec, why did Steven do it?'

'Apparently Watkinson used to taunt him, nothing nasty, he just used to joke with the kid. But it got under Steven's skin because he didn't do it to anybody else. Then, one day, he just cracked, kept hitting Watkinson. He's a strong lad, it wouldn't have taken many right hands to finish the guy off.'

'Poor Steven . . .'

Cooper huffed. 'He made Mackmin work for it, I can tell you. The guv'nor kept at him for hours – as much as he dared with the social worker there, anyway – but the kid wouldn't give an inch.'

'So Mackmin wore him down . . .'

'No, he promised him a cup of tea.' Cooper laughed. 'Steven kept on about wanting some tea, and Mackmin said he could have some as soon as he'd finished telling the story. After that the floodgates opened and you couldn't stop him talking.'

Karen let out a heartfelt sigh. 'Billy Mason did confess to shield Steven, then.'

'That's about it. They got the body in the boot of Mason's car and took it to the scrap yard after dark. Mason thought they were in the clear after that, but then Steven realised he'd lost one of his model cars he'd had with him on the night. By that time word started spreading that Watkinson was missing. Mason probably panicked and thought it best to give himself up – he knew he hadn't got long to live – so we wouldn't be looking for anybody else.'

'How's Mackmin taking all this?' Karen asked.

'Remarkably well, I'd say – outwardly, at least. Forensic have confirmed that the thumbprint on the model car found at the crime scene belongs to Steven, so he's been charged.'

'I wonder why Mason didn't go back to look for the car,' Karen thought aloud.

'Perhaps he did,' Cooper said. 'Perhaps he was disturbed before he could find it. Who knows?'

Karen's thoughts were racing. 'There's something not quite right about all this, Alec. Mackmin's always been so sure that Billy Mason was the murderer. I just never put him down as the type of man who'd capitulate so easily.'

'He'd got no choice, really, he had to charge Steven. Although I did hear him saying to Spencer that things weren't going as planned.'

'So, what do we do, now?'

'We wait,' Cooper said. 'Sooner or later, somebody from the Organisation will show their hand, and then we'll know what they're really after.'

'And Mackmin,' Karen said, hurriedly. 'How are we going to get him?'

'Listen,' Cooper whispered down the phone, 'if you ask me,

this is to do with Watkinson's work. There're probably some unpublished manuscripts that the Mob can't find. Now, Mackmin's going to have to come up with them, otherwise he won't get paid.'

Karen frowned. 'I don't understand any of this, Alec.'

'Trust me, Karen, please. It's so important that you do.'

She was about to reply when Matthew's key could be heard in the lock. Bringing the call to a hasty conclusion, she replaced the receiver as he hung up his coat.

'Who was that?' he asked.

Karen turned to find him standing in the doorway. 'What do you mean, who was that? I don't have to give an account of everybody I speak to. We're not married, you know.'

'For God's sake, Karen, what is it with you? Every time I open my mouth you jump down my throat.'

Karen knew she would have to break with him. It was for his own sake; for hers, too, in a way – she couldn't bear the thought of Mackmin getting his hands on him. So, if that was the way it had to be, then now was as good a time as any. Burying her feelings deep, she turned on him.

'Ever wondered why I keep jumping down your throat, Shelley? Eh? It's because you don't give me any space, you keep hemming me in.' She tried to ignore his crestfallen expression. 'By the way, Steve Mason's been charged with Watkinson's murder. He's made a statement admitting it.'

'Wow,' Matthew said, waving his arms expansively. 'I bet you're feeling very proud of yourself. Just think of the exclusive story you'll have, now. Can't you just see the headlines? I tracked down the real killer.'

'Oh, carry on,' she said, sneering. 'You're only jealous. I've been proved right and I've stolen your glory.'

She expected him to be riled and lose his temper, but something close to disgust darkened Matthew's face as he turned to go.

'For Christ's sake, Shelley,' she cried. 'Just for once in your life, get mad and fight.'

He remained with his back towards her, his shoulders slightly hunched. 'I don't want to fight with you, Karen. What's the point?'

'I think it's time we parted company, Shelley.' She pretended to search for something in her shoulder bag so that she wouldn't have to look at him. 'I'm going to be really busy from now on and, well, I simply don't need your services any more.'

He shrugged. 'Fine. I'll send you my bill for the work I've already done.'

Karen felt salty tears sting the back of her eyes. 'You'll drop the investigation, then?'

'Well, nobody's paying me, so it'd be pretty pointless carrying on. And, anyway, there's no more investigating to do, is there? You've already solved the case.' He spun round and cast her an irksome glance. 'I'll pack my gear and move back into my own place.'

It was Karen's turn to show her back. She moved away, sad in the knowledge that she would have to offend him, make him hate her, so that he would focus on that rather than on the case.

'It's far from over, and you know it,' she said, in a scathing tone. 'But, to be honest, I never really thought you'd have the character, the plain old-fashioned guts, to go up against these people.'

But Matthew refused to be goaded. He moved rapidly towards the telephone and lifted the receiver. Karen wore a puzzled frown while he punched out a number of digits. He listened for a moment and then held the receiver out at arm's length.

'1471,' he said. 'Do you want to know the last number to phone here?' He slammed down the receiver with considerable force. 'It was the police station. You have the gall to talk to me about guts, when you've already joined the opposition?'

'But it's not like that – '

'Isn't it?' he shouted back. 'Even if I gave you the benefit of the doubt, I'd say you've picked the easiest option.'

Matthew went into the bedroom, slamming all the doors after him. When he reappeared, five minutes later, he was clutching two carrier bags – all that was needed to haul his meagre belongings.

'It's been nice knowing you,' he said, with a sneer. 'Perhaps you'd like to tell your new friends I'll be making an application to see Steven.'

181

'But you can't,' she said, trying to hide her alarm. 'Mackmin would eat you alive if you did.'

'Huh, I'm not frightened of Mackmin.' He pointed a finger. 'You don't know me, Karen. You don't know anything about me.'

She refused to meet his eyes. Instead, she zipped up her shoulder bag and dropped it by the side of the settee. 'Why do you want to see Steven, anyway?'

'I want to offer him my apologies. After all, if it hadn't been for all my digging about, you wouldn't have found him.'

He disappeared into the hall, and when the front door slammed Karen cursed herself for the bungled way she had handled him.

But at least Matthew was off the case, now. Or was he? Her demeaning words could well have had the reverse effect, could have made him all the more determined to find those missing answers.

29

Matthew's office telephone remained unmanned for yet another day, and Roland Parr was forced to make a quick decision. He had to make his flight, no matter what. But there was still the little problem of the manuscript. An idea was forming in his mind, but he would have to wait until dark. Best not to take chances at this late stage.

No sooner had the last traces of light disappeared in the west than Parr was pulling on his thick quilted coat. He picked up the brown padded parcel containing the manuscript, his letter in an envelope attached to its front, and tucked it inside the coat before zipping it up. He studied his image in the full-length mirror in the hall and, satisfied that the bulky package did not show, let himself out of the cottage.

The thought that they were out there, watching him, brought a chill to his spine. In recent days they had chosen to show themselves – only briefly, from a distance, but those sightings always had the desired result. Parr would hasten away, his errands forgotten, and arrive back at the cottage, shuddering with fear. He knew who they were – that madman, James, and his partner, Nick.

Digging his hands well into the pockets of his coat in order to keep the package secure, Parr slowly negotiated the steep steps in the cliff that led down to the beach. The roll of the waves was gentle on the ear as he trudged along, damp sand pulling at his shoes at every step. Gazing up at the sky, he mouthed a prayer of thanks for the banks of black cloud that so skilfully obscured the moon, making it no more than a bright patch beyond the swirling mass.

All of a sudden Parr froze. He could hear something: a soft padding sound close behind him. He turned and peered desperately into the darkness, searching the dunes but seeing nothing. The noise came again and his stomach turned, panic rose in his throat.

Clutching the parcel to his chest, Parr began to run. Every few steps he glanced back, his lungs already heaving from the effort it took to run on wet clinging sand. Then the moon broke free of its black shroud and the beach was awash with a pearly radiance. Parr risked another backward look and almost stumbled, so shocked was he. For the moon had picked up a figure in the distance and cast its shadow long across the sand. Was it a man? And was that long object in his hand a shotgun?

Parr increased his speed, grimacing at each new intake of air that was so icy his throat ached in protest. But he had to go on, for that insidious sound was still behind him and getting louder. Once again the moon was trapped behind a veil of cloud and total blackness descended. Parr staggered along, losing direction in his haste, and he uttered a feverish cry when he stumbled into the water's edge, the weak waves lapping at his ankles.

Pad, pad, pad. The sound was closer, now.

His legs felt leaden and unreliable, as if they would let him down at any moment. Every step required a gargantuan effort that Parr's flaccid body was hard pressed to find. A sharp pain shot across his chest and he cried out, a whimpering cry of fear that barely reached his lips.

Pad, pad, pad. The noise was at his heels. He could hear strong rhythmic breathing.

Parr pitched forward and rolled on to his back. Sweat oozed from his every pore, but was dried instantly by the bitter night air. He was about to plead for his life when an alsatian dog dropped a long stick at his feet. The dog was trembling with excitement, saliva dripping from its mouth while it waited for Parr to enter into the game.

A man's voice sounded along the beach. 'Winston. Winston!'

The dog retrieved the stick, its tail wagging furiously, and went galloping off in the direction of its owner's impatient yell.

Parr was gasping for hreath. He tried to push himself up on to his elbows, but collapsed back into the sand. For many long minutes he lay there, oblivious to the hostile conditions, waiting for sufficient strength to seep back into his legs so that he might be able to stand.

With the parcel still safely in his grip beneath the quilted coat, Parr made a tentative effort to get to his feet. He staggered, took a few moments to get his bearings, and then set off in the direction of the village. He walked slowly, fearing another pain in his chest, brushing the sand off his clothes as best he could.

The quaintness of the village always evoked in Parr a sense of journeying back in time, but the illusion escaped him this particular night. He scurried along the main street, casting furtive glances all around, eager to reach the safety of Tom Harris's Newsagents and General Store.

Tom was in the process of closing the shop. The door had been bolted and his day's takings were before him on the counter, ready to be bagged and deposited in the bank's night safe. When Parr banged hard on the half-glass door, Tom shot him a puzzled glance and ambled across to open it. Parr tried the handle, but the door remained steadfastly shut.

'Hold on, Mr Parr, hold on,' Tom called, with much irritation. 'I haven't done the bottom bolt, yet.'

Parr waited, becoming more and more vulnerable with each passing second. But then the door was flung open and he was able to slip inside the shop. Tom instantly noted the man's frantic expression, viewed with alarm the hard-packed sand on his clothes, the water mark on his trousers that reached up to his shins. He said nothing, however, even when Parr edged towards the counter, his haunted gaze returning again and again to the darkness beyond the large window.

'Sorry about this, Tom,' he said, panting, 'but I'm here to beg a favour.'

'Anything I can do, Mr Parr, you know that,' Tom said, his curiosity aroused. 'But I was just bagging up my money ready for the bank.'

'I'll only keep you a minute, I promise.' Parr withdrew the parcel from the folds of his coat. 'Could you post this for me, first class, tomorrow?'

'But, Mr Parr,' Tom said, bemused, 'the post office is only two doors down – '

'I know, I know,' he blustered, 'but I don't want anyone to see me posting it.' He took out his wallet and removed two five pound notes. 'This should be ample for the postage, and please keep the change for your trouble.'

Tom's eyes twinkled as he relieved Parr of the money and then the package. 'Always glad to help,' he said. 'Now, I'll just put this over by the till, so as I don't forget. My memory ain't what it used to be, and that's a fact.'

Parr caught his arm. 'It's very important that the parcel gets posted, Tom, and I'd rather you kept it to yourself.'

'My lips are sealed,' Tom said. He put the ten pounds with the rest of his money and tossed the parcel on top of the ice cream freezer that was behind the counter, well out of reach of the local children.

'Thanks, Tom,' Parr said, backing towards the door. 'Thanks a lot.'

'My pleasure,' he replied, moving to lock up again. The bolts were thrown and he headed back to the till, scratching his head with bewilderment. 'Them townsfolk baffle me, they really do,' he murmured.

Matthew wasn't exactly trembling at the thought of facing Chief Inspector Mackmin, but by the same token he wasn't seeking a confrontation, either. So, when he turned up at the magistrates' court, next morning, he decided to keep well away from the man.

He was there for Steven Mason's first appearance. As in all such cases the hearing was short with Steven needing only to confirm his name and address. Matthew watched from the crowded public gallery and when Steven was brought in, flanked by two uniformed officers, he was deeply disturbed by the boy's distressed appearance.

Steven was remanded in custody for two weeks. When the magistrates rose from their seats Matthew dashed around to the court entrance and managed to catch his solicitor as he was leaving.

'Hi, I'm Matthew Shelley, a private investigator.' He handed over his card. 'You're Steven Mason's lawyer – Adrian Summers?'

The solicitor hardly glanced at the card before handing it back. 'Yes, what can I do for you?' he asked, sharply.

'I'd like to see Steven, if that's at all possible.'

Summers raised an eyebrow. 'Oh? For what reason?'

'I think I can help him.'

'God knows, he needs all the help he can get,' Summers said, casting his eyes to the heavens. 'With a signed confession and forensic evidence against him, it would take the intervention of the Almighty to get him off. And I take it you are not He?'

'Not quite,' Matthew said, with a rueful grin. 'Mr Summers, do you think Steven's guilty?'

The man gave a guarded smile. 'His guilt is irrelevant, really, unless it can be proven.'

'I *know* he's not guilty,' Matthew said, stabbing a thumb at his own chest. 'And how can it be irrelevant? You said yourself it'd take a miracle to get him off.'

'That's certainly true. At the moment, the best I could do is place a plea of diminished responsibility. But even if I pull that off, Steven would still spend the rest of his life in secure accommodation, so either way it seems to matter very little.'

'It matters to me,' Matthew huffed.

The solicitor studied him carefully. 'Why is this so important to you?'

'It's important because I believe Steven's innocent and I believe I can prove it.'

Summers let out a short laugh. 'I don't see how. Steven confessed, and the social worker who was with him throughout the interview said that no undue pressure was put on him to do so.' He spread his hands. 'Quite simply, Mr Shelley, I'm just trying to fix him up with the cosiest billet I can get.'

'You don't care, do you? Not really,' Matthew spat. 'Steven's just another legal aid payment to you, isn't he?'

'All right, keep your hair on,' Summers said. 'Actually, I'm on my way to meet Steven now. I'll ask him if he wants to see you.'

The shop had been open since five o'clock, the time when Tom Harris took delivery of the morning newspapers. So, by eight thirty he was more than ready for the mug of tea brought through to him by his wife, Hilda.

'By, girl,' he said, after his first sip, 'you know how to make a cuppa, and that's a fact. I reckon the spoon'd stand up in this.'

She chuckled. 'I should know how you like your tea by now.'

'Aye, and everything else,' he said, grinning, as she made her way back to their living quarters.

The bell above the door tinkled and Tom put down his mug with much reluctance while a group of schoolchildren traipsed in, their faces rosy with cold.

'Two choc ices, please, Mr Harris,' a little girl said.

'What, in this weather?' Tom asked, his hands on hips.

The girl giggled at his surprised expression. 'We put them in the fridge at school and eat them at lunchtime.'

'Fridges at school?' He shook his head. 'It was never like that in my day, young lady.'

The bell tinkled again. 'Your crisps, cigarettes and lemonade, Tom,' a delivery man shouted from the doorway.

'Right, Ben. How many boxes?' Tom asked, backing towards the freezer.

'About thirty. And I could use a hand, I'm a bit behind today.'

'Right you are, I'll be with you in a minute.'

As Tom lifted the lid of the freezer, his head still turned towards the delivery man, Roland Parr's package slid from it and disappeared down the back of the cabinet. It hit the floor with a dull thud, but the sound was covered by the excited chatter of the boisterous youngsters. The choc ices were found and handed across, and then Tom followed the children out to help Ben unload the lorry.

30

Steven agreed to see Matthew. Adrian Summers led him down to a tiny cell below the court.

'I can let you have five minutes, that's all,' he said.

Matthew nodded, and waited until the door was closed by the uniformed officer stationed outside.

'Do you remember me?' he said to Steven.

'Yes.'

The word was hardly audible, and Steven's face was a mask of misery as he stared at the cup of tea on the table in front of him. He pushed the cup to one side.

Matthew pulled up a chair and sat facing the boy. 'Don't you want your tea?'

Steven pointed to his wrist-watch. 'Tea's at eleven, it's not time, yet.' He turned his puffy eyes towards Matthew. 'Have you got any fags?'

'I have, as a matter of fact, I bought you some.'

He reached into his pocket and took out a pack of twenty. He watched while Steven pulled off the cellophane wrapping and tugged out a cigarette. Placing it between his lips, the boy waited while Matthew struck a match and held it out.

'Do you know what's happening to you, Steven?'

He nodded, inhaling deeply. 'They're going to lock me up, and I didn't do it.'

'Then why did you make a statement saying you did?'

'Tea's at eleven,' he said, taking another drag of the cigarette.

Matthew exhaled loudly. 'If I'm going to help you, Steven, you must talk sense. I know you're capable of it.'

'Tea's at eleven,' was the only reply forthcoming.

'Did you kill Glen Watkinson? I want the truth, now.'

'No,' he said, looking down at his hands. 'I've never killed anybody.'

'How did one of your model cars find its way to the murder scene?'

'Don't know,' he said, shrugging.

'Steven, listen to me. You're in very serious trouble. They're going to lock you up – have you any idea what that means? It won't be like the hospital you've been living in, nothing like it. You won't be able to go out for days in the town. You'll have people watching you all the time, and you'll never be free again. Doesn't that bother you?'

Again, the boy shrugged; an aimless, hopeless gesture. 'I don't have a choice.'

Matthew glanced up sharply. 'Why don't you have a choice?'

'Because nobody wants me.' He drew on the cigarette until its tip was a fiery red. 'I worked it all out. My dad loved me, I know he did, but he didn't want me, not enough to take me home. That's why I had to live in the hospital.' He made a face. 'It'll be the same wherever I'm sent. When you look like me, nobody wants you.'

Matthew got to his feet and leant against the door, hands in his trouser pockets, his watchful gaze on Steven's face. 'And none of that bothers you?'

'Why should it? That's the way it is – nobody cares what happens to me.' The statement was made without self-pity or anger; only a total acceptance of the situation showed in his voice.

'I care,' Matthew said, quietly.

Steven shot him an astonished look and let out a high-pitched laugh. Matthew made no response to that reaction as he regained his seat.

'I'm going to ask you some questions,' he said, 'and I want you to give me honest answers. Okay? Steven?'

The boy remained tight-lipped. He stubbed out the cigarette and flicked the cork tip across the room.

'Can I keep the fags?' was all he'd say.

189

'For God's sake,' Matthew said, thumping the table. 'Okay, listen. Don't just accept this, help me to find out what really happened.'

'Can I keep the fags?' he repeated.

'Yes, of course you can.' Matthew sighed. 'Did you kill Watkinson?'

'No, I've already told you.'

'Then how did one of your model cars turn up at the scene of crime with nobody else's fingerprints on it but yours?' The question was met with a blank stare. 'Think, Steven, it's so important, just think.'

The boy frowned as he thought hard, and Matthew dared to hope that he was at last getting through.

'I knew it had gone,' Steven said. 'But I didn't see who took it.'

'When did you first discover it had gone?'

'It was when Dad took me to Glen's house,' he began, slowly. 'There was another man there, he seemed to be in charge of everything. I took three cars with me, but when it was time to go back to the hospital I'd only got two.'

Matthew leant across the table. 'What was this other man like?'

'Dunno.'

'Think, Steven,' Matthew implored.

The boy started playing with the ashtray, pushing it away with one hand and stopping it with the other. Matthew feared that he had lost his attention and was about to offer a rebuke, when Steven said, 'He'd got grey hair, thick and combed back like this.' He pushed his fringe off his forehead. 'He was about as tall as you, and he'd got a suit on, even though he wasn't working.'

Matthew took a moment to picture the man. Then, he said, 'Do you know what happened to Glen Watkinson? Do you know who killed him?'

Steven shook his head, his attention span fast running out.

'Then, why did you tell the police that you did it?'

Steven clung to the table's edge and rocked it back and forth, back and forth, the ashtray and cigarette sliding first one way and then the other.

'Tea's at eleven o'clock. Tea's at eleven,' he chanted loudly.

Out in the corridor the duty constable bristled at the sudden outburst. He flung the door open and burst in. 'That's enough, Steven,' he cautioned. 'Calm yourself down, son.'

But Steven wasn't about to capitulate easily. He lifted the table for a few seconds more and then slumped in his chair.

'I think it's time you left, sir,' the constable said, beside the open door.

With one last despairing look at the boy, Matthew left the room. Outside he paused for thought. Steven's description of the man at Watkinson's house fitted Giles Abbot exactly. What had he said? The man seemed to be in charge of everything. Now, that was interesting.

Matthew spent the rest of the day tracking down the social worker who'd been present at Steven's interview, and then he went to see Dr Masters. It was six thirty when he sat down on a bench in the local park to eat two egg and cress sandwiches, his first meal of the day.

He now knew why Steven had confessed, and as he munched his way through the not-so-fresh bread Matthew wished that Karen was there with him. How he would relish the chance of telling her how wrong she was ... and that policeman boyfriend she now had in tow. How could she possibly fall for a vain, self-important clothes-prop like Cooper? He thought she'd have more sense. Still chewing, he dropped the sandwich packaging into a litter bin and made his way across the park while dusk descended rapidly.

Matthew didn't drink very much, but he needed one, now. He found the nearest off-licence and while waiting in the queue he realised he should give up the case. But then, there was nothing to give up, was there? He'd already been dropped. Nobody was paying him, and nobody would. His bills were swiftly mounting and would soon be replaced by summonses. He'd hardly got enough money to pay for the scotch and dry ginger he was clutching.

He *should* give up the case, but something was driving him on, something he didn't fully understand. He gave a mental shrug.

Perhaps he just wanted to get even with Karen for letting him down.

'Yes, love?'

The less than dulcet tones of the checkout girl broke through his thoughts. Matthew put the bottles on the counter and while the girl placed them in a bag he took the last ten pound note from his wallet.

Weather conditions drifting in from the Continent were producing a swirling mist and, not for the first time, Roland Parr offered up thanks to the heavens. His flight was booked, hotel reservations made; now all he had to do was get to Birmingham airport, and the restricted visibility would cover his departure perfectly.

Nervously pacing inside the cottage, he glanced first at his watch and then through the window. The mist was quickly becoming a fog; he would have to allow extra time for the journey. Whistling a tune Parr switched off the lounge lights and stepped out into the swirling vapour. It clung to him, formed an icy dew that instantly dampened his clothes and face as he carefully negotiated the route to his car.

In the driver's seat he turned the ignition key and flicked on the heater. The fog twisted and eddied beyond the windscreen like a crowd of tortured souls vying to get in.

'It should clear when I get inland,' he told himself, selecting first gear and edging gingerly out on to the road.

Less than a hundred yards away, a car was parked on the grass verge. James peered through the windscreen and picked up the faint red glow of Parr's tail lights.

'He's away,' he said, his voice cold and flat. 'Do we follow?'

A man leant forward in the back seat. 'Yes. If he's leaving he must have the manuscript with him.'

For a change Matthew entered his digs by the front door. He wasn't sure how much rent he owed Mrs Perkins, and he didn't really care. He was fed up with forever being on the defensive, walking a mile out of his way to avoid any sort of confrontation.

192

He'd had enough of it. Now they were all about to see the other side of the coin.

He let himself into his room, threw his anorak on to the bed, and got ready to pour himself a drink. His new image was dented straight away, however; he couldn't get the cap off the ginger ale bottle. He persevered, though, applied as much pressure as he could, and then came that satisfying fizz. The drink poured, Matthew switched on the hi-fi and selected an album. Soon Dusty Springfield was belting out 'Son of a Preacher Man'.

He sat at the table, sipping his drink, letting the music wash over him. By the time the first track had ended and Dusty was slipping into 'You Don't Have To Say You Love Me', Matthew was on his second measure. And when that was half finished, he could almost visualise Karen sitting on the settee.

'Oh yes, Karen,' he said to that image while Dusty worked her magic in the background, 'you may think you're very clever, but to my way of thinking, you're not. Nowhere near it.' He held up his glass to the empty settee. 'For once in your life just listen and you might find out how to conduct an investigation.' He inclined his head. 'Thank you. For a start off, one of the things that bothered me was how clear and concise Steven's confession was. You've met him, you know he's incapable of making anything like that up, so the conclusion has to be that's how it happened.' He leant forward and slowly shook his head. 'Wrong ... with a capital W. I talked to the social worker, and do you know what? She was adamant that Steven kept on denying everything at first, over and over again, wouldn't admit to a thing. Then, after a couple of hours, he started to get distressed, started pouring out the story.'

He waggled a finger at the settee, and then paused for effect while he topped up his glass. 'But when I questioned the woman further – perhaps led her a little, I have to admit – it seems the story Steven told was the one the police had been feeding into him, bit by bit, for the previous two hours. You know how it goes, Karen ... So, young man, you started hitting him and you couldn't stop – is that how it happened, Steven?'

The needle scratched around the inner groove of the record and Matthew tutted. He wandered across on unsteady legs and replaced it with one by Bob Dylan. Back in the chair he listened to 'Blowing In The Wind' for a few moments before turning back to the imaginary Karen.

'Then,' he said, trying to focus, 'when I talked to Dr Masters about Steven's confession, all became clear . . .'

Parr kept his fog lamps trained on the edge of the grass verge as his car crawled along the narrow winding lanes. As expected, the fog was thinning the further inland he drove, and trees in the fields either side of him appeared as dark twisted shapes against a murky white background.

So intent was he on watching the road ahead that he had failed to notice the car behind. Its dipped headlights were two pale specks surrounded by the drifting fog. He glanced into the rear-view mirror, his eyes seemingly drawn to it, and his mouth went dry. Automatically, without need for thought, he stabbed down on the accelerator and the car lurched forward. His speed increased to forty miles an hour, and he was travelling blind.

A sharp bend in the road caught him unawares and he had to wrestle with the steering wheel to stay on course. On the other side of the bend he straightened the car out and glanced again into the mirror. The headlights were still there, neither gaining nor losing ground.

Bob Dylan had moved on to 'Like A Rolling Stone', and Matthew had progressed to his fourth drink. Karen's image was still there on the settee, but it was moving now, shifting about, never quite coming into focus.

'Oh yes, Karen, Dr Masters was most helpful,' Matthew slurred. 'He explained a lot about Steven. It seems he likes to do the same things in the same way at the same time, every day. It's part of his make-up. And being institutionalised, as Steven is, makes it all the more pronounced.' He drained his glass and swallowed a burp. 'And that's why he confessed, basically. You see, in that interview room, when the hands of his watch finally came round to four o'clock, Steven asked for a cup of tea. It's a comfort thing, I suppose, tea's always at four; it's something he

194

can hang on to in a strange and hostile environment.' Matthew gave a vicious snort. 'But your friend Mackmin wouldn't let him have one. He said Steven could have a cup of tea after he'd told them all they wanted to know. That poor kid would've admitted anything rather than break his routine . . .'

31

Sweat trickled down Roland Parr's forehead, despite the bitter cold conditions. The fog was dispersing fast. It was sticking to the hollows, creeping along the ground like a vast grey carpet, but on higher ground a light breeze was pushing it away.

That car was still behind him, slowing down when he slowed and speeding up whenever he did. But up ahead Parr could see the snaking lights of a dual carriageway that would lead him on to the M6, and a glimmer of hope kept him going. Those tiny specks of light that arced into a flowing curve offered him a small degree of comfort, for they signified contact with other people, other vehicles speeding along to who knew where. Their very presence afforded him some guarantee of safety.

He took the slip road. The other car took it, too. And for the first time Parr could see that it was a Nissan.

Matthew was no longer aware of the Bob Dylan record. He was hardly aware of anything as he sat in the chair, chin slumped on his chest, nostrils expanding slightly as he took in a sluggish breath.

'I'm going to prove you wrong, Karen,' he mumbled, on the edge of sleep, 'because I know what really happened.'

Parr tucked himself in behind a slow-moving lorry and willed the Nissan to overtake. But it stayed where it was, just a few yards behind; so close that he could see the repugnant face of James, his lips stretched back in a predator's grin.

The miles slipped by. Every so often Parr would glance at the open atlas on the passenger seat. He was doing just that when the lorry in front signalled that it was taking a left, and when it slowed to turn off Parr had to brake hard to avoid running into the back of it. With the lorry out of the way he saw that the road ahead was empty, and a quick check in the rear-view mirror confirmed his worst fear: the only car behind was the Nissan.

His leg was trembling as he pushed down the accelerator to take on the steep rise that was coming up. The Nissan dropped back a little, and Parr's hopes flourished as he topped the hill for the valley below was thick with fog. He knew from the map that an exit lay about a mile ahead, and he calculated that the fog would easily stretch that far. If he could keep up his current speed he might lose the Nissan for a while; and when he left the dual carriageway he might lose it altogether. It was his only chance.

The fog was hanging in a low cloud. Parr's vehicle plunged into it and was instantly swallowed up. He was going faster, the needle of the speedometer touching sixty. It was madness, but his highly creative mind kept throwing up images of the tortured Andrew Dickens, and Parr wanted more than anything else to put distance between himself and the Nissan. Visibility was at an all-time low but for Parr the fog was no enemy, it was a friend, concealing him from his pursuers. In any case, whatever lay ahead had to be better than that which waited behind him.

He turned to the rear-view mirror, hardly daring to look. No faint glimmer of headlights showed and Parr let out an ecstatic whoop. Oblivious to the dangers now, he pushed the car harder. Sixty-five miles an hour. Seventy. The grasping mist swirled in front of the windscreen but Parr didn't see it; he was concentrating on the road markings. A large white arrow curved to the left – the turn-off was coming up.

Faster, he must go faster. He pushed the accelerator pedal down to the floor and the speedometer showed seventy-five miles an hour. Another white arrow. Parr swung the steering wheel hard to the left. Still no sign of the Nissan. Soon he would be at the roundabout and then lost in a maze of country lanes. He was giggling like a lunatic, spittle flying all ways.

But there was something up in front, hurtling towards him. It took a moment for his brain to register that the shape was a tower of bricks, now clearly visible. Parr hit the brakes and felt the car's tyres bite into the road surface. He clung to the steering wheel while the chassis bucked and swayed, its rear end threatening to veer round.

The world seemed to slow, time was suspended, and in a few fleeting seconds Parr took in details that should have taken minutes to absorb. The smell of burning oil that stung his nostrils, the criss-cross mortar between the bricks, the way the bonnet of the car buckled and parted as it smashed into the support column of the bridge. Parr let out an agonised scream.

A mass of scarlet flames sprang from the car, the heat from them intense, and plumes of black smoke were swiftly eaten up by the waiting fog. By the time the Nissan cruised past, the bridge support was already scorched, the car a burnt-out wreck.

James pulled into the outside lane and slowed his speed. He chuckled. 'If the manuscript was among Parr's luggage, it wouldn't have survived that.'

'You leave too much to chance,' the man in the back retorted. 'We'll go to the cottage and conduct a search.'

'You're the boss,' James said. 'But if it's not there, I don't know where we look next.'

Matthew opened his eyes, then winced and covered his pounding head with the pillow.

'My God,' he grumbled, 'I've got to be dead . . . I've got to be.'

He lay like that for several minutes and then pushed the pillow aside. He blinked; even that slight movement hurt like hell. Over on the table he could see the whisky bottle, only a third full, and he fervently wished it was still on the shelf in the off-licence.

He writhed about on the bed for a while, moaning in distress, and then struggled to his feet. A wave of nausea hit him and made him gag, but he staggered to the kitchen recess and forced himself to gulp down a mug of tea with two aspirins. Ten minutes and three more teas later the unbearable thirst was still with him. It seemed that no amount of liquid could wash away the thick fur that lined his mouth.

Matthew had a token wash in the bathroom, but decided that shaving was beyond him. Half an hour had passed, two more aspirins had been taken, and that blinding headache hadn't budged, so he thought he'd try and work it off.

He would call Jocelyn Charlton first. He was tired of being told who he could phone and who he couldn't. He reached for the mobile. Might as well use it until the rental lapsed. The connection was made almost immediately.

'Mr Charlton, good morning, this is Matthew Shelley.'

There followed a moment's silence, heavy with surprise. 'Mr Shelley, I did ask you not to get in touch with me again.'

'I remember, but this is important,' was Matthew's curt reply. 'I want some information about Roland Parr.'

There was a quick intake of breath. 'Parr? You've heard, then?'

'Heard what?'

'Roland Parr's dead, Mr Shelley. He was killed in a car accident last night. It's in the morning papers.'

'Parr's dead?' Matthew rubbed at his temples; that little shock had done nothing for his headache. 'And it was an accident?'

'That's what the papers say.' There was a pause. 'Mr Shelley, I've no wish to be rude, but I'm no longer paying you for your services and therefore I'd be grateful if you'd leave me alone. You remember, I hope, the threats I received from the Organisation. Well, I am definitely going to mind my own business in future, and if you know what's good for you, you'll do the same.'

'With all due respect, Mr Charlton, it *is* your business.' Matthew made no attempt to disguise the contempt in his voice. 'The people involved in all this are actually running your business for you, and they're covering up something that's probably costing you a lot of money. Don't tell me that doesn't bother you?'

'Not as much as dying does, and that's the nature of the threats I received.'

'But can't you see, Mr Charlton, they're the ones who're scared. They're running round like headless chickens trying to conceal something, and I know just what it is.'

'Oh, yes?' The man sounded sceptical. 'And what exactly have you unearthed?'

Matthew smiled into the mouthpiece. 'You're not paying me – remember? So, like everybody else, you'll have to wait. There is just one thing, though ... Roland Parr – was he writing books for your company?'

'No, he wasn't,' Charlton said, puzzled. 'Why do you ask?'

'It's just that when we were at Manfield House there was a set of proofs on the desk and Parr told me it was his latest book.'

'No, they would have been the proofs of Glen Watkinson's current book. Parr handled everything of that nature for Glen.'

'So, why would he say it was his?'

'Pride, maybe?' Charlton suggested. 'The man had been a reasonably successful author in the past, but had now come down to working as a secretary.'

'Could've been pride,' Matthew mused. 'Or a slip of the tongue.'

'Sorry?'

'It doesn't matter. Now, I know Watkinson's next book hits the shops in a few weeks ... When are the following ones due to be published?'

'I've no idea, Mr Shelley, I leave that side of things to other people.'

'Maybe you should ask those people. You could be in for a very nasty shock.'

Without waiting for a reply, Matthew disconnected the call.

32

Tom Harris was the first in the village to read the news of Roland Parr's death. It made just a few lines in the latest news section of the morning papers but it fair took his breath away, as he later told his wife.

It was only the day before the crash that Mr Parr had been in the shop. Last thing in the evening, it had been, while Tom was cashing up. He remembered the wet sand on the man's clothes, remembered thinking that it took all sorts. But, wait a minute . . . what was it he'd come in for?

Tom shrugged as he cut the tape holding together a bundle of tabloid newspapers. He started to arrange them along the counter. First thing in the morning was the worst part of the day as far as Tom was concerned. Having to stand behind the counter with all that time on his hands, being able to smell the cigarettes and the cigars and the ounces of tobacco on the shelf. What he wouldn't give for one small drag . . . Still, his doctor had said he'd be dead within two years if he didn't give up, and Tom wasn't willing to take chances.

Mr Parr used to come in for cigarettes. The man must have chain-smoked day and night to get through the number he bought. They didn't seem to be affecting his health, either. Good for business, Mr Parr was. It must have been cigarettes he wanted the other night. He only ever bought cigarettes and newspapers.

Tom sighed and rested his back against the freezer. Why did he bother to open at six when his first customer never turned up till nearer seven? An hour of torment, smelling the damned tobacco.

Tom jolted forward and leant heavily on the counter. He'd remembered. Parr hadn't wanted cigarettes that night, he'd come in about the parcel. Tom hadn't taken much notice, if the truth were known, he'd been too busy cashing up. And then Parr told him to keep the change out of ten pounds. He'd calculated the parcel would cost around six, so that would leave four, a tidy little profit for taking a few steps up the street to the post office.

But what happened to the parcel? He remembered putting it on top of the freezer and then he never saw it again. Hilda must have posted it. Yes, she must have done.

His thoughts were interrupted by Mr Gibbins, first customer of the day. Tom automatically reached for twenty Bensons and folded a copy of the *Sun*. Very fond of his page three was Mr Gibbins. After a ten minute chat, mostly about the girls who graced that inside page, Tom was alone again.

He set about tidying the sweets display but he couldn't rest, there was something nagging at his mind, something to do with poor old Mr Parr. It was that parcel. Hilda couldn't have posted it because she didn't know it needed posting. Tom moved quickly to the freezer and searched around. It couldn't have walked off on its own, so where was it?

'Oh, no,' he exclaimed, as he peered behind.

Sliding a hand down between freezer and wall Tom retrieved the parcel, now covered in a thin film of dust.

'Don't seem much point in posting it, now,' he muttered, brushing it down. 'The man's dead, so he won't be asking for his money back.'

It never rains, but it pours.

That thought kept running through Matthew's head, along with the little man wielding the sledge hammer, the one who paused every few moments to deliver a stunning blow to the inside of his skull. Not only had the aspirins failed to take away his hangover, but it was also an unusually bright day for the time of year and the sunlight was hurting his eyes.

It never rains, but it pours. That was the sort of thing Karen's mother would say. He could almost picture her saying it.

Matthew was on the top deck of a bus, with the window above his seat fully open so that the oncoming breeze could hopefully, clear his head. His thoughts were of Karen. Of course, if she knew what he was working on now, she'd say, 'Flying pigs.' He just about managed a grin.

'Well, watch the sky,' he said to himself. 'There's about to be a fly past.' The woman in the next seat shot him a sideways glance and moved further down the bus, muttering something about junkies.

Despite his hangover, there was a definite spring in his step when Matthew jumped off at his stop. He meandered through the street market, making time to chat to several of the traders. They helped to take his mind off his headache, and Matthew was starting to feel quite human again by the time he set off for the office.

He was about to cross the road when he stopped in his tracks.

A familiar figure was standing in his doorway. Should he carry on across or simply walk away? He decided to face it like a man and snaked a path between the slow-moving traffic.

'Hi, Karen.' He tried to sound upbeat.

Her face was bright with anticipation when she turned to him, but her jaw dropped when she saw his unnatural pallor beneath the untidy chin stubble.

'Jesus, Shelley, you look awful.'

'Oh, thanks,' he chided. 'You know, Karen, every time I see you I walk away feeling like a million dollars.'

'You are so thin-skinned, Matthew Shelley. I only meant – '

'I can see you've been missing me,' he cut in sharply. 'At a loose end, were you? Thought you'd drop by and hurl a few insults about?'

Karen reeled from that verbal attack. 'What? I wasn't . . . Oh, God, you're impossible.' She flounced towards the office doorway.

'*I'm* impossible?' Matthew yelled. He backed away, cradling his aching forehead and vowing never to shout again. 'Look, I don't need this, Karen. Was there a reason you called by, or did you just feel like a row?'

She exhaled loudly and took an envelope from her shoulder bag. 'I brought you this. It's a hundred pounds. You can take it off my final bill.' She thrust it towards him. 'Go on, take it. I owe it to you.'

Matthew snatched the envelope and stuffed it into his pocket. 'Thanks,' he grudgingly muttered.

'So,' Karen said, trying to smile, 'what are you doing now you're off the investigation?'

'Ah, so that's why you're here. You wanted to make sure I wasn't poking my nose in.' She opened her mouth to speak, but Matthew shouted her down. 'If you must know I'm not off the case. I've almost put this puzzle together, and when I have I'll be selling *my* story to the highest bidder. Tell that to the people you're working for, they might be interested.'

'You're being stupid, Shelley.' The words were spat at him. 'You're dealing with people who'd crush you as soon as look at you. And do you know why you're doing it?'

He sneered. 'I bet you do, and I bet you're going to tell me.'

'Yes, I bloody well am,' she shouted, attracting the attention of passers-by. 'You're doing this, Matthew Shelley, to get at me.'

'No, I'm not,' he said, quite composed. 'You might not understand this, but I'm doing it for some kid who, because of what he is, has never had an even break in life. You lot are just handing him around like he's a piece of meat.' He pushed past her, but turned on the bottom stair. 'Oh, and I'm doing it for me, Karen. For the first time in my life, I need to know that when the going got really tough, when it really mattered, I didn't run away.'

When Karen watched him race up the stairs she felt an almost overwhelming urge to chase after him. But she couldn't. She had engineered this situation, and she had done it well. Too well. Matthew hated her now, saw her as one of the enemy. She so wanted to tell him the truth, that she had behaved in that way to protect him. She wanted to tell him that Alec Cooper had passed on his suspicions to the Chief Constable who was even now ordering a special undercover team to watch Mackmin. She wanted to tell him how she felt about him. But she couldn't.

Matthew didn't take long with the mail. The water company was threatening to cut off his supply unless he paid up pronto. And NatWest were offering him a loan. Matthew managed a laugh at that one. They wouldn't be too keen to throw money at him once they knew his financial circumstances. The letters were screwed up and hurled at the wastepaper bin, and this time he didn't miss.

He dialled the number of the police station and asked for an extension number, smiling warmly when the connection was made.

'Hello, this is the police canteen – Ethel speaking. How can I help you?' Her telephone voice was quite grand.

'Hello, Ethel, it's Matthew Shelley.'

'Oh, hello, love, I thought you were dead.'

'I may well be,' he said, putting a hand to his throbbing temples. 'I'm phoning to ask for a favour, Ethel, and it's a big one.'

'I'll help if I can,' she said, brightly.

Matthew told her what he wanted, expecting her at any moment to say it was impossible.

'No problem,' she said when he'd finished. 'First of all I'll get that lot out of CID and into here for their breakfast. Then, Bet, the cleaner, can have a look at the files. Give me half an hour.' The line went dead.

Matthew grinned as he replaced the receiver. It was fortunate for Britain that Ethel didn't work in Whitehall, he reflected, otherwise state secrets would be at the mercy of her band of cleaners and washers-up.

Ethel phoned back dead on the half-hour with the information Matthew needed. Suddenly he realised his headache had eased, and he wondered whether he should phone the Leeds address she had given him, or pay a personal visit, tomorrow. A personal call would be better. After all, the information he wanted from the dentist wasn't confidential, but the man might be a little reluctant to part with it.

Matthew sprawled out on his chair and closed his eyes. In his imagination he could see the face of Roland Parr, his mouth wide open as it had been that day at Manfield House. He could see every tooth in the man's head. And he could also see the gaps where the missing ones had once been.

33

Karen's nerves were taut. Shaking her head ruefully she paced around the flat, examining her anxieties. Deep down she sensed that Shelley was in real danger and guilt flooded over her. If only she hadn't provoked him, hadn't fed his insecurities with her harsh words, he might well have left things as they were. But now, God alone knew what he was preparing to do.

And there was Steven to worry about. Karen at last realised – had realised for some time, if she were honest with herself – that Billy Mason going to jail to protect his son was a far too simplistic solution. And yet because of her interference Steven was in custody – a desperate situation for any innocent man, but for

Steven, cut off from the only home he had ever known and the people he had come to love, well ... the boy must be utterly distraught.

A knock came on the door and brought a startled cry from her lips. Chiding herself for behaving like a frightened rabbit Karen hurried into the hall.

'Who is it?' she called through the door.

'Alec Cooper.'

Karen slid back the bolt and let him in. He checked the corridor, left and right, before crossing the threshold.

'Hi,' he said, his gaze travelling hungrily over her features.

'Hello, Alec.' Karen deliberately kept her tone neutral; she was beginning to worry that his interest in her was going beyond the Mason case.

'I just called round to see if Shelley was behaving himself.'

'You make him sound like a child,' she snapped, heading for the lounge.

Cooper followed her as far as the doorway. 'You seem a bit touchy today.' She said nothing. 'Have you heard about Roland Parr?'

'Heard what?' She found herself dreading the answer.

'He's dead.' Cooper shrugged. 'Looks like a car accident, but who can tell? That's why I'm worried about Shelley. There're others showing an interest in him, apart from Mackmin.'

'Oh yes ... who, exactly?'

'Hazard a guess.' His expression was non-committal. 'Karen, do you know what Shelley's actually doing?'

She gave a dismal shake of the head. 'I haven't a clue. All I know is he thinks he's found out what really happened.'

'That's bad.' Cooper crossed to her, stood very close. 'Listen, I've got a bit more clout now, I think I can get a tail on Shelley without Mackmin finding out.'

His warm breath on her neck was making Karen cringe. She moved quickly to an armchair and sat down. 'Can't you just warn him off, Alec? I think I'd rather have him in prison than dead.'

'It's not quite as simple as that.' He stooped down in front of her. 'If I'm going to nail Mackmin, I'll need proof. As things stand we've got a stalemate. With Steven Mason charged with

Watkinson's murder it looks like end of story again. But Shelley's digging around might just reopen the book.'

'You're using him,' Karen accused.

'A little, yes.' He caught her distasteful look. 'I need a break, Karen, I've got to use whatever or whoever I can.'

'I want out of this, Alec.'

He took her hand. 'Trust me, I won't let anything happen to Shelley . . . or to you, for that matter. Do you know what line of enquiry he may be following?'

Karen broke free of his grip and folded her arms. 'I've no idea.'

'But he must have said something,' Cooper urged. 'Anything you can tell me, however insignificant, might help.'

She turned her forlorn gaze towards him. 'I know he's all fired up about Steven being charged with the murder. He feels it's his fault.'

Cooper's eyes narrowed. 'Has he ever mentioned a typescript, a manuscript?' he asked, lightly.

Karen frowned. 'I don't think so. Why?'

'Oh, it's nothing,' he said, straightening up. 'Just some idea I had.'

'What's going to happen to Shelley?'

'Like I said, I'll put a tail on him – that should ensure he comes to no harm. And if he contacts you with anything, just give me a bell.'

'Okay, I'll do that.' She got to her feet, keeping the armchair between them. 'You'll have to excuse me now, Alec, I want a bath, and . . .'

'Of course.' He gave her a smile, but disappointment showed in his eyes as he headed for the door.

A good night's sleep saw off the residue of his hangover, and Matthew felt more like his old self when he woke up a little after 7 a.m. He devoured a plateful of eggs and bacon, washed down by several cups of tea, because he anticipated a busy day and the likelihood of his eating again before evening looked remote. He shaved, managing to nick himself twice, and was almost out of the house before remembering to remove the tiny pieces of tissue from the cuts.

On his way to the railway station Matthew failed to notice a small slight girl keeping some fifty yards behind him. He was too busy thanking God that Karen had given him the hundred pounds – travelling on trains was an expensive business.

Throughout the journey, with the plain-clothed woman constable sitting two seats behind, he dwelt on Karen, on how she had let him down. She had called him partner – well, some partner she'd turned out to be. As green spaces punctuated by towns and villages flew past the windows, he decided that women were not for him. One had walked out on him – well, two had walked out on him – but this was his chance to come good.

Throughout his dreary reverie another thought kept bursting to the forefront of his mind: What would he do with the damning evidence, once he had it? He could hardly go to the Handwell police, and if he went to another town they would simply refer it back to Mackmin. Perhaps Jocelyn Charlton would be his best bet. The Mob, the Organisation, whatever it was, must be taking the man for millions, so Charlton would be as eager for the truth as Matthew was.

A hundred-mile journey was a hell of a jaunt, and by the time the train pulled into Leeds station Matthew's joints were stiff and another headache threatened. He didn't function well in unfamiliar surroundings and it took him three hours to find the dental practice.

Behind him, the policewoman was alternating between muttered oaths aimed at his back and bitter curses directed at her aching feet; and she was much relieved when Matthew ran up the stone steps in front of a large Victorian town house. She waited until he had vanished through the door and then wandered past, taking down the name of the practice in her notebook. The pavements were lined with mature horse chestnut trees, and she hid behind the nearest.

'Half an hour's walk, and it took him three hours,' she grumbled, easing off first one shoe and then the other. 'When he comes out of there I'm going to give him directions back to the railway station.'

*

Matthew took a chair in the waiting-room and flicked through a copy of *Country Homes* with unseeing eyes. A thin partition was all that separated the surgery from the waiting-room, and he could clearly hear the ominous whirr of the drill, could even hear the saliva being sucked from the victim's mouth. The sounds set his own teeth on edge. After what seemed like hours but was only five minutes the door separating the two rooms opened and in walked the dentist.

'Mr Shelley?' he asked, extending a hand.

'Yes,' Matthew said, discarding the magazine and getting to his feet. 'It's good of you to see me, Mr Shepherd.'

The dentist was a large man, with a gentle expression and a firm handshake. He smelt of antiseptic, and tiny dots of red were spattered across the lapels and breast pocket of his white coat. A gauze mask now rested around his throat.

'When you phoned, yesterday, Mr Shelley, I did have doubts, I must admit. But, having thought it over, I don't see any reason why I shouldn't supply you with the information you require.'

'I'm very grateful,' Matthew said.

The dentist ushered him across to the chairs. 'We'll sit here, I've got at least ten minutes before my next appointment. It's about Mr Watkinson, you said . . .'

Matthew nodded. 'You told the court at Billy Mason's trial that you definitely identified work carried out on the two teeth found at the scene of crime as yours. You also confirmed that the teeth were Glen Watkinson's.'

'That's correct.' The man frowned. 'You're not challenging my testimony, are you? Only I see from the papers that this whole business has blown up again.'

'Oh no, nothing like that,' Matthew quickly assured him. 'I just need a description of the man you carried out the work on. I want you to tell me what Glen Watkinson looked like.'

The man emitted a puzzled laugh. 'Well, one wide open mouth looks very much like another,' he quipped. 'Actually, Mr Shelley, I did very little work on that particular patient, but I'll try.'

*

By the time they arrived back in Handwell the plain-clothed policewoman had had enough. Seconded from the uniformed division, this was her first stint with CID and she was far from impressed.

'Give me back my cap and badge and let me face knife-wielding hooligans,' she muttered ruefully. 'It's got to be better than following some half-wit all across the country.'

She left him at the railway station car-park and headed back to the police department. Matthew still totally unaware that he had been followed, cut across town to his office. The street market was closing down for the day and he had to thread his way between transit vans being loaded with unsold merchandise. He picked up a Granny Smith apple, courtesy of the fruit and vegetables man, and was munching it as he crossed the road.

His doorway was unattended, no waiting Karen, no hovering bailiff, but as he made to go through the door the tailor who rented the space below his came dashing from his shop.

'Matthew,' he said. 'I took a parcel in for you.'

'Cheers, Joe.'

With the parcel under his arm and the half-eaten apple between his teeth, Matthew ran up the stairs. In the office he ignored his mail and tore instead at the letter attached to the parcel. He read it, intrigued, and ripped open the padded envelope to retrieve the manuscript. Taking the apple from his mouth, Matthew tossed it into the wastepaper bin and settled down to read.

Three hours later he turned to the final page. He stared for a long time at the stack of papers before him, his mouth open in disbelief. All that running around and chasing about he had done, and in the end the truth had landed in his lap. Matthew touched the manuscript as if it were a priceless object. As it might well be, for within its chapters lay the final pieces to the puzzle, and they fitted together perfectly.

34

Never in his life had Matthew felt more vulnerable than he did the next morning as he made his way to the office, tightly clutching the precious manuscript. He knew all too well that those pages beneath his arm had led to three deaths, one of which had been a cold and calculated murder. And the realisation that he, too, could easily be on his way to the morgue did little to cheer him. When Matthew reached the office he found Joe outside his shop; he was talking to some of the market traders.

'Hey, Matthew,' Joe called. 'There's been a couple of blokes looking for you.'

'Proper hard-looking geezers, they were, an' all,' said one of the traders.

'What did they look like?'

'Hard, as Jim said,' Joe replied.

'They weren't, by any chance, driving a blue Nissan, were they?'

Joe gave a nod. 'They're the ones.'

Images of James and Nick flashed through Matthew's mind, and sweat broke out on his forehead. 'Are they still there?' he asked, hesitantly.

'No,' Joe said. 'They went up to your office, but after about ten minutes they came down again and drove off.'

'Right . . . thanks, Joe.' Matthew started up the stairs.

'Matthew, if you're in trouble,' the trader shouted after him, 'just let me know and I'll get some of the lads to help sort it.'

'Thanks, Jim,' he shouted back.

Even though he knew they were no longer in his office, Matthew's step still faltered when he reached the top stair for his door had been kicked in and was hanging on one hinge. He stood on the threshold and surveyed the carnage. Drawers had been ripped out of the filing cabinet and the desk, their contents strewn all around the floor. Pictures had been ripped from the walls and deliberately smashed. Everything, it seemed, had been broken or damaged. When they had failed to find what they were looking for, they had obviously destroyed for the sake of it.

Matthew picked a path through the wreckage, stooping once to rescue a treasured picture from its shattered frame.

'I'm not going to let them do this to me.' The words were spoken through clenched teeth, while tears of anger stung his eyes.

Dickens and Parr had both made a mistake, he reasoned. They had tried to run, or to be more precise, they had attempted to conceal their whereabouts. Well, Matthew had no intention of repeating that mistake. He would tell as many people as possible about his discovery and then, if anything should happen to him, the Organisation would have questions to answer.

He searched around for the telephone, finally locating it beneath his desk, and was amazed to find it still connected. The first number he dialled was that of Giles Abbot. Soon, the man's smooth voice was filtering down the line.

'Abbot, here. What can I do for you?'

'It's Matthew Shelley.'

'Why, Mr Shelley, what can I possibly do for you?'

'I have a manuscript, here, and I think it might interest you.'

There was a moment's silence. 'Really? And are you prepared to divulge its contents?'

'If you're willing to meet me at your publishing house in, say, two hours.'

'I'll be waiting.'

Matthew cut off the call. When the dialling tone sounded he punched out Karen's number but stopped, midway. He tried three times in all, but could not bring himself to complete the number. Steeling himself, he dialled a fourth time, forcing himself to tap in all six digits. He listened to the ringing tone, his heart beating madly.

'Yes?' Karen's abrupt tone jumped into his ear.

'It's Matthew.'

'Shelley? Oh, thank God.' Her relief was almost palpable. 'I've been on the point of ringing you so many times. Look, I didn't let you down, or run out on you – okay? Mackmin was saying that if we didn't pull out of the investigation he'd fit you up for something, make sure you'd go to prison. That's why I did it,

Shelley, I had to get rid of you. And then Alec Cooper told me a number of officers had been put in to investigate Mackmin, and I saw it as a possible chance to lie low and clear this whole mess up.'

'Don't trust Cooper,' Matthew warned. 'And don't pass what I'm about to tell you on to him. You must promise me that, Karen. Promise?'

'All right, I promise, of course I do.'

He condensed the contents of the manuscript into a few terse sentences.

'Jesus,' she exclaimed.

'Listen, Karen, as long as I've got the manuscript and they can't find it, I'll be safe. But with bent coppers and the like, it's becoming impossible to trust anybody, so I've just got to play it by ear, and hope.'

'Be careful, Shelley. Please be careful.'

He rang Ethel next, explaining everything as quickly and as simply as possible.

'Well, you've really got a story, there.' She sounded impressed. 'It should do your agency the world of good.'

'But I don't know where to hide the manuscript, Ethel.'

'I might be able to help you there,' she said, after a moment's thought. 'See, our Albert – he's married to our Daisy – he works in the lost property office at the railway station. I can't see anybody going there to look for it – can you, Matthew? Anyway, I'll give Albert a ring and let him know you're coming.'

'Just one more thing, Ethel – do you know a copper I can really trust? I feel out on a limb here and I could really do with somebody on my side.'

'None of this lot,' she said, in a truculent tone.

'I had thought of going to Saltley, but they'd only refer it back to Mackmin.'

'Tell them not to, you silly bugger, tell them you don't trust him.'

'Huh, they're hardly likely to take any notice of me.'

Ethel gave a loud sigh. 'Matthew, there are times when you seem to have about as much sense as a pork pie. What you do is, you ask for the name of the officer you're talking to. It makes them think twice, you see. I mean, if they just referred the call to Mackmin and anything went wrong, they'd be for it, wouldn't they?'

'Thanks, Ethel, I owe you one . . . or maybe ten.' He replaced the receiver.

Then he rang the police at Saltley.

The lost property office no longer existed, as such; items were handed in and Albert issued tickets and stored them in the rear of the office.

'If it's not claimed in six months, it's yours,' he said, cheerfully. 'Mind you, nobody hands anything of value in, nowadays; they keep it, the greedy beggars.'

Grateful that Albert had shared his views on modern society, Matthew left the station.

With the last of his cash Matthew took a taxi to Charlton Publishing. He watched the meter very closely, and when it showed the amount he had left, they were still two blocks away from the publishing house.

'Let me out here,' he told the driver.

'Right you are, mate.' The cab drew to a stop. 'That'll be four pounds twenty-five.'

Matthew counted it into the driver's palm and scrambled on to the pavement.

'Thanks for the tip,' the man called as he pulled away from the kerb.

But Matthew scarcely heard him. He was planning the best way to spring his surprise.

He found Giles Abbot in the reception area. The man was pacing about and he seemed nervous, ill at ease, when he saw Matthew approaching.

'You'd better come through to the office,' he said.

Without a word, Matthew followed. As expected, Judith Ward

was already there, seated behind the huge desk. The door closed silently behind them and Abbot went and perched on the desk, to the right of Judith.

'Well, Mr Shelley,' the woman said in a terse voice. 'You've certainly caused us a lot of trouble, one way or another. I take it your trip to Leeds, yesterday, meant you were chasing your favourite theory...' She laughed. 'Did you really believe that Roland Parr was writing the books, and Glen was merely the front man, put in there because he looked right?'

Matthew's nod was half-hearted. Without being invited, he sat in the chair facing them. 'But from the dentist's description of the patient he treated, it was obvious that the Watkinson who ended up mixed with steel was the same as the one whose pictures appeared in the books. I confess I was close to giving up.'

'But then the manuscript turned up and you saw a chance of making some money,' Abbot ventured.

'Is that all you people can think about – money?' Matthew retorted angrily.

'If you're not here to talk a deal,' Judith said, 'you're very ill advised to be here at all.'

Matthew snorted. 'Andrew Dickens tried to talk a deal with you, and he ended up dead. And no doubt Roland Parr tried the same thing.'

'I did talk to them,' Judith admitted. 'I did my best to make them see sense, as I hope I can make you.'

'Manipulation, manipulation,' Matthew scoffed. 'It comes as second nature to you lot.'

Judith's face reddened beneath the make-up. 'We've no proof that you actually have the manuscript, Mr Shelley.'

'Oh, I've got it,' he assured her. 'And to prove it, I'll give you the title. *Forty Years Of Crime* by Billy Mason.'

The pair exchanged a brief glance.

'Billy had quite a life,' Matthew went on. 'Before he moved to the Midlands he was real big league. His gangland boss was one Sonny Chambers.'

'Jesus Christ,' Abbot muttered.

Matthew grinned. 'Sonny boy committed a number of murders

during the sixties, and those cases are still unsolved. Now, Billy was no fool; he knew he was dying and he needed a lot of money, he had dependents to think about. His wife was used to the good life and he wanted to leave her well provided for. His son, Steven, would need a small fortune if he were to spend the rest of his life in that expensive hospital. Now, Glen Watkinson was an ambitious man; he didn't just want to churn out slush fiction so he agreed to ghost-write Billy's autobiography. At that time I'm sure he had no idea that the gangsters he was naming were actually publishing his own books.'

'No, he didn't,' a stony-faced Judith agreed. 'And he was such an arrogant, vulgar man that even when he was told, it didn't matter a jot to him.'

'So, he ended up being crushed to death.' Matthew held her gaze. 'You know, one thing's always puzzled me ... I could never work out how anybody could force Billy Mason to confess to a murder he hadn't committed. But that's not how it happened, is it? I'd imagine everything possible was done to talk Billy out of it.'

'He was offered a lot of money not to write the book,' Abbot interjected. 'But he was a strange man. The more you tried to push him one way, the more he wanted to go in the opposite direction. He was convinced the book would be a gold mine.'

'And, of course, Watkinson had to be murdered because he knew too much,' Matthew threw in.

They nodded.

'And that's when the plot was hatched: if Mason went ahead and had the book published, his son, Steven, would be framed for Watkinson's murder. But Billy pre-empted that by confessing himself, and in doing so created a stand-off. True, he couldn't have the book published because if he did, Steven could still be implicated. But by the same token, you couldn't chase the manuscript because there was a risk Billy would tell his side of the story.'

Abbot squirmed on the desk. 'Do you know the real identity of this gangland boss?'

But Matthew refused to reply; he held up a hand for silence. 'Once Billy was dead, though, the hunt for the manuscript was really on. But then came the pressure from all those campaigners shouting about a miscarriage of justice, which was why Karen and I were hired.'

'Yes, I admit that,' Judith said. 'At first your job was to convince the public that the facts, as they had been presented, were true.' She shrugged. 'But neither of you believed that to be the case, and you started going off at angles.'

'Do you know who the gangland boss is?' Abbot asked again.

Matthew ignored him. His gaze was still on Judith. 'And when I discovered Steven Mason, the feeling must have been: Why not? If he goes down for the murder it'll silence everybody who thought his father was innocent and would give a very plausible reason for his confession.'

'You're very clever, Mr Shelley,' Judith said. 'You've worked it out to the last detail.'

Abbot moved from the desk. This time he was determined to be heard. 'Shelley, do you know – '

'For God's sake, shut up,' Judith yelled. 'Of course he knows.' She turned back to Matthew. 'You were a fool to come to us with this, Mr Shelley.'

'I don't think so,' he replied in an easy tone. 'The police know I'm here.'

Judith gave a hollow laugh. 'The police? You don't know how funny that is.'

The knock on Karen's door was urgent.

'Who is it?' she called from the hall.

'Alec Cooper. For God's sake, open the door, Karen.' He was inside the moment the safety chain was removed. 'We've intercepted a call Shelley made to Saltley police, and thank God we did. He told them of his reservations about Mackmin. He also said he was going to Charlton Publishing.'

'I know,' she stammered, studying his worried expression.

'You know? Oh, Christ . . .' Cooper grabbed her arms. 'Karen, has he found the manuscript?'

Dumbly, she nodded.

'Oh, Christ,' he repeated. 'Do you know where it is?'

She shook her head.

'Karen, I want you to come and meet the investigating officer in charge. You've got to help us. We have to get Shelley out of there before he gets killed.'

'I'll do anything, Alec.' She broke away from him, her actions frantic. 'I'll get my coat.'

Cooper was silent during the drive to the police station. In the car-park he manoeuvred the vehicle as close as possible to the back entrance.

'Follow me,' he said, hurrying across the tarmac.

Sensing the urgency, and worried about Matthew, Karen almost ran to keep up with Cooper as he strode along corridors and bounded up flights of stairs.

'In here,' he said briskly, opening up a door.

But Karen paused on the threshold, her mouth gaping open in horror, for the office was occupied by Chief Inspector Mackmin. He was seated at a desk, a wolfish grin on his face.

'But I don't understand . . .' she stammered.

Cooper placed a hand at the small of her back and pushed hard, sending Karen staggering into the centre of the room.

'Get in,' he ordered, harshly.

She rounded on him. 'You bastard, you've stitched me up.'

Mackmin was still grinning when he left his seat and positioned himself in front of her.

35

'What's funny about it?' Matthew asked Judith, with a superior smile. 'I took the precaution of contacting Saltley police. I thought they might be a little less corrupt.'

Her hollow laugh came again. 'That makes no difference. Your message wouldn't have got through to those who could help you.'

'I think it did.' Matthew cast a glance at Giles Abbot. He had returned to the desk and was running nervous fingers through his hair. 'You asked me who the big boss man was, Mr Abbot. Well, to be honest, when Steven Mason described the man who possibly took his model car, I thought how well that description fitted you. But then I saw the photographs that came with Mason's manuscript and I realised it was none other than Jocelyn Charlton.'

For a second or two the silence in the office was absolute. Then Judith slumped in her seat. She fixed Matthew with a dispirited stare.

'You may have worked everything out,' she said, 'but you've still made a grave error of judgement coming here.'

'I don't think so,' Matthew replied, quite relaxed. 'For a start off I don't think you two were ever really involved in all this. You didn't know about Watkinson's murder until after the event, and the deaths of Dickens and Parr must have raised questions in your minds, as would some of the things you were asked to do. Trouble was, you didn't ask those questions because you're both in highly paid positions and you didn't want to jeopardise your careers.'

Matthew had, for the most part, been working on assumptions, but when he glanced at Judith's shamefaced expression he knew that those assumptions were correct.

'It's different now, though,' he went on. 'I've told a lot of people I was coming here to talk to you. So if anything happens to me there'll be more questions asked, and if you two stand back and let it happen, you'll be accomplices.'

'Very clever, Mr Shelley.'

The voice came from the doorway. Matthew spun round to find Jocelyn Charlton standing just inside the room. Behind him, at either shoulder, were James and Nick. Charlton shot contemptuous glances at both Judith Ward and Giles Abbot. And when he motioned for them to leave, they did so without a word.

Charlton and his henchmen approached the desk. Matthew quickly left his seat and crossed to the far wall, keeping as much space between them as he could.

'Right, Mr Shelley,' Charlton said, grinning, 'now we'll talk business, and I want to keep it brief.'

Matthew leant against the wall, trying hard to look cool, as he faced the three men.

'You have something I want, and I'm willing to pay for it,' Charlton said. 'Thirty thousand pounds seems a reasonable sum to me.'

Matthew gave a derisory snort and slowly shook his head.

'Don't overestimate its value, Mr Shelley. Others have made that mistake.'

'It's not for sale,' Matthew countered. 'It's staying where it is.'

'At the railway station?' Charlton chuckled at Matthew's wide-eyed expression. 'With my network, Mr Shelley, I couldn't fail to find out where it was.' The chuckle faded. 'I'll tell you again – thirty thousand pounds.'

'You can't buy me,' Matthew spat.

Charlton sat in the chair before the desk and stared at him for many seconds. Finally, he said, 'I can either buy people, Mr Shelley, or if that doesn't work, I can put the fear of God into them.'

Matthew's amused gaze took in James and Nick, and then it came to rest on their leader's face.

'Bottom line is, you don't frighten me,' he said.

Anger bought a flush to Charlton's cheeks. 'I don't allow talk like that, especially from the likes of you, Shelley. You're a nothing and a nobody – '

'That's right,' Matthew interjected, angrily. 'Just like Steven Mason – a nothing and a nobody.'

'A sentimentalist ... that's all I need,' Charlton muttered. 'Shelley, the Mason boy will spend the rest of his life in an institution. Does the type really matter? I doubt he'll even notice the difference.' His features suddenly hardened. 'Now, go and get the manuscript and I'll pay you the money.'

Matthew could feel a hot rage building inside him; it was tinged with a fair amount of fear, it was true, but it still burned his middle. He looked at the three impassive faces in front of him, then bowed his head and made for the door. When he was clear of them, when he was no longer cornered, he turned around.

'Go to hell,' he said, very quietly.

A vein throbbed in Charlton's temple, and his lips pulled back in a snarl. 'Shelley, when I was looking for someone to do this job, you were described to me as a first-class tosser . . .'

'Well, maybe I am, Mr Charlton, but I'll promise you one thing – I'm going to do my damnedest to keep you here till the law arrives.'

Chief Inspector Mackmin strode across reception at the offices of Charlton Publishing. His expression was grim, and when the door to Abbot's office failed to open he took a step back, raised his foot and aimed a mighty kick at the handle. Such was his bulk, the door immediately flew open, banged against the inner wall and bounced back again. He gave it a hefty push and viewed the carnage inside the room.

Matthew was fighting for breath, his back propped against the wall. There was a gaping cut over his left eye, his nose was bleeding profusely, and he was leaning to the right as if to protect his ribs. In his hand was a leg from one of the broken chairs that littered the floor.

That wooden leg was responsible for the shattered teeth that were hanging from James's bleeding gums, and for the network of weals that covered his face. Nick, meanwhile, was lying in an uncoordinated heap by the desk, and Charlton was standing, white-faced and disbelieving, at the rear of the office.

Mackmin picked his way through the broken furniture and scattered papers. 'Put it down, Shelley,' he said, indicating the chair leg.

Charlton brightened straight away, while Matthew raised the makeshift weapon above his head, getting ready to attack.

'He just stormed in here and went berserk,' Charlton said. 'He kept raving on about a book Billy Mason had written.'

'Shut it,' Mackmin snarled. 'You three are nicked.' He returned his attention to Matthew. 'I said, put it down. Who the shit do you think you are – Bruce bloody Willis?'

Matthew let go of the chair leg and it clattered to the floor as uniformed officers swarmed around the room.

'Read those three their rights, and get them down to the nick,' Mackmin barked. He crossed to Matthew and kicked away the piece of wood. 'I'll give you one thing, son, you've got guts. No bloody brains, mind you.'

It was all Matthew could do to stay upright. The pain in his side was restricting his breathing to a serious of shallow gasps. Through the veil of agony he spotted a frantic Karen working her way around the mass of moving bodies.

'Oh, Shelley,' she cried, her face ashen. 'What have they done to you?'

'I'm all right, I just got mad this time.' He tried a smile, but his swollen lips refused to pull back. 'It didn't make any difference, though. They still knocked hell out of me . . . it just took them longer.'

'There's an ambulance on the way,' she told him. 'And you're a hero, Shelley. Chief Inspector Mackmin and his team are helping with an investigation of the police, both here and in Saltley, that was set up after the Watkinson murder. They knew Mason wasn't the killer, but they couldn't prove it.' She desperately wanted to touch him, to throw her arms around his neck, but she dared not for fear of hurting him. 'You did actually help to foul up his marriage, but I think after this he may forgive you.'

'Thank God for that,' Matthew breathed. He wanted to slide down the wall and go to sleep. He was so weary.

'Over here,' he heard Karen shout.

Then he was being helped on to a stretcher. He lay back and allowed his head to loll to one side.

'Can I go with him in the ambulance?' Karen was asking.

'No . . . no,' Matthew mumbled, trying to get up.

'Lie back,' the paramedic advised. 'We'll strap you in.'

Karen's face appeared above him; her eyes were moist and she was chewing on her trembling lower lip. 'Shelley?' she said, softly. 'Shelley, can you hear me? I want to go with you.'

'No . . .' He shook his head and winced.

'But, why not?' she asked, through her tears.

Matthew looked at her, tried to focus. 'I want you to pay the water bill. They're going to cut me off if it's not settled today.'

'Oh, Shelley,' she said, laughing and crying at the same time.

Karen walked with him to the ambulance and then followed him in, fussing until he was comfortable. Then she jumped on to the pavement and, heaving a relieved sigh, she watched the vehicle set off for the hospital.

She had to admit that Matthew Shelley was different from any

221

other man she'd ever met. He would leave the hospital, hobbling and wincing, making far too much of his injuries. And she would be there, waiting for him.

'Right . . . water bill,' she murmured, searching her bag for her cheque book.